"Have you heard the terms of my father's will?"

Clair shook her head. Nick's words, "give your house back," echoed in her head, the rasp of his tone burrowing deeper into her mind.

"Jeff left everything to me," he said absently, as if he'd forgotten she was listening. "But there were stipulations. He said I have to marry. Fall in love and marry within twelve months."

Only Jeff Dylan would be arrogant enough to believe he could regulate love. "What do you want?" she asked.

"I want you to marry me. If you pretend to be my loving wife for twelve months, I'll sign your house over to you."

"You must know other women. What's wrong with them?"

He laughed without joy or happiness. "I know other women, but I don't want to marry any of them. I don't want to start a marriage with someone who'd expect it to last. Can you imagine you'll want to stay married to me?"

Her stomach knotted. "No."

"Then you're the wife I want."

Dear Reader,

I grew up in a loud, loving, extended family. My aunts and uncles continue to love me as if I'm theirs, and I can't really tell my cousins from my own siblings. I know how lucky I am.

How many of you live away from your family, as I do now? Clair, my heroine in this book, shares my longing for hearth and home, for seeing the faces of people who belong to her as she belongs to them. I hope you'll enjoy reading about Clair and her not-so-convenient husband, Nick Dylan. Out of a marriage contract, they build a life and home and best of all, an extended community family of their own.

If you'd like to share your thoughts on this story, please feel free to write to me at P.O. Box 801068, Acworth, GA 30101 or annaadams@superauthors.com

Sincerely,

Anna Adams

The Marriage Contract
Anna Adams

HARLEQUIN®

TORONTO • NEW YORK • LONDON
AMSTERDAM • PARIS • SYDNEY • HAMBURG
STOCKHOLM • ATHENS • TOKYO • MILAN • MADRID
PRAGUE • WARSAW • BUDAPEST • AUCKLAND

ISBN 0-373-70959-5

THE MARRIAGE CONTRACT

To Sylvia, in memory of Becky.
I hope that soon the joy of her life
eases the pain of your loss.

CHAPTER ONE

NICK DYLAN lifted his glass to the orange sun that glinted through his father's library window. No. His window. He'd buried his father that morning. Uneven panes of glass twisted the October light, destroyed his perspective of the coming sunset, much as his father's life had twisted Nick's outlook on his own existence.

But not on his future. Senator Jeffrey Dylan had no right to Nick's future.

The library door opened behind him, and a man's footsteps preceded a gruff voice. "Dr. Dylan, why didn't you accompany your mother to Mr. Thomas's office?"

Nick's temples throbbed. "Leota went without me?" He turned away from the window. His mother's decision to go alone didn't surprise him.

He looked at Hunter, who'd run the family home here in Fairlove, Virginia, since before Nick was born. Stubble etched the older man's face. Though he wore his usual, perfectly pressed navy suit, Hunter's inattention to his beard was as good a sign as any of the grief that darkened this house.

Grief Nick couldn't feel. He mourned his father's lifelong disappointment in him, mourned the relationship he'd never won. Maybe he'd been wrong not to compromise more, not to find a way to be the son his father had tried to make him.

"I saw the limo turn out of the driveway. I thought you were with her, sir," Hunter said.

"Maybe she didn't want to wait for me. You know she likes to be early for her appointments." Nick tried to cover up the unease between himself and Leota. Her anger, a freewheeling, almost tangible entity, had grown with every passing second in the three days since his father's death. When Hunter had called to tell him about the brandy and sleeping pills he'd found on Leota's nightstand, Nick had moved back into this house. Though Nick and his mother were not close, he loved her. He wanted to care for her.

"I assumed she'd want your support, sir." Hunter straightened. "Perhaps she needed a moment to herself."

Crossing the Oriental rug, which muffled his footsteps on the wide plank floor, Nick tossed back the Scotch he'd poured himself. He set the tumbler on the tray that always stood beside his father's favorite leather armchair, grimacing as the alcohol scalded his throat. "Maybe I can catch up with her."

"Sir—"

"I wish you'd stop calling me that. Nothing's changed between us since Jeff died."

"I feel awkward calling you Mr. Nick."

At thirty-two, Nick had almost forgotten the title Hunter had used when he was a child. "Try just 'Nick.' You've managed not to call me anything for the year I've been back in town."

Hunter's self-conscious smile looked sad. "I'll try."

Nick fought an overwhelming urge to hug the other man. He'd last hugged Hunter on the morning his father had sent him away to boarding school. Hunter, the only man who'd shown him affection. Far more of a father to him than Jeff had ever been.

"If, for some reason, Leota didn't go to Wilford's office and she calls here, will you let me know?"

"She'll be there." Hunter sounded certain. "Despite her grief, she must be curious about your father's last wishes."

Or else she dreaded finding out what Jeff might have planned for them—the housemaid he'd married because she was pregnant and the son who'd almost been born a bastard. Nick grunted agreement. He glanced back at the older man as he curved his hand around the ornate library door frame.

"Get some rest," he said, uncomfortable with Hunter's sorrow. How deeply had he cared for his difficult employer? Nick had never discussed Hunter's feelings for Jeff, because he couldn't define his own.

The older man had been a refuge of stability for Nick. His presence had buffered Nick from Jeff, who'd found Hunter difficult to criticize.

Nick paused in the wide parquet-floored hall. He owed Hunter more than a caution to rest. He should ask straight out how the other man felt. A normal caring human being would ask the question. And once he crossed the final emotional minefield of his father's will, he believed he could begin to live like a normal human being. If he survived without a mortal blow, he'd come back here and ask Hunter to join him in a beer.

Nick hurried through the double front doors and then strode down the brick steps to his battered Jeep. The old green car was parked on one side of the curving drive like a poor relative, hoping for a kind welcome. Last night, after the limo driver had brought them back from the family visitation at the funeral home, Leota had suggested Nick hide his eyesore of a vehicle in the garage, or better yet, in one of the empty barns on the property.

Putting the Jeep in the garage would have made it appear he'd come home to stay. And though he'd never admitted it to another living soul, home wasn't a place where he felt comfortable.

He pushed his key into the ignition. As the engine coughed to life, he watched the lights starting to come on in the town below. From up here on Dylan property, Fairlove looked quaint and warm.

Appearances were deceiving. Since he'd come back to Fairlove, Nick had lived in a small house just two doors from Saint Theresa's—the church parking lot was where Hunter had taught him to ride his bike. For the past twelve months, Nick had attended countless school-board meetings and potluck suppers. He'd "doctored" townspeople who came to him only as their last resort, and he'd tried to turn himself into one of Fairlove's ordinary citizens. But the townspeople couldn't seem to forget he was a Dylan and therefore the last physician they wanted to treat their sore throats, arthritis or lumbago.

As the pole light above the Jeep came on, Nick put the car in gear and started down the winding road into the town spread out below him. Movement on the street in front of the high school drew Nick's gaze to the kids escaping at top speed from band practice.

Car lights flickered on as the parents who'd waited for their children started their engines and began to head for the tidy rows of federal-style houses. Some of the buildings had been built before the American Revolution, but some were new construction, erected according to the town's covenants. Nick had bought one of the newer houses. He'd lived in a historical monument long enough.

At the bottom of the hill, he checked for traffic on his left, then his right. The sight of the Atherton house provoked the usual momentary pang of helpless guilt. Derelict, forgotten, except by his father, the house called The Oaks was slowly falling down.

Nick looked away from his father's trophy. Jeff had destroyed the Atherton family while Nick had been away at college. If he'd been home, would he have tried to end the vendetta before the family disappeared from Fairlove? Or would he have sided with his mother's wounded pride and stood aside while his father took vengeance on the man who'd married Sylvie Atherton, the woman Jeff had truly loved?

Nick pressed his gas pedal and tried to put the past he couldn't change behind him. He had to concentrate on the here and now, on Leota, who seemed to be self-destructing, and on the will, which might contain a last, posthumous blow.

He passed his own dark house and the church before he turned in front of the courthouse. His father's black limo took up two of the hotly contested parking spaces on the square in front of Wilford Thomas's office. All around the limo, reporters and cameramen waited, their equipment at the ready.

Nick found a space as far away from them as possible and dodged through the evening traffic on foot. Wilford had arranged this after-hours reading to avoid the reporters who'd been following Leota. Obviously his ploy had failed.

"Dr. Dylan! Nick!" As he reached the door to Wilford's office, a man behind him shouted his name. He ignored the voice and yanked the door shut behind him.

Wilford immediately came out of his inner office. In his mid-fifties, he had white, perfectly coiffed hair and wore a suit as appropriately conservative as Hunter's. "I thought I heard a commotion. Come on in. I'll lock this door until we finish. I had the sheriff come by and give the press a talk about trespassing."

Leota looked up from the far side of Wilford's desk, slender, blond, perfectly made up and emotionally frozen.

"I thought we planned to drive together," Nick said to her.

"Why don't you all stop treating me as if I'm a lunatic on the verge of a breakdown?"

Nick, taken aback at her response, moved to the chair beside hers. He leaned toward her and lowered his voice. "I only meant you don't have to do this alone. You and I are still family."

Leota flashed him a look that fairly sizzled with

rage. Nick made a conscious effort not to show his bewilderment. Jeff's death seemed to have released all the demons she'd formerly held at bay.

"Can I get either of you a coffee?"

Nick turned to Wilford. The attorney's nervous tone boded bad news. "I'm fine." He glanced at his mother. "Leota?"

"No. Let's get on with it."

"Do you want word for word, or the gist first?" Wilford asked.

Nick tried to corner the attorney's shifting gaze. "Why don't you tell us what's making you uneasy?"

Wilford Thomas subsided into his chair, fumbling with the knot on his silver-blue tie. "I'm sorry, Nick." His glance flickered to Leota. "Don't look like that. Jeff hasn't left the house to a stranger or anything, but he's made an unusual stipulation."

"We're waiting." Leota's voice cut like a knife.

"You have the use of the house for the rest of your life, Leota, and you also receive a generous income. I'll go over the details in a moment, but first, I want to go over the bequest that concerns Nick."

"Jeff always wanted me to specialize rather than becoming a GP." Nick attempted a casual laugh. "Are you about to tell me I have to go back to school?"

"Worse, I'm afraid. All assets not mentioned elsewhere, the bulk of the estate, really, go to you, Nick, but—and this is the part that troubles me—he's stated a condition."

"Go on." Nick's pulse nearly choked him. He let

go of all hope that Jeff had finally forgiven him for the fact of his birth.

"He wants you to get married. Actually, the language states you must 'fall in love and marry within the next twelve months.' The marriage must exist for at least a year, and the other executors, along with your mother and I are required to ascertain your marriage is valid. Also, you must remain in the family home for the first year of marriage."

Nick lifted his hands as if he could stop the world from falling in on his head. "Don't finish." Standing, he dragged a hand through his hair. "Only my father would believe he could force me to fall in love with someone."

"And marry her," added Wilford, a stickler for details.

"And stay married for at least a year." Leota's voice was leavened with bitterness. "That's true love for you. Jeff's idea of it, anyway. Wilford, can we seal this will? Can we keep the papers from publishing it?"

Dumbfounded she could so easily accept his father's plans, Nick understood that her first priority was still protecting the family name. She'd sold vital parts of herself to hold that name.

He turned to Wilford. "Can his terms be enforced?"

"You'd have to go to court to fight them. And, Nick, your cousin Hale inherits if you don't meet the conditions."

Leota sprang to her feet. "I won't let you contest your father's will. You can't broadcast our private family matters to...to—'' she pointed through the windows ''—to them!''

Her hysterical tone betrayed her pain, but he wouldn't go along with a farce of a marriage like the one his birth had caused. ''Jeff still wants revenge because you got pregnant with me. I won't let him have it, and I don't care who finds out.''

''I know you, Nick. You do care—about people you've never even met. People who believed in your father. Look at those happy family pictures your father's office distributed to any newspaper or magazine who'd run them. You could have stopped posing for them.''

''That was politics. I'm his son. You know this doesn't compare.''

''What about me? I care what happens to his name. I don't want anyone to know Jeff the way we did. And what about the house? Do you want to lose everything?''

He didn't put a comforting arm around her shoulders. They never touched each other that way. ''You and I will be all right.'' But could he just let Hale take over?

Leota grabbed his arm, her gaze haunted. ''Promise you won't contest your father's will. I couldn't stand facing any more reporters. And Hale—he'll turn our home into an amusement park.''

Wilford's chair squeaked as he leaned forward. ''Let's get back to Jeff. I don't understand what you're trying to hide about him.''

Leota tightened her hand on Nick's arm as she met the attorney's gaze, a sheen of moisture lighting her eyes. "Jeff and Nick and I were a family. Our lives are no one else's business."

"You can't expect Nick to marry someone in the next twelve months just so he can keep the property and money?"

"I can."

She dropped smoothly into her pattern of subservience to Jeff's wishes, as if she were a drowning woman who'd grabbed a rope. She didn't know any other way, and Nick feared what it would do to her if he forced the issue.

"I don't expect my son to marry just anybody," she said. "We know plenty of suitable women. He'll fall in love with a woman of good breeding and quality who would have made his father as proud as she'll make me."

Nick's concern for his mother overwhelmed his urge to break free of Jeff, but he had to point out the obvious. "You want me to just pick a woman and fall in love with her?"

"I want you to do what your father asked." Leota lowered her voice to a hiss. "For once, carry out one of his dreams for you."

Dreams, hell. He refused to allow Jeff to turn his life into a nightmare. His father's idea of a suitable woman piled insult on injury. "I never made a choice he liked. Now would be the worst time to start."

Wilford stacked the pages of Jeff's will. "One thing I think Leota's right about, Nick. Are you sure you'd want to go over this in front of a courtroom? Whatever drove your father to make these demands would come out. Do you need to ruin his reputation? He was, after all, a United States senator."

"And how about my reputation?" Leota said.

Her broken tone reached him. Hadn't she suffered enough at his father's hands? "Why do you still care?" he asked, more honest with her than he'd ever been.

"He was my husband."

She lifted her chin, perfectly formed through expensive surgery she'd undergone because she'd never looked good enough for Jeff. In his eyes or, consequently, her own. Nick's knowledge of her pain weighed much more than his concern for name or money.

"I can't decide this now." But he was pretty sure he'd already decided. To help Leota he would force himself to give in to Jeff. "I'll call you, Wilford, to schedule a time so we can go over the rest of the will."

He didn't look at Leota again as he unlocked the office door and stepped into the anteroom. As soon as he closed the door behind himself, another woman rose from a straight-backed chair.

"Nick?"

"Mrs. Franklin." Selina Franklin and her husband, Julian, known around Fairlove as "the judge" ran Franklin House, an upscale bed-and-breakfast. "Can I help you? Are you sick?"

She shook her steel-gray head. "I have a question to ask you." She opened her purse and plucked out a yellowed piece of paper. "Read this first. I received it almost twelve years ago."

What now? Barely holding on to his patience, Nick took the paper. The writer had typed the words and hadn't signed the note.

"If you value your husband's career," it read, "you'll stay out of my plans for the girl. And if you tell anyone about this, it's your word against mine. I'll enjoy ruining the judge while we find out I'm more credible."

Nick didn't need a signature. He knew the tone intimately. "What girl?" he asked.

"Clair Atherton. After her mother, Sylvie, died, I tried to get her out of foster care and adopt her. Someone kept blocking me, no matter what I or my husband tried. When I realized who was behind our problems, I spoke to a few other people in town. After I visited with Mayor Brent, I received this note. I knew the mayor and every other man your father owned would line up to say I'd typed it myself."

She was right. Mayor Brent and Jeff had fished, hunted and apparently practiced extortion together. Jeff's eulogy at Brent's funeral had won him his fourth term in the Senate.

"Where is Clair Atherton?" Anger produced a note in his voice he didn't even recognize. He didn't want to believe Jeff could hurt a child.

Selina didn't answer. He'd known her most of his life, but since he'd come home, she'd treated him with icy deference. Now he understood why.

"Are you like your father?" she finally asked.

"What are you talking about?" He wanted to tear someone apart, not stand around discussing whether he would persecute little girls. Clair Atherton must be in her twenties now. Surely old enough to take care of herself.

"I'm going to invite Clair back to Fairlove. If she comes and you try to harm her, you'll face all of us who had to let her go. We were afraid we couldn't protect her any better than we protected her parents, but you don't have your father's political clout."

Deep in Selina Franklin's eyes burned guilt as strong and relentless as Nick's own. He felt her start of surprise as she also recognized his secret shame. Turning away from her, he started toward the door on legs that felt as stiff as iron pokers.

He glanced over his shoulder, but didn't allow himself to meet Selina's gaze. "Clair Atherton has nothing to fear from me," he said.

Two days before Halloween, Clair turned off the interstate at the Fairlove exit. Immediately, the trees seemed more lush. She rolled down her window to breathe in the crisp air of home. A small green sign directed her toward town. Within seconds, she came upon Shilling's Gas 'n' Go.

It looked pretty much as it had the day she'd left. The same sign displayed gas prices in bold black letters. Twelve years ago, she'd stared at that sign through the back window of a social worker's van.

She didn't need a map to find her way from here. She could have driven to Franklin House with her eyes closed. This hour of the day, breakfast cooking in Selina Franklin's kitchen lured anyone with a sense of smell.

Clair suffered from even stronger appetites. Mrs.

Franklin's invitation had answered a longing Clair had never satisfied. Her mother's old friend had said she'd found her through the "white pages" on the Internet, and she'd wondered if Clair ever thought of the old town.

Clair hardly ever forgot. The house she'd lived in might have fallen into ruin after all these years of neglect. Often, she'd dreamed of Jeff Dylan demolishing it with a big yellow crane and a wrecking ball. But she couldn't forget the place where she'd known love, unconditional and ever-present, love whose memory made her hungry for the place she'd felt it.

But she was no longer a naive child, and she had to wonder why Selina Franklin had suddenly remembered her. Her parents' dearest friends, Mrs. Franklin and her husband, an ambitious attorney whom Clair's father had nicknamed the Judge, hadn't been the only ones to look the other way when Social Services had cast around for someone who might take Clair in. None of the people she'd thought were like family had found room for her.

Which made Mrs. Franklin's invitation all the more suspect. She'd asked for whatever time Clair could spare. Clair reminded herself to be wary. People rarely made such generous offers without an ulterior motive.

She slowed her car at the small elementary school, and memories assaulted her, of books and paper, overheated children who played hard outside at recess. Her memories had never left her, had, in fact, grown more important to her, because they formed a lifeline back to Fairlove.

The bell at Saint Theresa's began to peal, a call to morning prayers, and Clair turned her car toward the sound. Those deep chimes had punctuated so many moments of her first fourteen years. She was glad she'd broken her trip from Boston in D.C. the night before. She'd wanted to arrive with the morning bells.

As soon as she rounded the corner into Church Street, she saw him. Nick Dylan. The man whose father had destroyed her family. Tall, lean and prosperous-looking in a dark suit and a long black overcoat, he was carrying what appeared to be shirts from the dry cleaners.

Clair began to shake as she saw him approach a Jeep and open the door. The long dry-cleaning bags twined around his body. She slowed as he tucked his laundry in his back seat.

Good. With any luck, he was on his way somewhere else. Since the cleaners was closed on Sunday, he must have brought the shirts from his house. Maybe Fairlove wouldn't keep him now that his father had died.

He straightened, and the wind lifted his jet-black hair. She glimpsed his sharply etched, aristocratic Dylan face, dark eyes that met hers and instantly flared. Clair looked away, but she couldn't help looking back at him. His pale, shocked expression struck her as she passed him.

Barely three feet separated them, a space poisoned by years of family enmity. Clair clamped her teeth together, to keep from shouting her frustration. How could she have prepared herself for a Dylan mundanely packing his shirts in a car?

Rattled, her heart pounding, she drove twice around the square. People stared, but no one else recognized her. To push Nick Dylan out of her mind before she saw Mrs. Franklin, she concentrated on the buildings.

A landscaper had taken over the old ice-cream shop. The local newspaper had bought out Mrs. Clark's sewing-and-crafts shop and added on to their property.

Clair fought back unwanted tears. The sheer, comforting familiarity of these streets and buildings brought her past back to her. Her memories hadn't just been myths she'd created to help her survive in foster care.

She turned down the town's outer road toward the high school where she'd been in her first year when her parents had died. Those rooms hadn't left a strong impression. Nor had the apartment block behind the school, where they'd lived until her father died, a victim of his own sense of failure after he'd lost their house to Senator Dylan. After her father's death, her mother lost interest in everything. Including her own life. Within months she'd suffered a heart attack and followed her husband to the grave.

Clair looked up the hill. If her home still existed, thick evergreens hid it from her, but the Dylan home remained as commanding as ever. An image of Nick flashed through her mind, but his stunned expression got all mixed up with his father's customary contempt.

She turned away from that house, determined to conquer the pain that still tore at her. She shouldn't have come this way. She drove straight to Mrs. Franklin's bed-and-breakfast, determined to live in peace with her memories of the Dylans.

Her other choice was revenge. A pointless exercise that couldn't bring back the parents and the home she'd lost.

Clair parked at the bottom of the steps in front of the bed-and-breakfast and climbed out of the car. She swung her backpack over one shoulder. Caution moistened her hands and dried her mouth.

She marched up the stairs and then curled her fingers around the cool brass door handle. Counting two quick breaths, she pushed the door open and stepped into a shadowy hall. Overhead, a fan's blades whiffed in rhythmic puffs of sound. She waited for her eyes to grow accustomed to the subdued light.

"Clair, you've come home."

Her heart hammered. Home. She knew this woman's voice—rich, ragged around the edges. Selina Franklin had been a frequent visitor at Clair's house. She'd brought homemade oatmeal cookies and sock puppets with black button eyes.

The shadow in front of Clair slowly formed itself into a woman who seemed too short to be Mrs. Franklin. Clair had last seen her through the back of that Social Services van. Her memory of her mother's friend was all bound up with a painful mantra the woman who'd driven her to D.C. kept repeating. "You can't stay. You have no one here to take care of you."

That memory had become a nightmare. Mrs. Franklin must have known how she'd felt. Old resentment she no longer wanted to feel rose in her and she swallowed convulsively.

The other woman lifted pale hands to her own throat. "Can you be Clair?" A slight change in the arrangement of lines around her mouth conveyed her welcome. "You look so much like your mother that for a moment I thought you were her. Sylvie was your age when I first met her, when she came here to teach. What are you now? Twenty-four?"

"Twenty-six." Clair drank in the other woman's delicate features, pale blue eyes she remembered laughing at her mother's jokes, a generous mouth that had grown thin after her parents' deaths. "How is the judge?"

"He lived up to your dad's expectations. The governor appointed him to the bench about ten years ago." Mrs. Franklin turned to pluck an object from a cubby behind her desk. "I'm so glad you've come. I've given you a room, because I thought you'd be more comfortable on your own than staying in my guest room." She slid a big old-fashioned key across the desktop. "I'm not sure how many of your friends are still in town. Most of our young people seem to leave these days. Except for Nick Dylan." Clair stiffened at her mention of the Dylan name, but Mrs. Franklin went on, her words tumbling over each other. "He took over Dr. Truman's practice last year, and he refuses to leave."

"Refuses?"

"Apparently. Because every time I go past his office it's empty. People don't go to him unless they need serious help fast. Maybe he should advertise."

Trying not to see his shocked face in her mind again, Clair reached for the registration book on its spindle. Mrs. Franklin spun it away from her.

"Don't bother. You're my guest. You know, you'll probably see Nick sometimes. You can understand the quandary folks find themselves in. Honestly, who wants to take her bunions to Senator Jeffrey Dylan's boy?"

Clair concentrated on Mrs. Franklin's widow's peak. Why did the woman go on so about the Dylans?

"I guess you heard about Jeff?" Mrs. Franklin said.

She meant the fact that he'd died a month ago. The nation had mourned him. Clair could not. She adjusted her backpack strap. "I heard." She searched her key for a room number, but nothing marred the smooth swirls of old brass. "Which room should I put my things in?"

"The Concord. A few years ago, I named the rooms for Revolutionary War sites. The tourists seem to like it." Mrs. Franklin patted the scarred top of her eighteenth-century accountant's desk.

Clair worked at a smile, bewildered by Mrs. Franklin's rapid chatter and the watchful gaze that vied with her light tone. "How do I get to the Concord?" she asked.

"Take the elevator to the second floor and turn right. Three doors down on the left."

"Thanks."

"You haven't said how long you plan to stay."

Had she been wise to come at all? "I'm not sure. I'm kind of between jobs."

A frown crisscrossed the older woman's forehead. "We'll talk about that when you come back down. I want to know everything you've been doing."

Clair turned away from the desk, cast adrift. The woman looked like Mrs. Franklin, but she sure didn't act like her. What had made her so nervous? Did she regret her invitation?

Clair glanced back with a smile as she stepped onto the elevator. As soon as the doors closed, she sank against the paneled back wall. She'd carried enough clothes for tonight in her backpack. Maybe she wouldn't stay any longer.

In the upstairs hall, a wide brass plate announced the third door on the left as the entry to the Concord. Clair opened it and stepped into a room with just enough clutter to feel cozy. She dropped her backpack on the bench at the end of the bed and crossed to the windows to pull back the velvet drapes. Sunlight spilled over a fragile writing desk, tracing patterns on the floor.

Clair laughed. In work boots and jeans and a thermal turtleneck, she was the room's jarring note. She opened the bathroom door and promised herself a soak in the claw-footed tub. She took a soap from the marble dish on the counter and sniffed its fragrance. She was washing her face when she thought she heard a knock at the door.

Straightening, she blotted her face with a towel and the tapping was repeated. She crossed the room, still holding the towel as she opened the door. It was Selina.

"You probably think I'm a nut," the other woman said.

"Different from how I remember you," Clair admitted, smiling to soften her words.

"I haven't been honest."

Clair dropped the towel. After a nonplussed moment, she scooped it up again. "Do I want you to be?"

"I have to tell you the truth, because I'd like you to stay in Fairlove."

Dread weighed on Clair's shoulders, but she'd perfected a knack for floating with unexpected punches. "What's your secret?"

"Your parents' other friends and the judge and I—" Selina broke off, clearing her throat. "We let Social Services put you in foster care."

She'd known her family's friends hadn't stopped her from leaving, but she'd never imagined they'd decided not to help her. Backing blindly toward the bench, Clair managed to sink onto her backpack. Metal rings and rough canvas didn't hurt half as much as the truth.

"Why would you do that to me? Didn't you love my parents?"

"We loved you. We had to let you go."

CHAPTER TWO

"YOU LOVED ME, so you decided to make me live with strangers? My parents trusted all of you, but no one thought I might be better off with a family who cared about me?" Clair curled her fingers into the towel, wadding it against her stomach. Unbelievable.

"You don't understand. We weren't able to protect David and Sylvie, and we didn't think we could save you from Jeff Dylan, either."

Clair licked her dry lips. "You looked for me now because he died?"

"When you first left, I used my husband's influence to watch over you. I made sure you stayed around the D.C. area, and my friend in Social Services led all Jeff Dylan's inquiries astray. I know this may not comfort you, but we worked hard to keep him from finding you."

"He could have hired detectives."

"He did, but they always stumbled across the false trails my friend laid. She stepped outside the lines for me."

Clair turned and dropped the towel on the desk. "Maybe I owe you gratitude, but I don't know what to say."

"I don't expect you to trust me, but I'm glad you're

home. I'm sorry about the way I talked downstairs. I just knew you'd inevitably run into Nick Dylan, and I thought I'd test the waters, find out how you'd respond."

"I already saw him." She closed her eyes against that nagging image of his shocked face when he'd seen her. "I don't care about him."

"You don't?"

Clair shook her head, trying to convince herself. From the moment she'd accepted Mrs. Franklin's invitation, she'd wondered if it might be time to come home. She'd given her resignation to the landscaping firm she'd worked for in Boston. Whatever happened, she was ready for more-southern climates. "I don't ever have to see Nick Dylan."

"Don't fool yourself. He wants this community to accept him. He doesn't keep to his side of the Dylan hill."

"I'm not afraid of him." Clair lifted her chin, and Mrs. Franklin planted her hands on her hips.

"Why would you be with all of us behind you? We're on your side."

Clair considered. Why would she want to stay in a place where people she'd trusted had developed feet of clay?

Because she wasn't fourteen anymore. She could reason beyond a fourteen-year-old's pain, and she didn't care about clay feet or disappointment. She'd been happy in Fairlove. Her mother and father were buried in the ground her family had lived on for generations. She belonged in Fairlove.

She dropped her company manners. "Is my parents' house still standing?"

Mrs. Franklin looked puzzled, but Clair held her breath, waiting for an answer that meant everything to her. Jeff Dylan had stood in the dusty dirt driveway while she and her father and mother packed the last of their things into a rental truck. Jeff swore he'd never touch the house again. He just wanted to watch it decay until the earth claimed it.

He'd always talked like a hellfire-and-brimstone preacher.

"It stood for over a hundred years," Mrs. Franklin said at last. "It wouldn't crumble in a mere twelve years, but it looks neglected. Let me drive you out there."

Clair struggled to add kindness to her tone. She'd rather rebuild relationships than choke them all off just because they hadn't turned out the way she'd hoped.

"Thank you, but no. I need to see it on my own the first time." Living in foster care, she'd stopped depending on anyone for support. Truthfully, she wanted to believe someone on the face of this earth would back her up if she needed help, but she'd long since forgotten how to reach out and trust.

"If you haven't already had breakfast, I'll make it for you when you get back." Mrs. Franklin touched her throat again, a nervous gesture Clair remembered. "You'll come back?"

Nodding, Clair flipped open the top of her backpack and plucked out the small purse that held her driver's license. "I want to come back, Mrs. Franklin. And no, I haven't had breakfast."

"Clair, I'm so sorry about the past—about everything." The other woman folded her arms across her stomach.

Clair nodded, uncomfortable with her own need for a relationship as much as with Mrs. Franklin's. "You don't have to apologize. I think we both want to start again from here."

"I do." Eyes filled with surprising tears, Mrs. Franklin scooped the hand towel off the desk. "Go on, and I'll start breakfast. Good Lord, I forgot I have other guests."

She vanished through the bathroom door, and Clair made her escape. She'd like to forgive and forget, but she had to be sure she could before she made a move. Every breath she took here in Fairlove made staying more important to her. For twelve years, she'd taken action to keep from indulging in self-pity. Often action had translated into running away. She needed a more mature attitude if she was going to make a home here.

She drove out of town to the familiar road that led to her family's old house. She saw the roof first, rising above the trees. It looked surprisingly intact, but time, neglect and peeling paint had colored the clapboard siding a dreary gray. Clair nosed her car onto the old graveled drive, sparsely covered now in patches of thin grass. She got out and picked her way through ruts onto Dylan property, property that had once been Atherton.

Suspended above the oak door her grandfather had

carved, a wooden sign banged against the house. Normally this sign hung from an iron arm attached to one of the clapboards. Rust had decayed the chain at the end farthest from the house, and the sign had scraped a rut in the wood.

Clair read the sign, even though she knew every curlicue in the burnt engraving. The Oaks. An ancestor had named the house for the great gnarled trees that surrounded it. Clair's father had burned its name into the current sign one hot summer day when she was still too small to reach the top of his workbench. Once in every generation an Atherton had to make a new sign for their home. Responsibility for renewing the sign had passed down through the family with the house.

Fresh grief swamped Clair, but she choked back tears, unwilling to waste any more valuable seconds. She'd ached too deeply to surround herself with the familiar sensations, the sigh of the breeze that wound a loving embrace around the corners of her home, the click of branches that seemed to tap each other in secret conversation a human couldn't understand.

Ahead of her, something moved in the long uncut grass. A bird rose with a startled cry, and a wiry black feline sprang into the air.

"Hey!" Clair raced for the cat to shoo it away, but the bird had flown out of reach.

Clair stopped abruptly. Its original prey gone, the cat sagged into a crouch, seemingly more interested now in her than in the liberated meal that mocked him from the air.

"Go away." She firmed up her voice and wondered about rabies. Had this feral feline had its shots? The cat growled. Who knew a cat could growl? "Go away!"

Throwing its entire scrawny body into a hiss, the cat looked painfully hungry. Half its right ear was gone, and something had nipped out patches of its coat. Just as Clair began to feel a sense of sympathy for a fellow stray, it turned and streaked out of sight. The grass closed, and she stood alone.

She turned slowly in the new, unnatural silence. Wildlife rustled in brush that had taken over her mother's once carefully landscaped lawn. Twelve years of neglect gave the house a lost look, which Clair connected with.

She wanted to fix the house, make it a home again.

She could look all she wanted, but she was a trespasser here. She had no rights. She wasn't allowed to change anything—couldn't help a bird, feed a wild, hungry cat, or clean up the bits of trash that had blown against the kitchen wall.

Fighting a sense of futility, she understood the crippling failure that had hounded her father to his grave after he'd lost the house to Jeff Dylan. She didn't dare go close enough to peer through a dirt-stained window. Emptiness inside her left her unable to look at the bare spaces inside those walls.

WHEN SHE RETURNED to the bed-and-breakfast, Julian Franklin met her at the top of the steps. Decked out for court, he reminded her of the old days, when her father had teased him about his "litigious" wardrobe.

"Hello, Judge."

His smile, lacking his wife's nervous edge, greeted her. "Selina told me you'd arrived. I wanted to welcome you."

He held out his hand, and Clair clasped it. "Your house is lovely."

He turned toward the door and opened it for her. "All due to Selina's reconstruction plan. I always do what she tells me when she makes a plan."

Clair laughed. "You're subtle, sir. Are you saying she's made a plan for me?"

He took her hand again. "I don't have time to be subtle. I declared a recess to give myself a brief break from court. I wanted to tell you we'd love to have you stay here as long as you can." He let her go and reached back for the door. "God, you look like Sylvie. I've missed you and your mom and dad. There's been a hole in my life ever since you left."

"Mine, too."

Grinning, he looked back one last time. "You listen to my wife. She's rarely wrong."

Clair smiled back at him as he headed out. If Selina was never wrong, she'd been better off in foster care. Hard to believe.

She glanced into the dining room. It looked empty, but a man's husky voice came from around a paneled corner.

"I won't do it, Wilford. I don't care who finds out about the will or anything else Jeff did. You're an executor and my attorney. Get me out of this. Give everything to my mother."

"You know it doesn't work that way. Your cousin

will inherit and move her out like yesterday's rubbish.''

Clair leaned around the door frame, shamelessly curious, but when she met Nick Dylan's dark blue gaze, she almost lost her balance and fell. She fled—from him and the appalled-looking white-haired man he was talking to.

An image of The Oaks reared in her mind, peeling, anchored deeper to the ground by its aura of neglect. She'd lost everything to that man's family. She'd had to flee, or she'd say things that would force her to leave a town where Dylan word might still rule.

Crossing the lobby, she snatched a newspaper off the stack on Mrs. Franklin's desk and sprawled on the love seat. Footsteps made the floor creak. She knew when she looked up she'd see Nick standing in the doorway.

''Good morning,'' he said.

She nodded. He looked lean and barely leashed, as if the powerful emotion that darkened his eyes might explode from his body at any moment. Restraint furrowed strong lines from the aristocratic nose someone had bent for him to his surprisingly full mouth.

''Maybe we should talk.'' The husky voice that had drawn her into the dining room took on a deeper timbre.

He stepped closer. She held still while inwardly she strained to look indifferent. Nick Dylan would never best her as his father had.

''I don't need to talk to you.'' Her voice sounded smooth to her, and she took courage.

''I know who you are.''

"Because I look like my mother. You remember her?"

He took another step closer. Losing her grip on her composure, she pressed against the love seat's cushions.

"Are you afraid of me, Clair?"

"Your father bought our mortgage and bided his time until Dad got in trouble and he could demand payment in full. Jeff hounded my father into his grave, and why? For the sake of his sick, obsessive love for my mother. He destroyed my father out of vengeance. Should I be afraid of you?"

Nick yanked at his black tie as if it had tightened around his throat. "I'm not my father."

"Then give me my family's house. Do what's right." Her unreasonable demand poured out of her.

His desperate look reached inside her, made her feel for him. "I can't."

The other man had come out of the dining room. "Nick, your hands are tied until you do what your father wanted," he said. He took Nick's arm, but Nick pulled away.

"We'll talk somewhere else, Wilford." He turned back to Clair. "I can't give you that house. You're asking me to do what I cannot do." He turned and waited for Wilford to leave in front of him.

Clair let out her breath when the door closed behind his too-straight back. She resisted the sympathy she'd felt for his pain. His weakness gave her strength.

It seemed he wanted to give her house back, and she'd take it if he gave her the slightest opening.

She turned her face to the newspaper, visions of her empty home haunting her. What if she stayed? What if she found a job?

Assuming she could persuade Nick Dylan to at least sell her the house, she'd still never find the kind of money he'd want. How would she find a job that could pay her that kind of money?

She simply didn't have the qualifications to afford a falling-down, hundred year old house. After she'd dropped out of college, she'd been a ticket taker in a theater, she'd managed a Laundromat and she'd washed dishes in a diner. Then she'd found landscaping. She'd planted other peoples' yards from D.C. to Boston for the past five years. But without a degree, she couldn't command the kind of pay a qualified landscape designer could.

"Clair? Why are you sitting out here?" Mrs. Franklin had come out of nowhere—or at least from the shadows behind her desk. She set her mouth. "You're upset because you saw the house."

Clair didn't feel comfortable enough with Selina yet to share what had just happened between herself and Nick. She attempted a smile that trembled uncomfortably on her lips. "The judge met me at the door."

Selina smiled knowingly. "I thought he'd drop by. He's glad you're home."

Home? Clair wasn't sure yet. She changed the subject, lifting the paper. "Still published twice a week?" The pages rustled in her shaking hands. She flattened the paper on her lap.

"Thursday's edition still carries the classifieds."

Clair understood Mrs. Franklin's message. "I haven't said anything about looking for a job here."

"But you'd like to stay? You feel strong ties. The house wouldn't have bothered you if you could just leave."

"You make it sound as if I can turn my life around overnight." But hadn't she already decided to stay? The moment she'd received Mrs. Franklin's invitation? Hadn't she decided then?

Mrs. Franklin came around the desk, ushering Clair before her into the breakfast room. "At least think about staying."

"I'm thinking I can't buy my house back."

"What kind of work do you do?"

Clair stopped beside a small round table that glittered with crystal and china, and reminded her of the table her mother used to set. "Where do you want me to sit?"

"Wherever you like. You didn't answer me."

She hadn't because Mrs. Franklin's eagerness, after twelve years of silence, put her off. "Most recently I worked for a landscaper. I notice there's a landscaping business on the square." She pulled out a chair and sat while the older woman brought a coffee carafe from the sideboard and poured her a cup. She left the carafe on the table.

"Paul Sayers owns Fairlove Lovelies. Do you remember him? No, you wouldn't. He moved here about four years ago. Still new in town."

"Nearly a stranger."

Mrs. Franklin smiled. "We have a new subdivision going in by Lake Stedmore. The development company hired Paul to maintain the common areas. Why don't I call him?''

"Why don't I think about it first?"

"I'm crowding you.'' The older woman's cheeks flushed. ''You were part of my life, as much as I could keep you in sight without alerting Jeff Dylan. I care about you, and I guess I'm trying to make up for those years.''

Touched, Clair let down her guard. ''You have nothing to make up. I've made my own decisions for a long time.'' She grimaced, remembering some of them, a love affair with a professor that had, however unfairly, ended her college career, the jobs and towns she'd left because she hadn't belonged. She could have made herself a home in any one of those places. ''I'd like to stay, but I'd have to find a job and I'd have to face the fact that I'll never live in my house again.''

"Do you love The Oaks more than the town? People who care about you, people who hold your history in their memories live in Fairlove, and we want you back now that it's safe for you.''

Clair wanted to believe. ''I'm not sure I can stay when I'm afraid I'd be letting Mom and Dad down if I don't try to get the house back.''

"I'll ask Paul Sayers to come over. You just talk to him. You don't have to decide now.''

Agreeing to meet him meant she'd made a decision. Clair knew herself well enough to realize she'd accept a job if the landscaper offered it. She wanted to be sure before she took action, but she heard herself answering, "I'll call him if you'll give me the number."

Mrs. Franklin pursed her lips. "Let me do this one thing for you, and then I'll lay off." She clapped her hands together. "Now, do you want the continental breakfast, or can I make you bacon and eggs and home fries like your mama used to make?"

Clair set the menu aside, hungry after such an exhausting morning. "No contest. I'll take the bacon and eggs, thank you."

Mrs. Franklin turned smartly for the kitchen and Clair opened the paper. A man and woman came into the dining room so completely engrossed in each other she couldn't help watching them. She envied the couple their intimacy.

As they took the corner table, she tried to return her attention to the newspaper. The dry cleaners had an advertisement that promised they'd clean six shirts for a low, low price. So Nick Dylan had found himself a bargain.

"All right, I talked to Paul."

Clair jumped. "I didn't see you come back, Mrs. Franklin."

She set a plate on the mat in front of Clair. "Better start on this. Paul's coming over. He had some free time, and he said he wanted to talk to an experienced worker."

Clair felt a bit nauseous, but she picked up her fork. "This is a huge decision. I still think I should take some time to make it."

"Talk to Paul. Then think." Mrs. Franklin straightened the knife at Clair's right hand. Her gaze made

Clair uncomfortable. "You look so much like your mother."

"I think you've confused me with her. That's why you're so glad to see me."

"Maybe partly. I'm ashamed I couldn't do more for you, but maybe I want to know you better, too. And you have a right to live in the town where you were born. Fairlove can be a good place to live."

"If your name isn't Atherton and you don't attract the hatred of a Dylan."

"Jeff Dylan loved your mother once."

"Then he hated her, and he hated my father and me."

"I don't think Nick Dylan is like his father. If you can stand seeing him around town, you'll like living here again. Leota stays up at the house. She hardly ever comes down to town, and she won't have anything to do with the likes of you or me."

"You?" Clair was surprised. "You're a judge's wife. You're just the kind of people Leota Dylan liked."

"She likes most judges' wives." Mrs. Franklin turned away, and this time she was clearly hiding her thoughts. "We'll talk about Leota later. My other guests will think I'm ignoring them."

Clair welcomed time on her own to put her meeting with Nick Dylan behind her and think about her impromptu interview with Paul Sayers. About whether she should even consider talking to this man about a job in a town where Nick Dylan looked at her as if she'd risen from the dead.

Her breakfast went untouched as she stared at the

newspaper whose ink she'd smeared, but not read. Did she have enough courage to try to make a life in Fairlove?

"Excuse me. Are you Clair Atherton?"

She looked up. A tall man towered over her table, his jeans clean but stained, his belly a gentle protrusion above his wide leather belt. He pried a Braves baseball cap off wild brown curls sprinkled with gray and threaded his fingers through them.

"You must be Paul Sayers."

He nodded. "Selina tells me you have experience and you might be looking for work. I could use another pair of hands."

Folding the paper away, Clair pointed at the other chair. "Do you want to sit down?"

He sat and hitched his chair closer. "Do you have any references? I know you won't have them on you now, but you can bring them to me."

She nodded. "I worked for a nursery in Connecticut for about two years, and then I moved on to a couple of landscaping firms in Boston." She reached into her purse and pulled out a notepad. "I can write down names and numbers right now."

As she wrote, he said, "I'll take them, but first I need to know how long you think you'll be staying in town." He reached for a cup from the next table and poured himself coffee. "Not that I should ask, but I've had a hard time keeping people for longer than a season."

She hesitated for a long moment. He was asking for a commitment. And it scared her, but this was a commitment she suspected she'd been running to, not one she would run from.

"I've come home," she finally said. Paul Sayers didn't know her, didn't know her family. She didn't have to prove she belonged in Fairlove to him. "I lived here once."

"Good. Wait a minute. Atherton? Your family owned that old house in the oak grove at the bottom of the Dylan estate?"

She nodded.

"I hate seeing folks let a fine old place like that go. It's a beauty, or it could be if someone with a little elbow grease took it over. Do you plan to buy it back?"

She looked away, not wanting to show him how much the loss of her home hurt. "I'd need more than one job to manage that."

Paul nodded. "I sure can't pay you that kind of money, but the company's young. If your references pan out and you're a strong worker and you actually stay, you'd be helping me stake my business in this town. If the business grows, my employees grow with it."

"I don't have a degree."

At his crooked smile, Clair wished she hadn't felt quite so compelled to be honest. Her embarrassment amused him.

"Mine's over twenty years old," he said. "Thanks for telling me, but I'm happy to teach anyone who stays. I figure I'm grooming people who'll take ownership in my business." He picked up his coffee cup and sipped. "Do you think Selina would bring some breakfast for me?"

"Probably." His matter-of-fact attitude put Clair at ease. She freshened his coffee cup from the carafe. "How often does she arrange job interviews for her guests?"

"Not very." Paul took a sip before he said, "Between the two of them, I guess the Franklins know most of what goes on in this town. If you work out, I may consider paying her a recruiting fee. Why don't you tell me what kinds of jobs you've done for those other companies?"

"I have some sketches."

Clair drew her pad out of her backpack, and they talked work. Mrs. Franklin brought breakfast for Paul without being asked. Finally he pushed back from the table and stood.

"Why don't you drop your résumé by my office in the morning and meet my two associates. We'll assume you'll start on Wednesday, and I'll call you if I have any questions about your references."

"Thank you." As she stood to shake his hand, she noticed the familiar scent of mulch. "I think I saw your office on the square."

"I took over the Tastee Cone shop." He dragged his baseball cap over his hair and smiled crookedly. "I hear my neighbors miss the ice cream."

Clair wondered. She'd been too young to understand nuances, such as socially acceptable businesses for the square, when she'd left. What if she had come back to a place she'd made up to comfort herself? It looked the same, but so far the people hadn't turned out the same as she'd remembered them.

She refused to think that way. She'd decided to stay. Now she had to find out if she'd really come home.

"Mrs. Franklin thinks highly of your work, and I'm grateful you had the time to come by here."

Paul was buttoning his jacket as Selina Franklin came through the swing door from the kitchen. "You'll probably work with me the first few days— kind of a probation period. I want to see what skills you bring, and then I'll pair you with other staff who complement what you know. This being winter, you know we're mostly cleaning, preparing for the spring." He lifted his hand to Mrs. Franklin. "What do I owe you?"

"Not a thing. I'm glad you had a free hour. Did you and Clair finish your business?"

"To our mutual benefit, I hope. Thanks for everything, Selina. I'll see you Wednesday, Clair."

He left, and Clair turned awkwardly to her hostess. "I'd like to hug you, Mrs. Franklin, but I remember my mother telling me to keep my muddy hands off your dress."

"You always did like growing things, didn't you?" She dropped her arm across Clair's shoulders and squeezed. "What do you say you call me Selina, and I'll tell you what I propose for your living arrangements."

"What do you mean?"

"Sit down. I'll join you in a cup of coffee. We're not too busy right now."

"Mrs. Franklin, I can't let you do anything more for me."

"Selina. And I want you to do a few things for me. When we finish our talk, I'll show you my back garden. It's a jungle."

Clair stared in dismay at the third cup of caffeine Selina had poured for her. "That lovely garden?" she said. "I used to think it was a playground."

"It looked like one. The judge had more time to work with it back then, but his taste ran to the gauche." Selina crossed her legs. "And I'm being generous. Since he took office, I've hauled away the candy-striped poles. I took down the birds and the wires he used to make them look like they were flying. I even got rid of that horrible birdbath sculpture his mother insisted we keep in front of her window. You remember the Furies in stone? They were most indecent—looked like snake women writhing all over each other, but then, you know the judge had to get his taste from somewhere."

"Are you asking me to work on your garden?" Excited, Clair forgot her caffeine buzz and sipped the coffee. "I'd love to, but like Paul said, I can't do much more than clean and plant bulbs for the spring."

"Cleaning." Selina sighed in overstated relief. "Just what I need back there. You do what you can after your work with Paul, and I'll give you a room until you find a place to live."

"I'm not going to pretend I don't want to." A garden she'd loved as a child proved irresistible. "You have a deal."

"Great. Take today to rest. You can start tomorrow."

"Thanks." She set her napkin on the table and broached an uncomfortable subject. "Can I ask you one more favor, Selina?"

"Ask away. I'll do what I can."

"I appreciate your help, but I remember how this town works. Please don't make me some sort of a…community project. I'd like to start fresh."

"Don't worry. I haven't told anyone else I had any part in bringing you back here. As far as they'll know, you decided to come home."

"They? I don't think I want to know who else was in on your plan all these years."

Selina's mouth quivered, but she wound her arms around Clair. "You're going to be all right now."

Clair hugged her back. Maybe coming home really was the right decision.

Clair unpacked the rest of the things from her car and then checked Selina's gardening shed for tools. She made a list of things she'd need and slipped it into the pocket of her jeans to take to Bigelow's General Store.

As she shopped the garden section at Bigelow's, she found herself circling flats of pansies. Her mom's crocuses had heralded the end of winter every spring. In fall, she'd planted pansies in her favorite flower bed by the front door.

Clair wanted to go home and tell her parents about today, that she'd met Nick Dylan and survived, that she'd found a way to stay in Fairlove if she got the job with Paul Sayers.

Maybe she couldn't tell them in spoken words. Maybe she hadn't been able to force herself to look inside the house, but she could do something about the way the outside looked. Purple had been her mom's favorite, so Clair added purple pansies and soil nutrients to her purchases.

She parked at the end of the driveway again, got out and followed the path she'd made earlier, marked by the bent grass.

Taking tools, plants and bucket up to the house required a couple of trips, but contentment stole over her. She forgot about time as she pulled weeds and restacked the bricks that had fallen away from the retaining wall in a dry puddle of crumbled mortar.

She hummed to herself while she blended the nutrients into the black earth. She ought to leave this flower bed for another day or two, but she couldn't. One of the Dylan attorneys might turn up at Selina's and tell her to stay off Dylan property.

She planted the pansies, then brought water from the stream that ran behind the house to thoroughly moisten the bed. At last she stood back to admire her work.

The sad, chipped house paint nagged at her, but the past twelve years had taught her not to dwell on what she couldn't change. Her pansies gave The Oaks an air of hope again. She felt foolish about being too afraid to look inside earlier.

Clair marched around the house to the kitchen window and scrubbed at the glass until she could make out the white enamel sink. Because dirt filmed the other side of the window, too, she still couldn't see anything in the shadows.

"Clair?"

She recognized his voice. Slowly, she turned and found he'd taken control of his emotions, and he'd inherited the Dylan ability to gaze arrogantly at the rest of the world as if he understood its relation to him. Patience stalked behind his gaze. He could wait for what he wanted.

Would this Dylan know how to grind the family ax against her?

"I'm surprised to find you here," he said.

"Surprised I'd trespass?"

He gestured at the house. "Seeing this place has to hurt you."

Ashamed of the way she'd fled without looking back earlier, she put on some arrogance of her own. "It looks better now, with the pansies. They're trespassing, too."

"How much have you missed this house?" His unexpected question suggested he'd stumbled upon the solution to a mystery.

Uneasily, she headed back to the front of the house to collect her tools. "I've missed it enough that I won't promise not to trespass again."

"I didn't ask you not to come here." His voice came from close behind her.

His changed mood signaled a shift in the balance of power between them. She picked up her things in one armload for the return trip to her car. Nick stood behind her again when she turned. He nodded toward the house.

"Do you want to go inside?"

Her breath caught. She wanted to go in. More than anything. But he was Nick Dylan. The son of the man who'd taken hearth and home from her. She couldn't make herself beholden to him.

"I have to leave." Immediately, she cursed her foolishness. He was the one person who *could* let her into her old home. She turned back. "Maybe some other time, I could come to your office and pick up the key?"

"You know where I work?" He seemed surprised that she would have talked to anyone about him.

"It's a small town."

"Come to my office. I'll have the key for you."

She held back, feeling suddenly vulnerable. To think she would walk into her house again, touch the walls and floors her mother and father had loved, dispel her nagging sense of having dreamed her first fourteen years.

But how much of Nicholas Seton Dylan's character rose out of his father's gene pool? He must have ulterior motives.

She forced herself to take measured steps back to her car. In case he was watching her as his father had watched her mother...

CHAPTER THREE

CLAIR HAD BEEN WORKING with Paul every day for a week when she stood at his shoulder as he tossed a quarter into the air.

"Heads, you aerate, tails, I go across the street and try to sell our services to Mrs. Velasco," he said.

Clair clamped her hand around one of the aerator's handles. "You think I don't notice you're sticking me with this bone-shaker either way?" She turned it toward the front of the lawn. "How do you know Mrs. Velasco's name?"

"I read her mailbox." Paul's sheepish grin was infectious. Friendly and open, he lacked Nick Dylan's intensity. He shrugged. "I can't afford mailing lists, but she'll see you over here, giving me your all, and she'll beg us to help her."

"Giving you my what?" Clair asked.

"Your all to make a more beautiful lawn for her neighbors."

At his prim spiel, Clair had to smile. "I guess her leaves need mulching."

"I'll promise her the industrious young lady across the street will do the job."

He moseyed over, and Clair fired up the aerator.

At the end of her first row across the lawn she peeked at her employer in his salesman persona.

"Mrs. Velasco" turned out to be a man of dignified years. His white hair floated in the cool breeze. He looked frail enough to rustle like the leaves that glided across his yard. He lifted a hand to Clair, joining Paul in a wave. She waved back, but then latched onto the aerator before it took off without her.

Its tendency to act independently forced her to keep her mind on her task, but when she finished, she turned to find Paul leaning against his truck, his feet crossed at the ankles. Silence echoed in her ears after the aerator's roar. She worked her way around Paul to hoist the equipment back onto the trailer.

"What do you think?" she asked.

"You're a strong woman. You remind me of my wife before she told me she couldn't work with me anymore."

"Thanks." She tied the machine down with safety straps, guessing she could offer insight into Mrs. Sayers's reasoning. "But what I meant was, am I safe to work on my own, or are you afraid I'll single-handedly bring down the Fairlove Lovelies empire if you turn your back on me?"

"Every time you say our name I think you're making fun of my business." Paul jabbed at her forearm. "Don't mock the company that feeds you."

"Have you decided it's going to feed me?"

"You have some real authority issues, Clair, but you work hard." He held out his hand. "Congratulations. You're official. Probation's over."

"Thank you." She shook his hand and walked

around him again to open the passenger door. "I can use the paycheck."

"How do you feel about Mr. Velasco?"

"You promised me to him?" Paul didn't care whose soul he sold to lock down new work.

"You closed the deal when you tossed that branch. No man can resist a woman who can whip him in a wrestling match."

"Get in the truck, Paul."

"Could you come back and work up a design for him?"

She let honesty get in the way of her ambition again. "I'd work like crazy at it, but remember, I'm not professionally trained to draft a plan."

"I don't care about this college degree that seems to be sticking in your craw. Can you do the work?"

His confidence pleased her. "You bet I can. Will you go over it with me before I show it to Mr. Velasco?"

Instead of answering, Paul took a tape measure from his pocket. "I told him we'd look over the yard before we left. He's especially interested in reclaiming the back from nature."

Clair fell into step beside Paul. "I'd better warn you, I tend to be on nature's side."

"I figured that out already."

She enjoyed working with him. He'd quickly sized up her skills, and she'd learned from him during her probation period. They thought alike, and their working association had quickly become a friendship Clair valued. That afternoon, when they returned to the office, the others had gone home for the day. Clair took over Paul's drawing table and lost herself in her work.

BY PLANTING FLOWERS in her old yard, Clair had shown Nick a way out of his problems. Maybe he could offer her what she wanted and persuade her to help him. He'd just have to make her forget who he was. For a year.

He'd hired a detective to find out where and how she'd spent the past twelve years. Two weeks later, he'd come home from his volunteer shift at the Staunton clinic and found the detective's report in his mail.

The number of foster homes she'd gone through surprised him, and they'd all been in the suburbs outside Washington, D.C. How had she felt, living within a couple of hours of the town she'd left after her parents died?

After high school, Clair had won a scholarship to Wellesley, which she lost after the first year. The detective reported rumors of an affair with one of her professors. Nick dropped the report, frowning at the list of jobs she'd held before she settled down to work at landscaping.

She'd been troubled. Maybe she still was. Even if she wasn't still changing jobs, she'd left her home in New England to make her way back here. How stable was she?

The detective reported she'd known several men besides the professor. Nick assumed the ''known'' was a euphemism. He tightened his mouth. Had she tried to replace the love she'd lost because of his father's need to hurt a former lover?

He'd like to know more about how Clair's father had lost their house. He hardly remembered David Atherton. Older than Sylvie by more than twenty years, his very existence had been an insult to Jeff Dylan. Jeff saw him as a less-virile man who'd stolen the one woman Jeff truly loved. Jeff liked to forget he'd told Sylvie she wasn't good enough to marry.

After she'd moved on, Jeff's second thoughts had nearly destroyed two families. Jeff had searched for revenge against David and Sylvie, who'd truly loved each other, until he wound up with the Atherton mortgage. And then he'd foreclosed.

Twenty at the time, preoccupied with premed, Nick had never asked for details. To Nick, Jeff's anger at the woman he'd thrown away had been an insult to Leota and an emotional counterbalance to Jeff's disappointment with the son he'd fathered on the rebound.

Clair had found the healthier response—contempt for his father's "love." But the past still held her as tightly as it did Nick. Like sought like when pain struck this deep, and he'd recognized how hurt she must still feel.

He pictured her, lithe muscles straining as she'd planted those flowers at her house. Humming a song as she reclaimed a small piece of her past.

Maybe he was crazy, but he thought Clair might be the perfect wife. She certainly wouldn't want the position permanently, but she longed for the house only he could give her.

At a knock on his door he shoved the letter, report

and envelope into a drawer before he opened the door to Hunter.

"Dr. Dylan, I'm just on my way to tell Mrs. Dylan dinner is ready. I was concerned you might forget to come down again."

Nick felt a surge of warmth for the man who still treated him as the neglected child in a rich man's house. "Making sure I eat isn't your job." Gratitude roughened his voice.

"I'm concerned about your mother, as well." Hunter shrugged uneasily and pointed at the door. "May I come in?"

Nick stood aside. Frightened for Leota, he'd flushed the pills, poured out the brandy and told his mother he'd invite a therapist to live with them if she renewed her supplies. "What else has happened?"

"I don't know whether I should talk to you about Mrs. Dylan. Telling you what I think is going on with her might be inappropriate, but you know my loyalty."

"What is wrong, Hunter?"

"She stays in her rooms until lunch. She's never hungry. I find this most difficult to say, but her maid suspects she's begun to cry herself to sleep at night. Mrs. Dylan's pillowcase is still damp when she makes the bed."

Cold dread grabbed Nick low in the gut. He'd been reason enough for his parents to marry. He hadn't made Jeff love Leota, and Leota always seemed to wish her son would try a little harder to make Jeff's love possible.

But Hunter had been family to him when his own

mother and father couldn't help reminding him he'd failed as a son. Time he took the load off Hunter's shoulders. And time he found out if he could be the son his mother needed.

"Thank you, Hunter, for telling me. I'll bring Leota down for dinner." But doubt hounded him as he went to his mother's room. He could talk her into dinner, but could he persuade her to get help? Maybe—if he managed to keep their home.

ALONE IN THE OFFICE, Clair was working on her design when Paul came in to lock the company's cell phones away. "You still here?" he asked. "Don't stay any longer. Your idea's almost ready to present."

"I want to finish it tonight before I go."

"What are you trying to prove? I know you can do the work."

"I need to polish." She pointed her pen toward the dark outside the windows. "It's too late to work in Selina's garden tonight and—" A tall, dark-suited man walked into the light shining through the windows onto the sidewalk, and Clair's throat dried out instantly. "What's he doing here?"

"Who cares? Whatever he wants, we'll do it for him." Paul hurried to open the door for Nick. "Dr. Dylan, come in."

"I'd like to speak to Clair, if she has time."

Both men looked at her. *No* sprang to mind. She'd avoided Nick since he'd offered to let her tour her house. Tending her pansies later, she'd thought hard about him and his family. She didn't want to owe him for even the smallest pleasure, but Paul's pleading gaze told her he didn't share her lack of enthusiasm for Dylan business.

Paul, she owed.

"Go ahead." She shooed her employer toward the door. "I'll lock up."

"Don't stay too much longer." He slipped out. He'd "Velasco'd" her again.

"Can I offer you coffee, Dr. Dylan?"

Nick tugged at his tie. "I'd rather have a Scotch. Want to join me?"

Not even for Paul. "As you can see, I'm working. What can we do for you?"

He shook his head, his dark blue eyes serious. "I didn't come to ask you to work for me."

She declined to feel alarmed. "Then why are you here?"

"After we talked the other night, I expected you'd come ask for the key to your old house."

"Why look at decay I can't clean out?" An unaccustomed blush warmed her skin. She sounded melodramatic, but it was the truth.

"How would you change the house if you could?"

"Paint." Plans she'd never consciously made spilled out of her without warning. "After twelve years, I'd probably have to rehang doors, take down wallpaper, redo the floors—" She interrupted herself, appalled. "But I don't think about it."

One corner of his wide mouth tilted, and he looked human. "Maybe you should think."

"Want to explain what you mean?"

"What if I could make the house yours?"

Pain streaked through her body. She pressed her

hands to her cheeks. "Are you saying you'd sell my family's house back to me? I can't afford to make an offer you wouldn't laugh at."

"I'm not asking for money."

"What do you mean?" Either money or power fed the Dylans.

"Let's get a drink and talk seriously." He opened the door and reached for the light switch, but stopped. "Think how you'd feel if I could give your house back to you."

She didn't know she'd backed away from him until she bumped into the table. "Why would you?"

"Have you heard the terms of my father's will?"

She shook her head. His words, "give your house back," repeated over and over in her head, the rasp of his tone burrowing deeper into her mind.

"Jeff left everything to me," he said absently, as if he'd forgotten she was listening. "Land, investments, bank accounts, your house." He switched off the light. "But he made stipulations."

"Please turn the light back on."

"He said I have to marry. Fall in love and marry within twelve months, and stay married for a year."

Only Jeff Dylan would be arrogant enough to believe he could regulate love. She shook her head to chase the thought away, feeling too close to Nick in the darkness. They both knew too much about the effects of his father's illogical resentment. A sense of intimacy with Nick Dylan was the last thing she wanted. "Turn on the light."

"Every time you look at me I know you despise

me, but your voice—when I can't see your face—
your voice hates me more.''

"What do you want?''

"Clair, I want you to marry me. If you pretend to
be my loving wife for twelve months, I'll sign your
house over to you, and no one will ever take it from
you again.''

A gust of wind rattled the glass behind him.

"Do you think you're funny? I'm not laughing.''

"I saw that as a good sign. I'm serious. Give me
what I need, and I'll give you your house.''

"I want it.''

"I knew you did when I found you planting pansies.''

Suddenly safe in the dark with her own disjointed
emotions, she was glad he hadn't listened to her about
the light. "You must know other women. What's
wrong with you?''

He laughed without joy or happiness. "I know
other women, but I don't want to marry any of them.
I'm not seeing anyone right now, and I don't want to
start a marriage with someone who'd expect it to last.
Can you imagine you'll want to stay married to me?''

Her stomach knotted. "No.''

"Then you're the wife I want.''

The light switch clicked, and Clair blinked in the
startling brightness.

"Want to come for that drink now?'' he asked,
weariness in his voice.

"Someone might see us together and misunder-
stand.''

"We may need people to see us together. If you

want your house back, everyone will have to believe we want to be married to each other.''

"Stop using my house against me. You're trying to buy me.''

"I'll do what I have to," he admitted.

Silence lay between them. Why pretend she felt any differently? "If I said yes," she ventured, "I'd want our agreement in writing.''

"Wilford Thomas is my attorney. You won't want me to suggest someone for you, but I believe you know Judge Franklin?''

"I'm staying with him and Selina.''

"He'll suggest someone you can trust.''

Clair hugged herself more tightly. "How did you choose me?''

"I have to marry someone. No one else wants something I have as badly as you do.''

Clair thought of the Dylan mansion, the stables, the pools and tennis courts. The offshore bank accounts. "Use your imagination.''

He had a way of smiling that made him seem as if he saw his own failings. Clair looked away from him.

"I need to think," she said. "I never expected a chance to take my home back.''

"I'm trying as hard as I can to give you a chance.''

He broke off as another man stepped out of the darkness into the light from the windows on the sidewalk. Clair couldn't place his rugged, weather-lined features. He stared from the pediment over the door to the interior of the shop. Nodding at them both, he opened the door and came inside, looking at them with a curious frown.

"Something wrong?" he asked.

"What do you mean, Fosdyke?" Nick eyed the other man with surprise.

"I saw the lights go off and on. Thought you might be having a problem over here." He studied Clair. "I know you."

Nick moved closer to her. "I forgot you might not recognize each other. Ernest Fosdyke, this is Clair Atherton."

"I knew your mother," he said. "I'm the fire chief. You certainly look like Sylvie."

"Thank you." She didn't want to talk about her mom in front of Nick.

"I heard you were working for Paul Sayers."

She used her job to head off gossip about Nick's visit. "Dr. Dylan and I were discussing some work on his house."

"No problems, then? You know these old buildings and their electricity. I guess I'll move on. I was on my way home. Night, Clair. Nice to see you back in town."

"I'm glad to be home."

"Good night, Dr. Dylan."

Clair glanced at Nick. Ernest Fosdyke had all but made a subservient bow.

"Wait, Ernest. I'll come with you. I want to talk to you about the clinic in Staunton." Nick opened the door, but looked back at Clair. "I can't wait long. I need a decision."

Clair lifted her hand in answer to Fosdyke's brief wave, and both men disappeared.

She shivered. What better revenge could she ever

hope to take against Jeff Dylan? It was just that she'd decided before she came back home not to look for revenge. No one like the senator would ever take advantage of her again, but she didn't intend to let anger turn her into a version of him.

She'd like to understand Nick before she thought about his idea. Marriage, an idea? A plan? Why didn't he contest the will? She'd have dragged a worthless piece of paper like that through the legal system frontward, backward and sideways.

Just went to show how different people could be. She fought back when someone tried to hurt her. Nick Dylan was willing to contort himself into a knot to come up with a compromise.

She laughed shortly. If she was willing to seriously consider his proposal, they weren't so different after all.

LEOTA WAS CRYING. Nick heard her that night as he climbed the stairs to his bedroom. He followed the sound to the hall outside his father's door. He'd tended to see his mother as the softer-hearted of his parents, but he'd never heard her cry.

He knocked, but he knew she wouldn't ask him in, so he opened the door. Leota sprang up from his father's bed. Gold and silver bracelets jangled on her wrist as she brushed her smooth blond hair from her face. Lying down had wrinkled her silk blouse and dark green trousers.

Baffled, Nick met her wild gaze. "Are you all right? Can I help you?"

"Are you here this time as my son or as a doctor?"

"Why not both? I'm concerned about you."

"I don't need a keeper. If you don't like seeing me this way, go back to your house."

"And leave you alone? Even if I weren't your son, I couldn't."

"I don't need your interference. I need time."

"You're suffering from pretty severe mood swings."

"My husband has been dead for a month."

"But you won't talk about your feelings, and you aren't in control of them. At least trust me. Talk to me."

"How can I talk to you when you've always pushed us away?"

"I've pushed you?" She and Jeff had sent him to boarding school when he was eight. They'd disapproved of every major decision he'd ever made. Discussion had led to recrimination and finally, to silence. He rejected his own thoughts. Now wasn't the time to air his grievances. Whether or not she would admit it, Leota needed help. At least he could offer a watchful eye. "I'm not pushing," he said. "I'm asking you to put the past behind us and trust me to help you."

"You think getting me to see a therapist will help," she said sarcastically. "I need you to do what your father wanted. If you don't get married, we'll lose everything that matters to me."

Nick hesitated. His marrying Clair would drive her crazy, but at least he'd decided to comply with the will. "You're right. I have to get married, but you'll have to trust me to choose the right woman."

Leota wiped her eyes. "Thank God. Who are you thinking of? Someone I know?"

"You can't choose a wife for me." His parents' choices had been part of his reasons for avoiding marriage so far.

He didn't want to hurt his mother, but he couldn't settle for one of the women she and Jeff had paraded past him since college, all beautiful, with bloodlines Jeff approved of. Prepared to love him for his name and the wealth he'd inherit. Clair suited him better.

"I've met someone." Taking Leota's arm, he led her toward the door. He turned off the light as they went into the hall. "I'll introduce you to her before I make a decision."

"You have to look at the rest of her family, too, if you want your marriage to last. What kind of people are they?"

Distaste chipped at Nick's patience. Had she always been this way, or was she taking Jeff's stand? "You don't have to worry yet. Will you let me make an appointment for you with the therapist I told you about?"

"I'm all right now that I know we'll be able to keep what belongs to us."

Her relief wouldn't survive the mention of Clair's name. So Nick didn't tell her. She needed to rest. "Try to get a good night's sleep tonight."

"I'll be fine now."

No matter what he did, he'd hurt someone. He couldn't marry a woman he didn't love and pretend he cared for her, and Clair was the only woman he

knew he could trust to stick to such a ludicrous bargain.

CLAIR FOUND Nick's office down a side alley on the
opposite end of Main Street from Paul's shop. No one
sat behind the receptionist's counter or in the waiting
room. She knocked on the glass that separated the
reception area from the back office.

Nick appeared in a corridor to the left of the desk.
When he saw her, his mouth thinned, but he opened
the door for her.

"I didn't expect you."

"You don't have a receptionist?"

"She works part-time."

A muscle in Clair's cheek twitched. "I spoke to
Angus Campbell yesterday."

"Angus is a good attorney." Nick led her down
the corridor to a small, forest-green-painted office.
"Can I get you a drink? Coffee? Soda?"

"I'm fine." She wasn't sure she could swallow.
"Angus suggested you and I should discuss specific
terms."

He sat on the edge of his desk. She declined the
chair he offered, because she didn't want to sit at a
lower level than he. It put her at a disadvantage. As
if he understood the political byplay in her mind, he
sat in the chair next to her. Recognizing they were
finessing each other—and getting nowhere—she gave
in and sank into soft, tufted leather.

"Two terms," he said. "Marry me, and pretend
you want to."

She tried to picture him as a husband. A woman

couldn't glance his way once and forget him, even if his attraction had more to do with the passion that simmered just barely beneath the surface control. Tall and lean, he had a maleness that distracted her. She couldn't think of him as the man he was and go through with the marriage he needed. "How much do I have to pretend?"

His smile emphasized his strong jaw. Clair pushed her fingers down the arms of the chair. She ought to put more distance between them.

"In front of other people we'll touch each other. Occasionally." He swallowed. Talking about touching obviously bothered him, too.

"Selina told me you've moved back into your family home." Clair had assumed he still lived there, so she was already as accustomed as she'd ever be to the idea of living on Dylan property.

"We'll share a door," he said. "I'll make sure we have adjoining rooms."

She threaded her fingers together. Her turn to demand. "I want to start repairing my house now. If I leave before our...before the time's up, I wouldn't expect you to repay me for any work I do."

"If you leave?" He leaned forward. "What would make you leave? I don't want to marry you and have to start over again in a few months."

She tried to take his lead and think of marriage as a business deal. "I'm just saying if. I don't know why I'd leave. Some emergency, maybe, but I don't plan to leave."

"Do you need time to think? I can't make a mistake."

She took a deep breath and held it. If she thought too long, she'd realize a house and land couldn't be worth marrying the son of her family's enemy. She wasn't making dramas. She shouldn't eat lunch with Nick Dylan, much less marry him.

"I can't help it." She met his gaze evenly. "I want my home and my past. I want my memories back."

"You can't remember your childhood without living in the house?"

His interest startled her, but again she should follow his example. She had to find a way to live with Nick Dylan for the next year.

"I'd rather not talk about my past or your father."

Sitting back, Nick stretched his long legs in front of him. "I guess we have a few more terms to iron out before we meet with our attorneys."

She curled her legs under her and pulled her skirt over them. "I'd like to move home as soon as we sign the prenuptial agreement."

"But you'll move into my house after the wedding?"

"Yes. I can sand all the floors downstairs before we put a wedding together." Her skirt hid the way her knees shook every time she thought about marrying him.

This was the only way she'd ever get her home back.

"LISTEN, CLAIR, I wanted to talk to you alone because I have to assign you to a job at the Dylans'."

She blinked. When Paul had asked her to his office, she thought she might have done something wrong on an assignment. "What kind of a job?"

"You're the only person I have who has experience installing fountains, and Mrs. Dylan wants one. I gave her a catalog, and she's supposed to put in her order this week."

"You want me to work for her?"

Paul picked at the chipped top button on his shirt. "I have to ask you to do the job. I'm afraid I've heard the story about your family and the Dylans, but their business is important to me. I don't want to risk an untrained person making a mistake."

Clair knew her responsibility. "When do you want me to install the fountain?"

"Depends on when it arrives, but I need to warn you, Leota Dylan makes certain rules for people who work in her house."

Big surprise. "Like what?"

Paul cleared his throat. "She doesn't want us to mix with the servants or with her or Dr. Dylan." He licked his lips. "I know you'll dislike her caste system, and I'm afraid you'll tell me you won't do the job, but we're welcome in the greenhouse and nowhere else."

Clair had dreaded telling anyone about her upcoming wedding. If she didn't tell Paul now, he'd wonder why later. She'd agreed to make her marriage look real, but her heart pounded as if she were pointing herself headfirst over the edge of a cliff. "I'm marrying Nick Dylan."

Paul gaped at her, obviously trying to decide if her engagement helped his business or hurt it. "I guess Mrs. Dylan will have to modify her policy for you."

HUSHED TONES filled the church. A sibilant "she," repeated over and over, as the wedding guests spoke of Leota. "She's not coming. Her own son's wedding, and she's not coming."

Clair listened from the vestry. The undertones sounded almost like a laugh track from a bad TV sitcom. She didn't care so much for herself. She didn't embarrass easily, and she might have had to wrestle herself into the church if she were Leota. But Nick probably wanted his mother's approval. According to the discussions they'd had during the prenuptial negotiations, Leota was one of the executors they had to convince.

The lace cap on Clair's veil made her scalp itchy. She slid her fingers beneath and scratched, mindful that Leota Dylan didn't suddenly show up and catch her being unladylike.

With each passing second, escape looked more attractive than marrying Nick. She'd give Leota five more minutes, and then she'd beg the judge to run her down the aisle before she sauntered out there and called the whole thing off.

"Clair, she's finally here." Selina fluttered into the vestry, plucking at Clair's dress like a small bird trying to put its nest in order. "Are you ready?"

"Stop, stop." Clair caught her hands. "I'm so nervous, Selina."

"Brides are supposed to be nervous. Your wedding wouldn't feel real if you weren't. Can I tell the minister you're ready?"

"The moment Leota takes her seat."

"Let me peek outside and make sure the judge is ready to give you away. Oh, you look so lovely. I can't help thinking of my own wedding."

Clair slid a finger under her left eye, where a tear burned. Would she ever love a man enough to marry and mean it? Was she capable of real love?

Selina beckoned from the door. "Come on."

"You'd have made a great matron of honor."

"You don't need me."

"Not true." Clair hugged her mother's friend—her friend. "Thanks for your help. The church is beautiful." She grinned. "The judge is beautiful."

"Make him use his hanky if he cries."

Selina slipped out. Clair and Nick had agreed to forgo attendants except for the judge. She waited for Selina to take her place in a pew before she stepped into the aisle and took the judge's proudly offered arm. Clair returned his warm smile, but faltered as she looked at the man who waited for her at the altar. She hadn't prepared herself for Nick in a tux and candlelight.

He looked gorgeous. No other word for it. His black hair gleamed. His suit embraced him, defined the lines of the tall, strong body to which she was about to pledge her troth. The determination in his gaze pulled her up the aisle.

The music she'd chosen, a piece from Massenet's *Thais,* overwhelmed her. The traditional "Wedding March" hadn't seemed appropriate, but she loved this music. It seemed to flow into her body, making her powerful and womanly. She should have gone for the traditional. It might have been another lie, but it wouldn't have meant so much to her.

Nick came forward, and the judge pressed their hands together.

The minister spoke. Clair clung to Nick's heat,

wary of her own pounding pulse. During a small silence, she realized the minister had asked if anyone knew why she and Nick shouldn't be married. She looked into Nick's dark boundless eyes. No one answered, and the minister went on. Nick took her other hand.

A physical connection vibrated between them, startling Clair, increasing her uncomfortable awareness of him at her side. Dreading the kiss they had to share, she stole a glance at his full, firm mouth. In truth, she wanted to feel him against her, wanted to know how he tasted.

The minister gave his permission, and Nick slid his hands up her waist. As he grazed the swell of her left breast, Clair stopped breathing. He brushed his cool lips against hers. With a surprised breath that felt hot against her mouth, he pulled her closer.

"I give you Dr. and Mrs. Dylan."

Amid more whispers, the church doors banged open, and two men rushed inside. "Fire!" one shouted. Everyone froze. "Fire!" he yelled again.

Men and women in their Sunday best began to pour toward the exits.

"Here?" someone demanded.

"Where?"

"Whose house?" a woman shouted.

The first man answered, just loudly enough to make everyone stop and listen. "The Atherton house."

CHAPTER FOUR

"I've NEVER SEEN a place burn down around its own door before." Ernest Fosdyke nudged Clair, smearing soot across the sleeve of her waterlogged wedding dress. "But doesn't that oak door your granddaddy carved still look fine?"

Clair peered from the black streak at her elbow to the golden oak door standing tall in wet rubble. She turned blankly to the fire chief, blinding herself in his truck's headlights. "I've lost everything I loved most."

"Nonsense. You just married the man you love." Prodding his big silver hat back on his forehead, the chief squinted with relief at someone beyond her shoulder. "Dr. Dylan, over here! I found Clair, but she's not talking sense."

Nick. She'd tried not to think of him for the past eighty minutes. She'd married him for her house, and now her house had burned down.

He draped his heavy black overcoat across her shoulders and caught her arm, offering comfort Clair couldn't afford to accept. The unexpected passion they'd shared for that brief, confusing moment in the church threatened to change the way she looked at Nick. She was too smart to give in to physical need.

"Let's get you out of this weather," he said.

"I'm fine." Easing his coat off her shoulders, she caught it in one hand and offered it back. "You keep this."

"You're not fine." Mist from the spraying fire hose dotted his silky hair. "You're in shock. If you won't take my coat… Here, wait. Fosdyke, throw me a blanket."

One sailed out of the darkness into Nick's hands. With the same capable blunt fingers that had touched her breast, he wrapped the blanket around her. She stood completely still. If she moved she might fly apart.

The fire changed everything. Her hope had gone up in flames, but Nick's gentle touch made her want to sway toward him. So she pushed his hands away.

His expression froze, but then he smiled tightly, using a quick glance at the crowd beyond the fire trucks to remind her of their audience. "You're shivering." His tone cautioned. "Let me take you home."

She filled her lungs with smoke-scented air. She'd lost her house, and she couldn't find the cat who'd adopted her after she'd begun to give him food that didn't fly away.

"I can't leave without Kitty."

"I've looked everywhere. I shouldn't have left you alone this long."

"He's the one who might need help." Two strays, she and Kitty had entered into a bond Nick couldn't understand. Not that she mistook Kitty for a human connection, but she recognized a soul who wanted to trust on his own terms.

She wrapped the scratchy blanket around her shoulders. "I'll wait for him to show up. Feel free to go to your house without me." She couldn't call that Victorian mausoleum a home.

Nick's eyes glittered, half in admiration, which, dammit, she liked, and half in frustration, which she shared.

"I won't leave you alone on our wedding night," he said, "and I don't intend to kill myself with hypothermia in the hope your tomcat gets his fill of romance before morning."

She turned her gaze to the wet ground. Kitty wasn't the tomcat he'd been, and she still felt guilty about his surgery. "He's not looking for romance. I had him neutered, and—" She broke off, unwilling to admit how much she cared. Nick didn't need to know she could love. "I'm worried about him," she said flatly.

With a fierce meow of affront, a black streak sizzled from around the side of the ruined house. Kitty burrowed beneath her drooping skirts, sparing her a swipe with razor-sharp claws. Gasping, she caught Nick's forearm for support, but he flexed his muscles beneath her palms, and she let go.

"Kitty." He either didn't know or didn't care how silly the name sounded on his lips. He dropped to his knees and searched for the cat in her skirts.

Every Fairlove citizen old enough to rubberneck at a late-night fire had come to watch, and some laughed as Nick fumbled beneath her dress. They liked to keep an eye on the Dylans.

"Get up, Nick. Everyone's watching us."

"Do you want your cat? Is it still— Oh, no, you

don't, fleabag. Fosdyke, get me something to carry this feline in.''

''I have a burlap sack,'' Earnest offered.

Nick quelled him with a glance so powerful that it unsettled Clair. He'd been raised to expect people to hop to his bidding, and Ernest scrambled to find a make-do cage.

Nick stood, Kitty twined and hissing around his forearm. The onlookers cheered. ''Forget about them,'' Nick said, with the disdain she'd known he'd adopt sooner or later. ''Help me with— No, get his mouth, before he bites.''

Clair peeled Kitty off him and gingerly nestled the scared animal in her arms. ''There.'' She pressed a protective palm to his damp fur, against the heartbeat that pounded as fast as hers. ''I'm with you, buddy.''

She studied the people who'd driven straight from her wedding to the fire. Their faces melded into a flesh-colored blob, and Clair felt as if she'd stepped into the past. All those faces and no one who belonged to her. No one she belonged to. Except they all thought she belonged to Nick now, so she interested them.

''We can't do anything else here tonight.'' Nick looked impatient. ''Why do you care what they think?''

''I don't expect you to understand. They're either afraid of you or they revere you, but next year I'll move back down here with them. I have to care.''

He turned her away from her burned home. ''You live up there with me now.'' He pointed, but the estate, usually too well lit for her taste, hunched in darkness tonight.

She looked back at her house. A century of family history, twelve years of her hopes and dreams and plans—her final stab at making up for the loss that had claimed her parents—all of it smoldering, the smoke like a last gasp at living. She'd never be able to restore it now. She swallowed tears with a hard gulp.

Nick wrapped his arm around her shoulders, but Kitty growled a possessive warning, and Clair toned down a similar response. "Please don't," she said. "I'm all right, but I can't stand your hands on me right now."

He moved away. Even such a small concession should have eased her concerns about enjoying his touch, but she understood hurt feelings too well to ignore hurting him.

"I'm sorry." She smoothed Kitty's furrowed brow. "I'll try to get along with you, Nick, but I see your father every time I look at you." And she felt guilty for wanting or needing comfort from the son of her family's enemy.

His gaze, bullet hard in the headlights, told her only that he possessed strength to match hers. The thought unsettled her.

"Why can't we make this easy for each other?" he asked.

She stared at him across an emotional divide. "Your father left our house to rot so he could gloat every time he passed it. What can be easy between you and me?"

"I'm not Jeff." Nick caught her arm again, acknowledging her involuntary recoil with a harsh smile. "I married you because of Jeff's will, but I'm not capable of the things he did."

Clair's heart tapped against the soggy lace at her breast. He thought he could play her? "You don't have to be nice to me now. I won't leave and break our deal."

He tensed his fingers. She felt each one through the satin that covered her forearm. "You think I'd try to manipulate you?"

"Yes, to keep a legacy you want as badly as I wanted my house."

He started toward his car, where Ernest waited for a last word. "You're wrong." Nick tossed the words back at her. "I care that you're hurt, and you're making a mistake."

He had to be the one who was making a mistake. Changing the relationship between their families couldn't be that easy.

AT HOME, Nick waited beside Hunter while Clair negotiated the stairs in her wedding dress. Nick considered and discarded several husbandly remarks he might make to his wife. Tonight wouldn't have been normal even in a true marriage. He fished his emergency medical bag out of the front closet.

"Turn on the lights down here, Hunter. Where is everyone?"

"Mrs. Dylan—your mother—gave us the evening off. The rest of the staff hasn't returned."

"Listen." Nick started up the stairs, his tone pulling the other man behind him. He had fences to mend. "I'm sorry about the wedding invitations. I spoke to my mother when she arrived at the ceremony, and she told me she'd mailed them late. I didn't realize, or I would have made sure you all attended the wedding."

A small lie. Leota Dylan hadn't felt the people who waited on her every whim deserved to see her son get married. One more troubling act borne of her excessive rage since Jeff's death.

"Don't worry about it. I'll talk to the others, but I'm relieved she went. Did any of your wife's house survive the fire?"

"The door," Nick said. "You know, that oak door Jeff tried to buy from her grandfather?"

Hunter nodded. "Do you think we should ask Dr. Porter to look in on her?"

Nick gripped the doorknob of the room that adjoined his. "I'm a doctor, Hunter," he reminded the other man mildly. Not even Leota and Jeff had doubted his professional capability.

"You're also a husband."

Husband, enemy, specimen of manhood Clair thought she could grind beneath her heel to prove her independence. Not that she despised all men.

The night of their engagement party, he'd watched her lose herself in a dance with Paul Sayers. Town gossip described her and Paul as fast friends. Mrs. Sayers had smiled indulgently as they'd danced past, but Nick had wondered if Clair had told Paul the truth about her marriage.

"Shall I run a bath for Mrs. Dylan?"

Nick snapped back to the present. "Thank you."

He went in first, concerned by Clair's silence, wary of what she might say. He wouldn't try to trick her into staying, but despite what she said, could he trust her not to break the contract?

Barely two steps across the creaking, polished floor, he stopped, stunned at the sight of his wife sitting in front of the fireplace, her skirts billowing around her in tints of orange and blue and red from the flames. Kitty lounged in her lap, his ears flicking back and forth as she hummed a low song to him. Hunter bumped into Nick from behind with a mortified cough.

"Sir." The other man's strained voice belied his usual calm under duress. "Was the animal burned? Shall I telephone the emergency veterinarian?"

Clair looked up from caring for her mangy friend. "Kitty wasn't in the fire."

"He always looks like that," Nick added.

"Good heavens." Hunter straightened his tie. "When did you last dip him, Mrs. Dylan?"

She stared at the butler, her mouth slightly open as she decided how to answer. "Dip him in what? I've never had a cat before."

Nick steered Hunter toward the bathroom. "The vet probably dipped Kitty for fleas before the operation. Hunter, if you'll run Clair's bath, I'll see to her ankle. The cat's already scratched her once, and I don't think we need to upset it."

"Will you stop calling Kitty 'it'? He has a name."

Nick set his bag on the floor beside her. "His name's kind of delicate for him, don't you think?"

Nick could almost have sworn her eyes filled with

tears, but she ducked her head, and he felt as if he'd walked in on her naked. He tried to think of her as a patient—a particularly troublesome one.

"Where'd you first find Kitty, anyway?" He moved toward her carefully as he'd approach one of Jeff's skittish stallions.

"I think he was living off the birds in my yard. I fed him to keep him from chasing them, and he kept coming back. I got used to him."

He eyed the cat. "That's like getting used to Jack the Ripper." Sitting cross-legged in front of her, Nick opened his bag. "Do you want to take off your hose?" Opaque silk clung with a lover's tenacity to the curve of her calf. His mouth went dry. Ever since he'd kissed her in the church, he'd warned himself against thinking of her as a woman. He hadn't expected to want her. "Or I can cut them off."

"No." Scooping up her skirts and Kitty, she struggled to stand and hold the cat in her arms at the same time. She lost her balance, anyway, as she wove from side to side above Nick's head.

He flattened his palms on the firm curves of her bottom. He'd touched his patients before, but their bodies had never disturbed him as Clair's did. "Give me Kitty before you drop him."

She rubbed her grumbling pet's ears. "He'd eat *you* alive."

They had to discuss their marriage tonight, even if she wasn't ready. "I need to talk to you. Give me the cat and take off your hose."

"Talk about what?" Her green eyes went flat.

"About whether I can trust you not to back out."

"Of our marriage?"

"Sir, I've prepared Mrs. Dylan's bath."

Clair whirled toward Hunter, and Kitty sprang from her arms. The black wad of fur scurried under the bed, snarling a hostile warning.

"I squeezed him," Clair explained, rubbing her fist across her face. "And please don't call me Mrs. Dylan. You know my name. You used to lecture me for steal-borrowing apples."

"I can't call you Clair. You've married my employer."

"But I'm still the same person."

Nick curled his fingers into his palms. To Hunter, she'd never be the girl who'd stolen those apples again. Nick hadn't fully considered what his name or her possession of it meant to either of them. She'd be at least partly a Dylan for the rest of her life.

Her insistence that she hadn't changed reminded him how she'd had to, because of the events his father had set in motion. She'd left Fairlove a fourteen-year-old orphan whose parents had loved and sheltered her. She'd come home almost as feral about her independence as the cat who'd claimed her.

Hunter cleared his throat, and Nick tensed. It was important that even Hunter believe they'd married each other because they'd fallen in love, a purer love than the kind his father had felt for Clair's mother.

"Thank you," Nick said. "We'll be fine for tonight."

"Good evening, Mrs. Dylan." Hunter inclined his head.

"Good night." She closed the door behind him.

Nick pointed at her legs. "What about your hose?"

"If you have some antiseptic, I'll clean the scratch myself." She lifted her chin. "A doctor can't treat his own wife."

"I'm not playing with you." Nick climbed to his feet and held the bathroom door for her. "You won't win this argument, so don't waste your breath. Take them off, or I'll take them off for you."

With a smile that suggested he not try, she stepped around the door, but she didn't close it. Her rustling skirts distracted him. He imagined her long thighs in bride's garters, and the walls seemed to close in on him.

Her mother had once loved his father. Sylvie must have been in this house often. Had his father's need for her started like this—an unexpected, inconvenient desire? Nick stared at the expanse of tile floor he could see through the open door. Would Clair ever see him without seeing Jeff?

"Why did your father make you live in this house?" she asked abruptly.

"You mean in the will? He's still trying to force me to live what he considered an appropriate life, but I would have come back anyway. Leota has been..." He paused, belatedly reluctant to discuss his mother with her. Clair's main goal in life might be revenge on his family. He'd risked that chance for himself, but why give her ammunition against his mother?

"Leota?" Clair reminded him.

"She hasn't been well since Jeff died." Her decision to send Hunter and the staff away on Clair's first night was a prime example of the grief-driven rage that concerned her son more each day.

Heavy silence wafted from the bathroom. He couldn't blame Clair if she wasn't Leota's biggest fan. His mother had refused to speak more than a few icy words to her.

"I can't believe Leota let you move in here to look after her," Clair said.

She knew his family better than he'd realized. "Jeff's will didn't give her much choice."

"Why do you call them Jeff and Leota?"

He hadn't bargained for personal questions. They should have set limits on what they'd talk about. He took the flip way out. "They never seemed like a mom and dad."

She answered with more silence until she came back into the room, holding her skirts above her bare feet. "I admire you for taking care of Leota. The way she treats you probably takes a lot out of you." She made a big production of searching for her cat, who hadn't budged from his hiding place. "Any chance of finding a litter box for Kitty tonight?"

Nick didn't let her put him off. "I should have talked to you about living here, but I honestly forgot you'd have a say. I'm not used to being married."

Clair trained her green eyes on him like twin scopes on a high-powered rifle. "Don't take this marriage too seriously. I'm not really your wife, and a husband is the last thing I need."

"I wouldn't have married you if I didn't believe that."

"Good." She dropped her skirts and patted them into place. "Now, how about that litter?"

He flicked the toe of his shoe at the dust ruffle on her bed. "Any chance of sending him to the garage?"

"You want me to punish him after he's lost his home?"

This side of her interested Nick. She loved that shiftless cat despite its vast imperfections. "I think I can locate some sand and a box to put it in, but I'll do that after I take care of your ankle." He eased her toward an armchair.

"Wait, I'm filthy." She grabbed his wrists. With the balance of a gymnast, she held herself above the pristine upholstery.

"The chair can be cleaned," he said, finding sensual promise in the force of will that allowed her such control over her body.

"You rich boys don't understand real life. You won't be the one to clean it."

Speechless, he let her maneuver out of his hands. He'd expected her to hold a grudge against his father. He hadn't thought she'd make such unflattering assumptions about him.

"I'll get a towel," she said.

To keep himself from watching her walk away, he took a tube of antibiotic cream and a roll of gauze from his bag. He'd played mind games all his life, but she had a talent. He wished she'd show some sign of her feelings, instead of badgering him about his name and his family's position. She'd hate to know it, but tonight, she fit right in to this house.

"Turkish towels." Clair brandished one at him on

her way back to the chair "What luxury—but I took a small one. Plenty left for your bath when you're ready." She spread the thick pink cloth on the chintz armchair. "I'm surprised at your color choice."

"My bath is on the other side of my bedroom." Nick pointed with the antibiotic tube at the door that divided their rooms. "Through there."

"Hmm. I keep forgetting where I live now." She dropped into the chair. "Do your worst, Doctor."

He lifted her hem, but she snatched the fabric out of his hands, as if his touch on her bare leg felt too intimate.

It did. She was forbidden, but he'd always wanted what he couldn't have. His father's respect. Once upon a time, even his mother's love. Why shouldn't he want a woman he'd promised not to touch?

He pulled on gloves and carefully cleaned the thin cut where Kitty had slashed her. With the pad of his index finger, he smoothed medicated cream over the scratch, which spanned the delicate bones of her ankle. She shivered, and he froze.

For the first time since he'd come home to take over Dr. Truman's practice, he knew he shouldn't treat a patient. This patient. His wife.

He cut a piece of gauze and pressed it against her wound. Swiftly, he snipped two pieces of tape and secured the bandage. "If the cut or any of your lymph nodes begins to swell in the next day or two, tell me."

"I will." In spite of her brittle tone, she sounded brave, and he realized he didn't really know this woman he'd married.

Their unnatural situation had him off-kilter. The

wedding and then the fire. Knowing how hurt she had to be, he couldn't see her as his co-conspirator. They'd spoken wedding vows without meaning them, but they'd entered their contract together. Whether Clair or he liked it, she wasn't alone anymore.

She pushed her skirts down and stood, forcing him to back away. Exasperated at his own need, Nick turned to repack his medical bag, but suddenly realized she still needed to bathe. "I didn't think. I should have waited until you bathed."

She glanced down at her ankle. "I'll keep it dry."

"Fine. I'll check the gardening shed for sand. Go have your bath."

She didn't wait to be urged twice. With her eerie self-possession, she got up and went into the bathroom, closing the door on him.

In the stiff silence she left behind, he asked himself if he should have met the conditions of the will. He'd prefer not to go to the mat with Clair every ten minutes for the next twelve months. He'd stated his half of their prenuptial terms through Wilford, but he needed to persuade Clair that they had to pound out their own day-to-day pact for living together.

Once she told him whether she planned to stay.

He considered how to ask her as he searched the gardening shed for sand. Tossing gravel and grass seed relieved some of his frustration. He finally found a bag with a small amount of sand left in it, and he lined a wide flowerpot pan with plastic. Then he sprinkled an inch of the makeshift litter in the bottom, but discarded every idea he came up with for asking his wife if she planned to divorce him after a few hours of marriage.

Carrying the litter into the house and up the stairs, he was stopped just outside Clair's door by an unfamiliar sound. She must have lured Kitty out from under the bed. She seemed to be singing again, though the song sounded… Singing, hell. Clair was crying.

He burst through the doorway, spilling sand all over the floor, and set down the pan. Clair dragged herself to a sitting position on the edge of her bed, swaying beneath the large pink towel on her head. Horror flashed from her tear-reddened eyes. Another stretch of pink terry, slipping from the tops of her full breasts, made him stop. But her shoulders shook, and Nick stumbled toward her.

"Don't you know how to knock?" she demanded.

"You don't have to go through this by yourself."

She buried her face in the tails of her turban. He'd offered solace out of instinct, but like his father before her, Clair didn't want tenderness from him.

He should leave, but how was he supposed to turn his back on her? Her struggle touched him. She'd lost her reason for marrying him, but she hadn't reminded him yet that she could go if she wanted. Her strength impressed him, where his father's had left him cold.

Plunging into a major conflict of interests, Nick sank to the bed at her side and wrapped his arms around her. Surprising him, she leaned against him.

Though her response had to be unconscious, the solid, slender warmth of her body eased pain he wouldn't admit, pain at losing his father before he learned why he'd never been enough of a son, anguish at his father's last, posthumous strike, despair that he couldn't help his mother, because he still wasn't the son she needed.

He tucked the towel around Clair, careful to avoid touching her skin. "I was wrong to talk you into this marriage," he said.

"We made a bargain." She lifted her head from his chest, setting her jaw. It quivered again. "I'm sorry I cried. I thought I was alone."

"I should have knocked, but when I heard you...." He shrugged, and the tension between them eased. "My job involves a lot of helping."

"I just..." She shook her head, and her towel brushed his brow. "I don't know where we go from here."

"I asked you to marry me because I needed a wife and I had something you needed. I figured you'd say yes because of the way my father treated your parents, but I can't make you stay."

"You think I want revenge? I might have tried to hurt him, but who would I be if I made you pay because he hated us?"

"He loved your mother once."

"Yeah, and imagine how she must have felt when he told her she was beneath his class? Then, when she fell in love with my father, your dad married—" She broke off, choking on an embarrassed gasp at what she'd almost said.

Nick finished. "The housemaid. Maybe you weren't going to put it that way, but I know how people look at us. You must know he slept with Leota to get your mother out of his head. I was a product of Jeff's rebound.''

''No,'' Clair said. ''You're a Dylan. You don't understand what that means, because you've never been someone who doesn't matter. I remember the picture of you in *Life* magazine, when your father handed you your med school diploma.''

He gritted his teeth. The *Life* photographer hadn't captured the moment he'd told his mother and father he was coming home to take over Dr. Truman's practice.

He'd nearly come to blows with his father. Jeff had said he finally understood Leota's blood meant his son would never amount to anything more than a country doctor.

Leota had hated his announcement more than Jeff, but that he understood. He'd even felt sorry for her. Every time he made a decision Jeff considered unacceptable, Jeff took it out on Leota.

But they were the ones who'd preached social conscience in front of the microphones. Doing good where you could, with your name or any other asset you could cultivate. So many sound bites, rolling out of Senator and Mrs. Dylan's mouths.

None of his past mattered to Clair, but he had a sneaking suspicion he might owe her the freedom she had every right to.

''Do you want me to arrange an annulment?'' he asked.

She shook her head, and the turban fell off. He touched her hair, and the silky dark-auburn curls slid through his fingers as she pulled back.

"I said I'd stay." She sounded anything but certain.

Scratching sounds behind them distracted her, and Nick closed his eyes to hide how much he didn't want to start another bride search. A supremely irritated meow punctuated the scratching. He turned and found Kitty tangled in Leota's Battenburg-lace curtains, halfway to the high ceiling. "He wants out."

"So do I," Clair admitted. "What would happen if I left?"

"You know what would happen. I'd lose everything."

"You can find a new wife."

"Maybe, but our attorneys are the only other people who know the truth. I have to convince the other executors, including Leota, my marriage is real. If I install a swinging door on the church, it might be a problem."

She stayed quiet, but the moment he looked at her, she turned away, and her hair slid across her pale cheek. "We've had too much dishonor between our families," she said.

"Jeff treated yours dishonestly."

"And your mother resents me because I look like my mother. Maybe she thinks your father still loved my mom. I don't understand her, but I don't want to be like your parents. I don't want to hurt you just because I can."

He couldn't take advantage of her. "I won't hold you if you want to go, but if you offer to stay, I'll accept, so think hard, Clair."

She lifted her head, and he read resignation in her

tired eyes. Selfish relief made sweat break out on the nape of his neck. She'd decided in his favor.

She nodded at Kitty, who was still fighting for the top of the curtain. "Better pry him off there. I'd hate to upset Mr. Hunter."

Nick crossed the room and cupped Kitty's torso to balance him while he unwove a paw from the lace. Fending off sharp teeth, he worked at the other paw. Clair stood in a rustle of chintz spread. When he turned to hand her the wriggling cat, she was tugging the towel over bare skin.

His body responded to her hands tucking the towel into the vee between her breasts. Clair, completely at ease with being half-nude, had already begun to move on without him. He wanted her to be aware of him, as conscious and uncomfortable as her body made him.

He wanted her to feel his craving. He thought of the detective's report. She was no blushing bride, and he felt jealous of her ease, of its implication about her past with other men.

She'd become his wife, and he was Dylan enough to feel possessive.

"Why did you agree to stay?" he asked. "I can't force you."

"Force?" She narrowed her eyes. "I don't want to know what that word tells me about your life." She set Kitty on the rug. He shot back beneath the bed, and Clair straightened. "I want my land back so I can rebuild. You and I are married in name only. You know we can't fix anything for each other."

He started to ask her what the hell she meant, but he was afraid she'd tell him.

CHAPTER FIVE

CLAIR AWOKE from her restless wedding night in the grip of a chill. Shivering beneath the bedclothes, she couldn't tell if the cold came from inside her or from a faulty Dylan furnace. She felt around for her cat. "Kitty?"

No answer. Sitting up, she peered around the room, but the animal was either hiding or gone. She grabbed jeans and a sweater from a chair and yanked them on before she peered under the dust ruffle.

"Kitty?"

Usually he woke her with a hungry yowl for his breakfast. Not today. She searched the closet for her sneakers and some sign of her cat and called him again as she sat in the armchair to tie her shoes.

Leota wouldn't care for Kitty roaming free. The poor little guy usually beat a hot trail to his food dish first thing, but she didn't have a dish or food for him here.

Shoes on, she slid to the floor for a more comprehensive inspection of the underside of her bed. The dark, polished floor stretched away so clean and empty it looked like a hole. Such a lack of dust bunnies must have bored him.

"Kitty?" She peered around the room. No cat in

the curtains. He wasn't curled up behind the heavy clock on the dresser, a spot she'd plucked him from three times during the night. He'd scared her half to death, shifting the family heirloom to make himself more comfy.

She squeaked to the bathroom door in her sneakers. Last night, he'd dangled into the toilet for a quick sip. He wasn't there now.

Nick must have let him out of her room. No one else would have opened the door. They'd have to have a chat about privacy. For now, she'd better find Kitty before he persuaded Leota to evict him.

She had the doorknob in her hand when the telephone rang. She hesitated a moment, but Nick had put in a private number for their rooms. When it rang again, she hurried to the nightstand. Someone might want Nick for an emergency.

She put the phone to her ear, but she suddenly didn't know how to answer. Should she announce she was now ensconced in Dr. Dylan's residence?

"Clair? Nick? Hello? Is anyone there?"

"Selina." Clair sat on the edge of the bed, feeling pretty foolish. "I didn't know what to say."

"'Hello' is customary. Especially to put me out of my misery, since I've called you on the first day of your honeymoon."

"I seem to have lost Nick." Certainly no one stirred in his room. She'd heard him walking around in there after he'd left her the previous evening. "And Kitty," she said, carrying the phone into the bathroom. She opened the cupboard with her toes, but still no Kitty.

"What are you talking about, Clair?"

"I slept in. They must have gone downstairs."

"Leap back into bed. Nick's probably bringing you breakfast."

Clair couldn't repudiate that startling idea. "I'd better find Kitty. His charms won't be obvious to Leota."

"I won't keep you. I just wanted to make sure you were all right, after the fire."

"I'll learn to be."

"You worry me when you take that self-sufficient tone. You have friends around you now. And Nick. That you could fall in love with him…well, it has to be fate."

Clair rubbed her temple. Her newfound relationship with Selina, still in its infancy, needed honesty to grow. She didn't want to lie, but she'd promised Nick she'd keep their secret from everyone.

"I'd better look for him. Last night was stressful for him, too."

"Call me. I looked around this morning and found a couple of things your mother gave me. I'd like you to have them."

Clair held the phone in silence, glad that anything of her mother's remained. "I wish I'd left Mom and Dad's stuff in storage." She'd waited to take everything out and put it in the Atherton-family home until she'd felt sure the roof wouldn't leak and the walls wouldn't collapse. Her final, most expensive project would have been the electricity. "I'd be grateful for anything you could spare."

"Come by. I have a little pile of treasures for you."

"I'll see you soon." Clair stood, unaccustomed to so much emotion. She focused on her cat. She had to find him before Leota put him out. Maybe he'd headed straight home for his favorite food dish—the one fire had destroyed. He could hurt himself climbing the unsteady rubble.

She barely reached the door when someone knocked on the other side. She yanked it open. Nick, in jeans and a navy sweatshirt that made him look incredibly masculine, riveted her to the floor.

His sexy looks were none of her business. "Have you seen Kitty?"

"He's downstairs."

"By himself? Does Leota know I brought him?"

"We all expected he was part of the package." Pushing her door open, he backed her inside. "We need to set a few ground rules."

Reluctantly, she watched him close her door behind himself. His large hand on the dark wood looked proprietary.

"Last night was our wedding night." He waited, as if she was supposed to answer. Or maybe, as if he felt anxious about saying what was on his mind.

"I remember." She forced a bland note into her voice, but her anxiety rose on par with his. "Did you expect traditional events? I thought we agreed…"

"To make our marriage look real."

As in, sharing a bed? "How real did you have in mind, Nick?"

"We need to tell each other what we plan to do each day. Leota's one of the executors, and she'll guess the truth about our marriage if we live separate lives.''

His request, though reasonable, felt like an infringement. ''I'll try, but I haven't answered to anyone in a long time.''

He took her hand, rubbing his thumb over her wrist. ''We have to consider how we look to outsiders.''

Had he not considered that his thumb against her skin might feel too intimate? Clair held still, caught between a shiver and shoving him away. ''Would your mother tell the other executors if she suspected us?''

''Until we know whether Leota hates your family more than she loves Dylan land and prestige, let's make sure we both know where we're headed in the mornings. We don't need to make unnecessary mistakes.'' He looked down at her arm, purpose making his gaze more remote. ''Come over here into the light. I think you have a rash.''

He tugged her to the bathroom door. Clair grimaced at his back. Okay. She'd mistaken bedside manner for uncontrollable lust. She'd be wise to get a grip.

''What's wrong?''

He lifted her hand and brushed his fingertips over a series of small red bumps on her wrist. ''Bad news for you and Kitty.''

She pulled away before he could explain. No need for him to look so damned much like a husband when they were alone. ''Nothing terminal, I hope?''

''Fleas.''

Clair stared at him until she realized she'd left her mouth open. "I have fleas?"

"You can thank Kitty. You'd better arrange to have him de-fleaed again before he spreads them around the house. Hunter's on your side right now, and you don't want to lose him. He may be the only human in this place."

"A pretty stiff human." She scratched at her wrist as Nick frowned at her. "Sorry. I don't mean 'stiff' in a bad way. He's just correct. That's what my mom would have said. He's correct."

Nick's frown eased. "My father liked Hunter for his correctness."

Clair considered Nick's expression, thoughtful, backward looking. "Why didn't your father like you?"

Nick turned a sharp gaze on her. "I don't want to... Do you want the truth?"

She nodded, as surprised as he that she'd asked, more surprised that she really wanted to know.

"I'm not your mother's son. I was the reason he had to marry my mother. I carry 'common' blood. I'm not good enough, and once I was on the way, he had to stop begging your mother to come back to him."

Another inappropriate question seemed more to the point. "Why don't you hate him?"

"He was my father. I still wonder if I'll ever stop wanting him to—" Nick broke off, tension straining his facial muscles. "Let's not talk about Jeff. You probably want to see your house. I'll drive you over, and we'll see if we can salvage anything."

She didn't want him with her. "I'll be fine on my own. The insurance money on my house cancels out your part of our bargain, anyway."

"My father foreclosed on your family the first chance he got. I owe you everything we agreed to, every cent of that mortgage."

She wanted no misunderstandings between them. "The law allowed him to throw us out. My father got no favors from your family, and I don't want any, either."

"Let me do what's right." The jut of his chin made him look arrogant again.

And the cold inside her spread. "I won't take money from you."

"I'm not trying to pay you for services." As if he was allowed, he pressed the back of his hand to her cheek. "Did my family make you so cynical?" He caught her when she would have turned her head away. "Idiotic question," he said.

She absorbed the pressure of each long finger. "You're back in doctor mode. You think you can fix what's broken in me, but nothing's broken. I'm not sick."

"No, not sick." He exhaled a deep breath that stirred her hair. His guarded gaze told her he was willing to drop subjects she didn't want to discuss. "But you're trembling." He rubbed her hands between his. "This room is awfully cold. Would you like coffee?"

She tugged free. Coffee with Nick looked like something she ought to avoid—if she was the sort of woman who backed down.

"I'd love hot chocolate. Just half a cup. No whipped cream."

Opening the door, he looked back at her, his expression watchful. "Why deny yourself? Half a cup is more palatable than a full one? Self-denial doesn't make you strong. It's just denial. Take a full mug and top it with whipped cream."

He was talking about life, but Clair saw her grandmother's broken and charred Limoges cups. Just three days ago she'd unpacked them and settled them on shelves her father had built into the dining-room wall. She forced a smile and walked through the doorway in front of him. Pain revived her more comfortable hard edge. "I'm good at delaying gratification."

"But why would you?"

As if he was one to talk. When she turned to answer, she heard a tinkling sound. Clair recognized it—Leota's signature bracelets. On the third-floor landing, Nick's mother stood, frozen. She smoothed her black crepe pantsuit over her hips, still the perfect politician's wife.

"You found her. We certainly missed you at breakfast, Clair Atherton." Leota turned a hard look on her son. "She hasn't abandoned you?"

Clair tried to see the woman through Nick's eyes. He must care for her. He'd moved home to help her, and he put up with her condescension. Clair's respect for Nick's fairness didn't extend to sympathy for Leota. A wiser woman would find a way to appreciate a son who tried to take care of her.

"Cat got your tongue this morning, Clair Atherton?"

Nick looped his arm around her back and slid his hand into the hair at her nape with the loving touch of a real husband. Clair's breath whooshed out of her lungs. She forgot how to speak in the instant, unexpected pleasure of his massaging fingers.

"Let's not argue on Clair's first morning here, Leota." His kind tone compounded Clair's emotional confusion. His mouth, mobile and sensuous for such a lean-faced man, fascinated her. The restless need in his voice made Clair feel powerful, but she looked into his eyes and saw emotional bruises.

How many women would have married this man just to heal him?

She fought hard to keep from pushing him away. She'd come home to heal her own wounds, not to nurse his. Why couldn't he be the man she'd bargained for?

"I know you two are lying. You couldn't possibly care for each other after what Jeff did to Sylvie and David."

Clair pulled away from Nick. Revenge against Leota suddenly looked like a plan, but Nick caught her back, pressing his hand against her belly. He slid the pads of his fingers across her naval, drawing Leota's furious gaze, making Clair want to scream in protest. Sensual pleasure curled low and deep, despite her attempt to reject it.

Nick spoke again, a lazy tone Clair couldn't have managed in several lifetimes. "Cut it out, Leota, and consider my wife and her parents off-limits."

Just in time Clair remembered her promise to act like his wife. He had to touch her to make Leota and the other executors believe in their marriage. And this marriage had to last a year.

She looked slowly to the mother-in-law her husband considered in need of help. "Why not put the bad years behind us?" she said. "We all have to live here." She bit her lip, but knowing how Leota would have treated her mother gave her strength. Jeff Dylan's wife was not Clair's role model. "I don't want anything of yours. I just want to make a life—friends and family—of my own."

Ruddy color stained Leota's face. She turned her back on them. "Tell Hunter I'll take my calls and my meals in my room today."

The moment she slammed her door, Clair met Nick's flat gaze. "It wasn't my mom's fault your father was obsessed with her."

"It wasn't Leota's fault, either. She tried to be a good wife to him."

"My mom let your father go. Both your parents should have followed her example."

"You and I could learn from Sylvie, too."

Clair resented his quick answers, because he was right. "I don't like the way you touch me," she snapped in frustration.

"You know I have to."

"You enjoy putting your hands on me."

"And you don't?"

She was beginning to resent her physical response to him most of all. "We're lying to everyone we know. What we feel is a lie, too."

She searched his gaze but learned nothing, because where he was concerned her instincts deserted her. "I expect you to be completely honest with me," she said, "about everything. I don't want us to confuse ourselves."

"You're the one who's pretending not to feel anything."

"I feel plenty with you. I won't pretend I didn't kiss you back at our farce of a wedding, but I don't want to feel. Not with you." She'd lost this round. "I'll get my coat and head over to the house."

The moment she turned on her heel, she felt guilty. How was her behavior more excusable than Leota's? Was Nick to blame because she was lonely enough to desire a man who knew how to make a woman feel pleasure?

She waited in her room, giving him time to leave. Instead, she gave herself time to realize she'd taken out her pent-up frustration on him.

Going back into the hall, she stopped at the landing and leaned over the stair rail, hoping to find Nick. Her will to apologize faded with the passing minutes. Strangely, he was sprawled on the bench against the far wall, his legs stretched in front of him. His expression mirrored her disgust with their situation.

"Nick?"

He looked up.

"I'm sorry," she said. "I was angry with Leota, but I shouldn't have punched at you." She left the attraction between them alone. He was a man, she a woman. Both healthy, they naturally responded to the high emotions they provoked in each other.

"That's okay—" he paused for a grin that caught her like a blow to the chest "—wife."

He got to his feet and moseyed out of view. Clearly, he thought he'd won this round, too. Teach her to apologize.

Bemused, Clair descended the stairs into a pool of golden light that drew her gaze upward. Sunlight swept through the stained-glass window above the door and bathed the tall, ticking clock and the priceless, oriental runner in gold.

Appearances. This household dazzled with fairytale images of home and hearth that changed with the slant of the sun.

THAT AFTERNOON, Nick paced to the door of Clair's room and knocked. In his first twenty-four hours as a married man, he'd noticed details he should have considered when he'd asked Clair to marry him.

It was essential that anyone who walked in and out of their rooms on a regular basis believed their marriage was real. This morning he'd made his bed before he'd left his room, so it would look as if he hadn't slept in it. Maybe he and Clair should spread some of their belongings in each other's rooms.

He knocked on Clair's door again. When she still didn't answer, he went inside.

Her scent lingered. Deep purple satin splashed across the flowered chintz comforter on her unmade bed. Like a voyeur, Nick sifted the satin nightdress through his fingers. Its thin cord straps looped around his wrist.

His detective hadn't mentioned Clair's penchant for fancy lingerie. Nick resisted a primal urge to lift the satin to his face. Suddenly the phone rang, like an alarm bell. Nick dropped the gown as if someone had caught him doing something illicit. He picked up the receiver and said hello.

"Nick? Ben Wells, here. Selina Franklin gave me your new number. Is Clair around?"

He knew Ben, Clair's insurance adjuster. A man who prized his ability to spin a hunting yarn from tavern to tavern, all the way from Fairlove to Charlottesville. Ben hardly ever called the victim of a disaster first, but in Clair's case he'd have to pay out a large sum of money.

"She's not here, but I need to talk to you about the insurance on her former home."

Ben didn't answer. His silence said plenty. "You won't like what I have to tell you."

"What?"

"Your father never insured the house, but Wilford Thomas came by just after the senator died. He and I agreed to insure the house for worth, not replacement value."

Wilford had drawn up Jeff's airtight will. Basically a decent man with honed, lawyerly instincts, he'd also produced Nick's equally untouchable prenuptial agreement. Apparently, he'd carried on other business, too.

"Wilford and you agreed?" Furious and ashamed that Clair would suffer because he hadn't kept an eye on the insurance, Nick turned his anger on Ben. "You decided how to insure my house?"

"No, Dr. Dylan. Wilford made the decision."

Apprehension fluttered in Ben's voice. Nick had

never used the power of his name before, but he forced Ben to stutter on.

"Technically...well, it's part of the estate, and Wilford holds power of attorney until it goes through probate."

Nick cut to the chase. "The insurance won't cover rebuilding?"

"You know what that coverage would have cost you?"

"Why didn't you ask me, Ben? Who do you think the house goes to after probate?"

"Wilford handled it. He's eager to do a good job for you, and he said you weren't like your father. You don't have to poke your fingers in every pie."

Not like his father? He just hoped Wilford Thomas had soaked enough out of the estate to support himself in golden years that might not look so bright after this.

Nick glanced around the untidy room. Clair had marked it as her own, in the clothes she'd draped over the closet door, the twisted bedding and, of course, her gown. She'd agreed to honor their deal when she'd believed she didn't have to. She was so damned independent she'd live in a cardboard box before she'd let him turn over the money that would have come to her if he'd been paying attention.

He had to put that money in her hands.

"I'm on my way, Ben. Don't set foot out of your office until I see you, or I'll hunt you down."

Not like his father? He chose not to behave like Jeff. He'd never pretended he didn't know how.

PARKING HER CAR at the edge of the drive, Clair watched Paul Sayers turn from contemplating the smoking rubble of her house. She took Kitty out of the car and started through the wet grass to meet Paul. A friend who didn't make her heart race.

"Clair, I'm sorry." Paul was a further contrast to Nick, in faded jeans and a sweatshirt printed with a circle of text that read Fairlove Lovelies, *Your* Landscaping To Order.

She pointed at the words and raised her voice so he could hear her over the restless wind. "Too late for landscaping here."

He held out a tattered pansy. "I found this. All that's left of what you planted. Am I intruding? Amanda wanted to come with me, but she thought you might not want to be overrun today."

His wife, Amanda, had semi-adopted Clair and Paul's two other employees, feeding them after the hard days Paul put them through, reminding Paul they were human, rather than mere spawn of a farm-equipment manufacturer.

"I wish she'd come. You're both good friends."

He bent a rueful nod at the mess smoldering behind them. "We were saying this morning we couldn't imagine worse timing."

"No." They didn't know the half of it. Kitty tumbled over his wind-tossed leash, and Clair danced to keep him from choking himself. "I can't dwell on the timing or what I've lost until I clear the land and start over. I'm not sure I could function if I let myself feel it's all gone."

Paul tugged her close. "You have friends now. Lean on us."

"Did you see the crowds around here last night? No one cared twelve years ago when my family moved out, but from now on most people in this town will see me as Nick Dylan's wife."

"You are his wife, and the Dylan name has prestige, but people will eventually accept you as Clair, the hard worker. You don't put on Dylan airs. And if you take my advice, you'll stop being so mysterious about your past."

Clair pulled her hand away. She didn't trust even Paul enough to share information on her wandering years. She'd looked for love in the worst places, squandered her first love on an older man who'd treated her like the naive child she'd been. Worst of all, she'd thrown away her education, because the administration had stood with him when their affair came to light. After all, who would stand with Clair?

"What past?" She lifted Kitty to her shoulder. "I was always heading back here. I just didn't know it until Selina found me. Why aren't you working today?"

"I am." He tapped the beeper on his worn leather belt. "But Amanda and I wanted to make sure you were all right. Thought I'd stop by in case you were here." He handed her the crushed flower. "Where is your doctor?"

"His name is Nick, and I decided to come by myself." Turning toward her ruined home, she caught a piece of the fluttering yellow tape that had worked its way off a wounded tree. ''I wasn't sure how I'd react to seeing this.''

''I am imposing.''

''No.'' A silver glint caught her eye. She dropped the tape and moved toward the rubble where the kitchen had stood. Could that be a piece of her mother's silver? The morning of her wedding, she'd placed it all so carefully in the maple trays her father had made. She set Kitty on the ground and reached for the gleaming metal.

''Clair!'' Another masculine voice rang out. She turned. Ernest Fosdyke had driven his own car today, a sleek new Jeep she hadn't heard over the wind.

''Don't touch anything!'' he shouted. ''This may be a crime scene.''

CHAPTER SIX

A COLD CHILL fingered its way down Clair's spine. "What kind of a crime?"

Ernest Fosdyke nodded a silent, brusque greeting at Paul before he answered. "I asked an arson guy from D.C. to look at the place. He promised me his results by the end of next week."

"Arson?" Who'd set fire to her home? Who didn't want her in Fairlove that badly? "You think someone did this deliberately?"

"The timing is…interesting." Ernest reached for the banner of loose tape. "I have to make sure before I let you disturb possible evidence."

"Couldn't the timing be a coincidence?"

Fosdyke looked at Paul as if he'd rather finish this conversation without an audience.

Paul took the hint. "I'll go. Clair, call Amanda or me if you need anything. I guess you aren't going away for your honeymoon?"

"No, but I'd like to take care of the insurance and start cleaning up here before I come back to work."

Paul hugged her briefly. "Take all the time you need. You'll be okay?"

He meant with Ernest. "I'll be fine, thanks."

Nick's offer of help annoyed her. Paul's motives, she trusted.

Fosdyke waited for Paul to get in his car. "Be logical, Clair. I think I was the only person in this town who didn't attend your wedding. No one was likely to get hurt in this fire. I wonder if someone was trying to warn you."

"Warn me about what? I'm not important enough to warn. I don't know anything I need to hide."

"Just take it easy for a few days. Lie low while I work, okay?"

"I won't hide from someone who probably doesn't exist." She'd feared too much in her life already—being alone, never being loved again, maybe never letting anyone love her. She didn't indulge in fear anymore.

"'Probably' is a big word, under these circumstances."

"You don't understand. I took all my mom and dad's things out of storage." Her mother's china, her father's books. "The boxes are in there."

"I don't want to upset you..." Chief Fosdyke wound the tape so tightly around his hand the ends of his fingers turned white. Compassion threaded his voice, but he battered ahead. "Your boxes burned. You may find a piece of a frame here, a cup handle there, but don't get your hopes up. When we remove those ceiling beams that fell in the fire, we'll find ashes."

His distress touched her. Clair peered at him through suddenly misty eyes. He cared about her and he had nothing to gain. "I'm trying to accept my house is gone, but don't make me lose anything else that belonged to my family.''

"I was on duty last night. I'm supposed to find out what happened here and make sure I protect you. Help me do my job.''

"I wasn't here. How am I supposed to help you?''

"Tell me who'd want to destroy your place.''

"Someone who wanted to destroy me,'' she said without thinking. Leota's bangles jangled in her memory. "We had to delay the wedding for...'' She couldn't accuse Nick's mother of arson. She had no proof, other than the woman's irrational resentment. Besides, Leota might not be a popular woman, but she possessed the Dylan name, and the Dylan's still held all the power.

"Who?'' Chief Fosdyke dropped the tape at his side, and Kitty leaped at the trailing end. "Who came late to your wedding?''

"No one.'' Leaning down, she ducked his gaze while she removed the tape from Kitty's claws. "I shouldn't have said anything.''

But when she straightened, Ernest got in her face, dropping all pretense of the lovable, but bumbling public servant. "I'll ask the other guests who showed up late.''

Clair breathed through clenched teeth. "I don't know how many people came late. What about the ones who didn't attend at all?''

He grabbed her shoulders, his hands heavy. Where was the man who hadn't wanted to upset her with home truths about the fire? "Tell me, Clair.''

"You're hurting me.''

"Who do you suspect?"

"I have to be careful. People in this town see me as a failure's daughter. They liked my father, but no one had enough power or money to help him. Maybe some people were even relieved when I left, but my home is here. My family is buried on top of that hill." Yellowed granite rose out of the rise she pointed to, a soft knoll Leota had to face every day of her life. "My roots dig deeper than any Dylan's. We just never trampled on anyone to make our place here."

Ernest looked from the burial ground to the battered cat that wound around Clair's feet. "We hurt you in this town, didn't we?"

"It doesn't matter now." Since Selina had brought her back, she'd tried to look at the past through new eyes. "But Fairlove is my town, too, and I won't go away."

Ernest released her, his consent hesitant. "I won't force you, but if the verdict comes back arson, you'll have to tell me the truth."

Engine sounds from an already familiar car filtered through the swirling wind. Turning, the chief dropped his hand to his side, and the tape he was holding fluttered toward the road.

Nick's Jeep rocked up and down the ruts of Clair's driveway. Kitty leaped to the end of his leash for the yellow tape, and Clair followed, giving him slack.

"We're not through," Ernest said to her.

"Why do you care so much?"

"I've known Leota a long time, and I know about the troubles between your families." He lifted Kitty so she could pull the tape off several more claws.

"Leota's had enough bad luck. I don't mean for her to suffer anymore, and she will if her family's hurt."

Clair took Kitty back, cradling him on her shoulder. "What's between you and my mother-in-law?"

"You believe all her bluster? Look a little deeper, girl. She's hurting. She just lost her husband."

Unsettled to find he shared Nick's concerns, Clair looked toward her husband. In the long charcoal coat she'd like for herself, and a suit Mr. Blackwell couldn't have disparaged, he looked more like a stock mogul than a country GP.

He dressed like an ice-cold Dylan, but he'd shown more heart than his father had ever possessed. The strength of his belief in his mother had begun to make Clair review her cynical opinion.

The long grass parted before Nick's expensive pant legs as he strode toward them. Clair covered her suddenly jittery stomach with her hand. Men hadn't made her nervous in a long time. "How many days do you need to investigate the fire?" she asked Ernest.

"Investigate?" Nick echoed.

"Morning, Dr. Dylan." As before, the fire chief almost tipped an invisible cap.

"Good morning. I have a few minutes before my first appointment, so I thought I'd see what you're doing out here."

"I've just been bringing Clair up to speed. I asked an arson specialist down to run some tests."

"What tests?" Nick's stance changed from casual to fierce. "You think the fire was arson?"

"As I told Clair, I'm concerned because of the timing, but I have no other proof."

"I'll take care of this, Nick." She couldn't seem to make him understand she didn't want his help.

"The house belongs to both of us now."

Not on his life. "You know the house means more to me than to you."

He snapped her a warning glance. She'd forgotten her role. What would a loving bride do?

"Ernest," Nick said, "when do you expect your investigators to finish?"

Loving bride, hell. How dared he talk over her, as if she didn't count?

"By the end of the week. I should have waited to talk to both of you."

"I'd like to bring in a man or two of my own."

"What?" Clair wasn't sure she'd said the word out loud, because the chief's voice, barking "what" simultaneously, almost drowned her out.

"I understand you're anxious about your wife, but how many arson investigators do you know?"

Nick shifted his shoulders. "I'm not trying to go over your head, but I can afford a more thorough investigation than the town. I won't risk Clair's house—or her life. Why would someone burn this place if not to get at her?"

"I'm asking the same question." Fosdyke all but congratulated Nick on their little men's club as Clair reached flashpoint.

She opened her mouth to set them straight, but Nick's beeper went off, saving her, him and their makeshift marriage. With a tight look of impatience, he tilted his hip to read the number on his pager.

Her body jerked an unwilling response to his masculine movements. She either suffered from terminal loneliness, or he was the most unconsciously sensual human being she'd ever set eyes on.

She scooped Kitty into her arms and turned her back on her husband and the fire chief. With any luck, a medical emergency would whisk Nick out of her reach before she showed him his place in her world and gave their secret away.

"Don't be angry with Dr. Dylan. He shouldn't have to take calls on his honeymoon, but he's the only doc around here."

"Ernest, you startled me." She'd have welcomed a few minutes to compose herself, but Nick joined her, too, sliding his warm, confident hand around her waist.

"I have to go to my office. Luke Blevins cut his hand with his chainsaw, and I persuaded him to meet me."

"Now?" Ernest said.

Clair's muttered "okay" sounded a touch too strangled for a fond wife's.

Nick cut her another look of caution, but then he nodded a goodbye to Ernest and pulled her toward his car. Ernest would notice if she sidestepped away. The fire chief's powers of observation impressed her enough to keep her still in Nick's hard grip.

"Where have you been all morning?" Nick asked.

"I took Kitty to the vet. I wanted them to check him over after all that smoke, and Dr. Grant recommended a flea collar to use until I can get him dipped again. Why didn't Mr. Blevins go to the hospital? A chainsaw wound sounds serious."

"I'm lucky he'd agree to stitches at all."

She pulled away from him. "Then I'll see you later. I forgot to buy a litter box for Kitty."

"Why don't you follow me home, and we'll drop off your car. We'll go back into town together, and you can do your shopping while I treat Luke."

For the fire chief's benefit? Not a chance. She shook her head, fully conscious of letting stubbornness get the better of her. Something about Nick...

Fosdyke's disapproval burst out of him. "You two are the darnedest newlyweds I ever saw."

With an almost convincing laugh, Nick caught her to his side again. Annoyed at such rough treatment, Kitty jumped out of Clair's arms to crouch at her feet. She twisted her head to glare into Nick's frustrated gaze. Would his grip look like affection or a wrestling hold?

"Give in for once," he whispered. "I don't want to leave you alone if Fosdyke thinks someone burned your house."

"You're just trying to impress him."

"You're my wife. I have a legal right to worry about you. Besides, this is a good opportunity to play our roles. We'll look devoted."

"All right," she said, "but who's going to dog my every step while I buy cat litter?"

"Good point. You'll just have to wait in my office while I finish with Luke."

"No, thanks. You can drop me off at Selina's."

"Now that's more like it," Fosdyke said behind them.

Nick had figured it would be enough. Only newlyweds made up such time-wasting car games.

FURY FLOODED LEOTA'S THROAT with bitter gall. She
scanned the society section of the morning newspaper, skimming grainy pictures of her new daughter-
in-law. Clair looked too damned much like her
mother.

Her face brought back memories Leota had tried to
put behind her since she'd first learned the truth about
Jeff and Sylvie Atherton. Seeing Sylvie in town occasionally, straightening from her garden, strolling
down a sidewalk with an air of owning it, had been
torture enough. Facing Sylvie's daughter across her
breakfast table for who knew how long to come
nearly made her sick.

Studying the paper again, Leota couldn't say for
sure whether her son had fallen in love with that girl,
but the wedding photographer obviously bore her a
soft spot.

He'd positioned Nick like an actor hired to play the
groom, but each photo threw a new light on a pre-
viously unnoted angle of Clair Atherton's bone struc-
ture. That face…that face had branded her with pain
from the moment she'd realized her husband still
wanted Sylvie.

His hatred, borne of his own weakness for another
man's wife, hadn't extended to Sylvie's daughter. Revenge on David Atherton had spread to Clair only by
accident, and Clair's grief had caused him the only
second thoughts Leota had ever known him to suffer.
He'd never done as much for her, or for the son she'd

borne him, and she'd nearly left him when she'd found out how hard he'd searched for Sylvie's girl.

That ridiculous Selina Franklin had always thought he wanted to hurt Clair. Leota suspected his intentions lay more along the lines of doing penance for her parents' deaths.

In his twisted pain at losing the woman he'd really loved, he'd seen Clair as the daughter he might have had with Sylvie. He couldn't hide his deepest, darkest wish any more than he'd hidden his disappointment with the son he'd made with Leota.

Still, she smiled with satisfaction even she recognized as being unhealthy. Clair had never sensed the softening in Jeff's heart. She'd never know how many times Jeff had gruffly ordered their limo driver to go back and buy lemonade from her summer stand once they were out of the car. Clair would never hear about the twenty-four hours Jeff had shut himself in the study after Hunter dragged her in for stealing apples.

Leota slammed her paper on the breakfast table and snatched up her coffee cup. She hardly felt the heat that seeped through the china.

Why hadn't he loved their son? Why had his inability to love him tarnished her feelings for Nick?

Hearing an engine's growl, she went to the window above the drive as Nick parked in front of the door. Seeing his passenger, heaviness pinned her to the floor. Her fine leather slippers felt as though they were made of lead.

Nick opened the door to the back seat and reached in to pull out a shopping bag. Clair dropped her purse in her rush to grab her own packages and fend off his assistance. Leota tapped her cup. Something wrong with those two.

She'd just watch. And wait.

Straightening, Clair tossed back her hair. Like her mother before her, she couldn't claim perfection in every separate angle of her features, but the whole of her animated face arrested even Leota's gaze. Clair's beauty scalded.

Nick didn't have to say what he saw in his bride. Leota already understood the way male Dylans responded to Atherton women. She ran shaking fingers through her perfectly tinted hair and smoothed her cashmere sweater over her tucked tummy.

Had Jeff been right? Could her origins dilute a bloodline that ran back to the rolls of an Elizabethan army? She stared at her son, her passport to living in a world she'd never dreamed she'd enter. She'd made him no happier than she'd made his father, and now his moving back here with that woman felt like vengeance.

On the driveway below, Nick strode around the car and took Clair's packages. His coaxing smile only increased his mother's fury as he nodded toward the car again, and Clair leaned down to fish out a large gray animal carrier.

The cat. Leota set her cup on the wide windowsill. If they thought she'd allow that Gypsy feline to live in her house… Hadn't they already inflicted enough punishment on her?

She marched down the stairs to the front door. Cool air swept the pair inside, pushing the younger woman's hair across her pale skin, shielding wind-kissed, red lips that made Leota wish for a nice poisoned apple to offer.

"What's that?" She pointed at the carrier.

"Leota, I didn't see you there," Nick said. "Do you know if Hunter set up a spot for Kitty's things?"

"I hope he waited," Clair cut in, as the cat complained loudly from inside his plastic quarters. "I'd like to settle Kitty out of everyone's way."

Her troubled expression pleased Leota. Sad when a little thing like territorial anxiety made you happy. "I'm sure more important matters occupied Hunter's time today. Why have you brought that cat back?"

"His name is Kitty." Defiance only made Clair's expression more elegant. "You don't have to worry. I'll replace or repair anything he harms."

"You are your mother all over again. She thought she was important, too, but I guess Jeffrey showed her how much she counted, and I can do the same for you."

"Leota!" Unexpected anger reverberated from Nick's voice. "Never speak to Clair like that again. You will not insult her or try to diminish her rights in this house. She's my wife, and she belongs here. Now leave us."

Leota clenched her fists and then unclenched them, willing herself to speak in the controlled tone Jeff had forced her to cultivate early in their marriage. "Like it or not, you're my son, Nick."

"And this is my home. Mine and my wife's."

"And mine, for as long as I wish to live here. Remember that part of the will?"

Without waiting for an answer, she started back to

the sanctuary of her room. She waited for the laughter that would certainly follow her.

Clair's mother had probably laughed. Too many times to forgive.

"I need to feed Kitty. Do you think Hunter will tell me where the food dish and litter box would bother him least?" The Atherton woman's tranquil voice floated up the stairs.

Leota slammed her bedroom door. She mattered here, dammit. "I matter, Jeff." A familiar refrain she still cried to a man who no longer heard. Her words, her own broken voice, hung in the air.

Smothering her.

"WHY DON'T YOU put them in the mudroom behind the kitchen?" Distracted, Nick stared upward as his mother's slammed door reverberated throughout the house. "I ought to talk to her."

"I don't like her talking about my mom."

He felt torn. "I know, Clair, but this is her home. And I expect she's trying to push us, hoping we'll make a mistake she can use to prove we only married because of Jeff's will."

"I let you down with Fosdyke earlier, I know, but I'll try to make our marriage look real." A hint of contrition flavored Clair's voice. "I didn't realize how real it would feel just because we share the same roof."

He reached for her arm, but she flitted away, obviously unwilling to let him touch her. Nick glanced again toward the stairs. He didn't know what tack to take next, with his mother or the woman he'd married.

Clair leaned down and opened the door on Kitty's carrier. She stroked the cat, and he grumbled at her before he shot away from her toward the kitchen. Nick started up the stairs, but Clair's voice called him back.

"I don't want to make matters worse between you and Leota, but one of us should suggest she stop trying to frighten me away."

"Frighten you? What are you talking about?" But he knew. Deep down, he'd also wondered if Fosdyke's doubts made sense. Their late-arriving wedding guest had been Leota and everyone knew how much Leota disliked the Athertons. "You think she set that fire?" He never would have believed his mother capable of that kind of violence.

Clair looked ambivalent. "I don't want to think she'd burn my house."

"Did Fosdyke ask you point-blank about her?"

"No."

"But he made you suspect her?"

"I didn't say that, but I have to live with you for the next year, and...well, I'll tell her if you can't."

Her bland expression drove him to the end of his rope. "You're like her, you know."

Clair lifted her chin, like a boxer starting across the room. "Explain what you mean. And fast."

"You've been hurt, and you won't let anyone hurt you again, so you shut people out. Do you ever consider what you might be throwing away?"

Clair took a firm step toward him, her eyes glittering. "I keep myself safe. From now on, I'll be alone when I choose to be. No one will ever take my life from me again.''

''You're twenty-six years old, and you aren't fighting for pecking order in a foster home. You have your own place.''

''I've sold myself for my own place. I did what I had to do to take my home back. I couldn't have lived there, even for the past month, any other way. But I sold myself for the house, and I'm not proud of that.''

Nick started up the stairs without answering. They'd made the same unpleasant choices. On the third tread, he leaned over the banister, lowering his voice.

''You can choose to be proud. I only gave you what my family took from you. I used you to get what I needed.''

''We share a mutual lack of ethics.''

''That's how it looks to you? All black or white? No shades of gray?''

''None I can see.''

Her conviction made him want to pound the stair rail. ''How can you enjoy your house if the way you took it back was wrong?''

''Let me get it back first. Then I'll worry about enjoying it.''

''You and Leota—I'm trying to build a world I can live in, but you both try to break the world to suit you.''

Clair stood her ground, her expression enigmatic. His frustration almost sent him back down the stairs. Like Clair, he was trying to reclaim his home. Maybe he couldn't succeed until Clair left, or until Leota found a kinder place to live. Listening to his wife's hard, quick breathing, he turned away and began to climb the stairs.

CLAIR CLOSED HER EYES and willed her breathing to slow as Nick's footsteps took him farther away. At last, he knocked on a door above and waited only a moment before he went inside.

After the door snicked shut behind him, Clair exhaled. Break the world—ha. Who'd he think he was? Freud reincarnated?

She snatched up her packages, a litter box and litter, Kitty's favorite kibble. The bags slapped against her legs. A box's hard corner scraped her knee, bringing her back to reality.

She'd married the man, not agreed to take therapy from him. Next time she married someone for material gain, she'd demand a prenuptial personality profile.

She reached the kitchen door and found her cat. Prancing a circuitous path on the kitchen counter, he writhed all over Mr. Hunter's arm as the man tried to spoon a substance that looked like caviar into a crystal bowl.

"Mr. Hunter!"

He jumped and caviar dotted the pristine fridge door behind him. "Mrs. Dylan, please don't shout my name when I don't know you're here."

"What are you doing? I can't afford to feed my cat caviar."

"Mrs. Dylan considered this brand inferior. You may think of it as a gift. He wouldn't touch tuna."

Kitty didn't even look her way. He braced his two front paws on Mr. Hunter's arms and then heaved himself into a strange, rolling contortion. "Look," Clair said. "I'm invisible to him."

"Cats are like that, Mrs. Dylan. I hope you didn't expect loyalty." Without stopping to clean the fridge, Mr. Hunter spooned the rest of the caviar into the bowl as Kitty sat up, looking dizzy. "And I hope you don't creep around the house like a burglar all the time."

The concept of loyalty was starting to give her a headache. "Didn't you hear me coming?" She lifted the bags that had made a racket rubbing against her jeans.

"This cat of yours purrs like a machine gun."

"He does? He never has before." She dropped the bags and hurried to the counter to hear for herself. "Did he fall for you or the caviar?"

"The latter, I assume. Could you hold him back a moment so I can put the dish on the floor? I'm afraid he'll take my arm off when I try to move the bowl."

Kitty mistook Clair for a caviar provider and continued his affectionate seduction while Mr. Hunter whisked the bowl to the ground. With a low meow, the cat shot after his heart's desire, and Clair eyed Mr. Hunter with new respect.

"You like my cat?"

The palest pink stole over his perfectly groomed cheeks. "It was hungry."

"You called him 'he' when you asked me to hold him back. He's not an 'it' to you anymore."

"Don't try to persuade yourself that animal is lovable to anyone but you."

"I promise not to go overboard, Mr. Hunter. I'd better disinfect that counter. Kitty has many fine qualities, but I don't think he's germ-free."

"Thank you, but I let him up here. I'll clean the surface. May I put your packages away for you?"

The concept appalled her. "Let's get this straight. You don't pick up after me, and I'll make sure you don't notice I'm here."

He glanced at the source of even louder purring. "Let me counter. I will pick up after you, because that's my job. You clean his litter box regularly."

"I'll clean his litter box, because he's mine, but I don't want you treating me the way Leota and Nick..." She ran out of words that her contract allowed her to say.

Mr. Hunter shook his head. "You're an extremely important member of this household, the one who assures that my staff and I will keep our jobs."

"What?" The word exploded from her mouth like a bullet from a gun. Had Nick told Mr. Hunter the truth?

"A distant cousin of the family would have inherited if Nick hadn't married. He sent in a team to study the possibility of turning this home into a bed-and-breakfast. Come to think of it, Mrs. Franklin will probably get around to sending you a thank-you card."

Producing a smile, Clair sagged against the counter. Hunter knew only that someone else would have inherited. She looked around the room. Sterile restaurant fixtures and spotless, white ceramic tile counters repelled human touch.

Kitty's throaty ode to caviar threaded his pleasure into the air, but any self-respecting inn would include a charming cat to make its guests feel at home. She studied Mr. Hunter, who'd given Kitty crystal and caviar, despite his blue-collar origins. She didn't have the heart to point out a bed-and-breakfast atmosphere might improve the house. A sudden suspicion straightened her.

"Did you feed him because you want to keep me happy here?"

Mr. Hunter produced an economy-size container of disinfectant from beneath the porcelain sink. Squirting the bleach cocktail on the counter, he looked at her. "I fed him because he was hungry, and he's skin and bones, and I must tell you, even his skin is not terribly attractive."

Clair grinned. "You're a practical guy." She lifted the litter box. "Where should I put this? Nick suggested the mudroom."

"Good idea."

She left the door open while she set up Kitty's facilities. Mr. Hunter would know a few more of the answers she needed. "When I'm not here, would you prefer I move all this and Kitty to my room?"

"I beg your pardon?"

"You might not want him underfoot."

"This is your home, Mrs. Dylan."

Clair paused in the middle of pouring litter. Mr. Hunter seemed shocked she'd suggest tucking Kitty out of sight. She liked him better for his egalitarian mind-set.

"I wouldn't let him climb that counter too often," she advised. "Give him an inch, and he thinks he owns the place."

"I have access to plenty of disinfectant. He could use some pampering."

She snapped the lid on the litter box and set the bag of litter on a counter above a rack of colorful, hanging umbrellas. "Do you have any pets, Mr. Hunter?"

"To be honest, no one ever thought of bringing an animal here before. I believe we all assumed the family would disapprove."

"Nick never had a dog or anything?"

"A hamster that departed after he nested in the senator's briefcase. Dr. Dylan started boarding school when he was eight, so Kitty is his first pet since then."

Mr. Hunter's acceptance of her marriage cemented his acceptance of her and warmed Clair's heart. She went to the sink to wash her hands. Nick and Mr. Hunter had both been kind to Kitty. Maybe Nick's kindness came from Hunter, the man who had no qualms about showing his affection for Nick.

Clair dried her hands and pulled a slip of paper from her pocket. "I have a gift for you." She held it out so he could read the time and date she'd written down. "I made an appointment to have Kitty dipped again."

She didn't mention the fleabites Nick had found.

OBEYING A LIFETIME HABIT, Nick took his usual place on the uncomfortable period chair in his mother's sitting room. This time he wasn't a miscreant, sent by his father to discuss why his behavior hadn't measured up to Dylan standards.

"I don't want you to feel pushed out," he said, "but you have to accept Clair's place in my life."

"How did she persuade you to marry her? What can you possibly want from such a low-class, ill-prepared scullery maid?" Angry red color drew jagged lines from her throat to her cheekbones.

"Did my father's family call you a scullery maid?"

"Lay off the psychoanalysis and get her out of my house."

"She's here to stay. Why don't you tell me why you dislike her so much?"

"You've blinded yourself to all the reasons you shouldn't have married her." Acrimony pitched her voice higher. "Soon, I doubt you'll find time to worry about me."

"You don't want me to worry about you, but isn't that what families do? Do you want Jeff to run the rest of our lives?"

"Your father was a good man." Her eyes raked him.

"Be honest. If he'd been good, you wouldn't still resent me, and I wouldn't have grown up knowing he was trying to recoup the best he could find from an accident. Me." Unused to being so blunt, he stood and rubbed his damp palms down the legs of his trousers. "Don't force me to choose between you and Clair. Neither of us really wants me to do that."

A blast of cold from her gaze was obviously meant to shove him toward the door, but he held his ground.

"You and I can still make a relationship, Leota."

She blanked all expression from her eyes and stiffened her posture.

"Why do you want to fight?" What he really wanted to ask was, why didn't she want him as her son? He couldn't.

Nick chewed the inside of his cheek. She refused to speak, so he filled the gaps. Maybe she couldn't admit his father had been right about the woman he'd married and the son whose existence had forced their marriage. Maybe she had tried to use her pregnancy as a stepladder into a different class. Maybe Nick would never be anything more to her than a failed attempt at social high jumping.

"My wife and I expect you at dinner tonight." He opened her door and closed it behind himself, winded.

Leota might be right about one thing. He'd chosen a wife who contributed to their family war. But he felt responsible for Clair now. That part of their vows had become real. When he'd caught her contentedly planting flowers at her house, he'd understood how much she loved her home.

Her shock-blank gaze last night had affected him more than Leota's tantrums or his father's legendary ice-spiked disappointment. Clair expected nothing from him, but her refusal to make demands had shown him a different kind of woman. Her sense of honor contrasted sharply with the women he'd known—women he'd believed he'd loved, who eventually forgot to hide the fact that his family name and legacy mattered more than he did.

To Clair, his family was a liability. How did a man avoid falling under the spell of such a woman?

He looked at his watch. He still had time to call Ben Wells and make arrangements to meet in the morning. He'd had to cancel today's appointment so he could take care of Luke Blevins. Tomorrow he'd figure out how to make Ben help him cover up the insurance fiasco so Clair could rebuild her house.

TWO DAYS AFTER THE FIRE, the wind blew stronger than ever around the burned house that refused to give up its secrets. Ernest Fosdyke leaned into the gusts as he searched the site. The cold prodded at him, a nameless threat of more bad times to come.

He felt the hair on the back of his neck stand up. Something wasn't right. He'd worked fires for more than twenty years, and he trusted his gut. It never let him down. Today he wanted to retire his gut. He wanted to be wrong about this fire.

Caution tape snaked back and forth over the grass. Nothing about this puzzling fire offered a real hint of the truth.

Shrugging the weight of his frustration off his shoulders, he rewound the yellow tape around the singed trees, but he trained his eyes on the grass as he walked the perimeter of the burned house, not sure exactly what he expected to see.

Who'd want to hurt Clair Dylan? Only one name came to mind, but he didn't speak it yet. Not even to himself.

The feud between the Athertons and the Dylans reached back to his own teenage years, when Sylvie Moore and Jeff Dylan had become an item that had displeased Jeff's illustrious parents. The scandal in the town only burned brighter when Sylvie broke off with Jeff and eventually took up with David Atherton.

Not long after that, Leota married Jeff Dylan. Jeff's parents left the country for an extended visit anywhere else when Jeff brought Leota home. Seven months later, Nick arrived.

Jeff had never made Leota happy. But she hadn't complained. She'd stuck by her husband and shrugged off her friendships. Including her relationship with Ernest. He'd never believed the benevolent front Jeff put up for the voters, and he'd never forgiven himself for not saving Leota from the mistake of her marriage.

After he tacked the last piece of tape in place, he inspected the charred edges of the kitchen wall. He was as curious as Clair about what had started the fire, about where it had started. Looked to him as if the burning had been most intense around the old kitchen windows, but he was so close to this one he couldn't find his objectivity.

The Leota he'd known stubbornly returned to his mind, the girl who outran every boy in their valley among the blue hills, the girl who'd led them from pretend battle to makeshift fort. For the sake of that Leota, he prayed his suspicions were wrong. Why would she hurt a young woman who could match her pain for pain?

Unable to come up with an answer, he returned to

the Jeep and took a poster board from the back seat. He sprayed Keep Off in black enamel on the white surface and nailed the sign to a tree trunk. Wide branches would shelter the heavy cardboard in rain. He made two more signs and nailed them up.

Hammer in hand, he stared over the roof of his car at the mess. Damp wind blew the scent of smoke at him. He embarked on one last short search around the edges of the clearing.

He toed his way through the high grass again, looking for something he'd recognize only if he saw it. At a break in the trees, the grass looked bent over, as if someone had started a path. Ernest looked up. Thick evergreen trees hid the Dylan house from view, but this new path couldn't lead elsewhere.

Excitement rose with his dread, but he tried to stay calm. Clair must have come back and forth countless times since she and Nick had begun to see each other. Leota might come this way, too. She might have walked down here the day her son married the daughter of the woman she despised.

Parting the tall sharp fronds of grass, he hoped he'd find nothing. Common sense and experience took over. Just when he'd decided to go back for his gloves, he saw a small white square.

Off the path, but not too far. Far enough that someone might have tossed it. Casually. Not to hide it.

A matchbook. He yanked his shirt out of his waistband and lifted the matchbook with the hem. It fluttered out of his grasp. He leaned over, but his hand shook as he picked it up.

At the Jeep, he opened the back door and set the

matchbook on the seat while he pulled on gloves. Even through latex, the damp cardboard felt slick. He flipped the cover open, careful to touch only where he had to.

Someone had used all the matches. A sudden image of Leota sneaking her occasional cigarette jarred him. He'd passed her many times, parked on the side of the road with her car windows open, a circle of blue smoke twisting above the roof.

He read faint writing on the cardboard cover. Someone had scrawled the name Brandon Pembroke and a date and time. Rain had faded the ink, but Ernest could still make out the words.

Was the matchbook a clue or litter? Who was this guy? Whoever he was, someone had made an appointment with him for—Ernest checked his watch—thirteen days from now. He'd find the guy's address and be waiting at two-thirty to see who showed up for this meeting. And then he'd make his own appointment with Mr. Pembroke.

CHAPTER SEVEN

ON THE THIRD DAY after her wedding, lunchtime came and went without Nick. Leota kept to her room, and Clair started a territorial dispute with the Dylan's cook, Bonnie, when she cleared the table after her solitary meal. Mr. Hunter had broken up the argument with a look that suggested Clair had no business bringing her own dishes to the kitchen.

Clair had given in, then wandered the house until she grew so restless she almost called Nick's office to ask when he planned to come home. Instead, she checked Kitty's food, water and litter and drove to Selina's.

The judge greeted her from behind the front desk. "You're just the woman I want to see. Selina has a cold."

"I should have called before I came. I don't want to disturb her."

"Actually, I'd be glad if you could talk her into visiting your husband. Every year, she starts with this same kind of chest thing, and eventually, we do an emergency-room run."

Clair glanced toward the stairs that led to the family quarters. "She waits until she's that sick?" What grudge did Selina hold against Nick?

"Talk to her, Clair. Maybe you can make her see sense."

Selina answered her knock in a congested voice. Clair entered her bedroom expecting the worst, but Selina lay on a divan, in sweats with a book clasped to her chest.

"Hi, sweetie," she said. "I'm so glad to see you. Come sit with me."

Clair started across the room. "Your cheeks look a bit pink, Selina."

"Don't worry about me. Hey—see that brocade bag on my dressing table?"

Clair veered across the carpet to pick up the burgundy drawstring bag. She traced the gold threads embroidered in Celtic-looking designs. "It's lovely."

"Sylvie made it for me. While she was pregnant with you. You know, you came kind of late in their lives, and Sylvie was confined to her bed for the last four months of her pregnancy."

"Did you spend a lot of time with her?"

"As much as I could. I'd just started renovating this place. Open the bag."

Clair gently opened the top and turned the bag on its side. A rhinestone hair clip in the shape of a bumblebee fell into her palm. She held it up to Selina.

"She used to plant that right in the middle of her chignon. She gave it to me not long before she died, but you should have it." Selina took the bag and dumped the rest of its contents on her lap. A fountain pen in lapis lazuli, a yellowed calling card with *Sylvie Atherton* scrawled across the top, and a bent, silver sewing thimble fell on her knitted blanket. "She used the thimble when she embroidered the bag."

"I can have these?"

"These, and a pajama case she made for me when I lost Julian's and my child."

"Selina," Clair protested. She could only guess at the suffering the Franklins must have endured.

"I'm all right about it now." Selina rubbed the back of her hand across her nose. "But we always wanted children. I would have asked you to come live with us, but as I've told you I was so afraid for you. Go get the case. It's in the top drawer of that dresser."

Clair followed her pointing finger and pulled out a square of lawn material. She turned the case to the light. Her mother had used blue and silver thread, faded now, to embroider a sky of moons and stars and a woman in a flowing gown and a nightcap who yawned from her perch along the curve of a large crescent moon.

"She was creative, a dreamer," Clair said in wonder.

"But a practical mom."

"Are you sure you can part with her things? I know how much she loved you."

"She loved you more. I've never understood what took her from us, why she gave up on life and let herself fade away when she was still a relatively young woman. I remember her saying she knew David would die before her, and she dreaded being without him. Sometimes I wonder if she had always prepared herself to follow him."

Clair laid a hand on Selina's sleeve. "I wish she'd been stronger. I've always wondered why she didn't love me enough to want to stay alive."

"What do we know about the human mind? I think when your father died, she stepped onto a path she couldn't come back from. And then she had that heart attack. Maybe it was stress. Maybe grief." Selina pulled Clair into her arms. "I'd like to be your friend now, a better friend than I was to Sylvie. I couldn't convince her to fight for her life, and I couldn't keep you here when she died."

Clair fought tears that burned at her eyes. "I'm learning to understand why you let me go, but, truthfully, after all these years, it doesn't matter anymore. You're more important to me now." She kissed Selina's cheek, but then drew back. "You do have a fever."

Selina made an impatient face. "You sound like Julian. He didn't mention juice, did he?"

"No, but I'll get you some." Clair rested the back of her hand against Selina's forehead. "You're sick. Have you taken anything?"

The door opened behind them. The judge arrived, sporting a glass of orange juice. "She needs antibiotics. She's had this fever for two days now. Why don't you let Clair take you to Nick's office? I'll look after things here."

"I guess I could see Nick now," Selina said, sparking Clair's curiosity.

When her friend felt better, she'd demand an explanation. "Where are your socks and shoes?"

"I'll help her," the judge said. "Why don't you call Nick and see if he can fit her in?"

Clair dialed the number, and Nick answered right away. Mindful of her audience, she tried to soften her voice when she spoke his name.

"What's wrong?" he asked. "Have you heard from Fosdyke?"

"No. Selina's sick. The judge tells me she's had a fever for two days. Could you look at her?"

"Glad to. Are you bringing her?"

"Mm-hmm. The judge can't leave their guests."

"Bring her as soon as she's ready. I'll be waiting."

He met them at Clair's car and gave Selina his arm as he walked them inside. "Why don't you come in with us, Clair, if Selina doesn't mind? I usually call my receptionist, but she's at a soccer game today with her youngest."

"I ought to charge you for this visit, Nick Dylan. When people hear I've come to you, they'll stop staying away."

"I was thinking the same thing," Clair admitted.

Nick led them to the treatment room and helped Selina onto the table. "You can dictate your charges once we find out exactly what's wrong. Clair, will you take a robe from that bottom drawer? And step outside with me while Selina puts it on. I'd like an X-ray, Selina."

"I knew you would."

He was smiling as he shut the door. Clair leaned against the cool wall.

"What gives between you two?" she asked.

"She remembers my father as fondly as you, and

she's right. If people find she's used my practice, they'll start to come in. Unless she calls them off. How did you persuade her to come?''

"The judge suggested I bring her, and she reluctantly agreed. She hasn't been rude to you before, has she?''

"Not when you're with us," he said, and knocked on the door.

"Just a minute," Selina called. "I can't find the ties on this thing.''

Nick brushed Clair's hair away from her face. She turned her cheek toward his hand, seeking his warmth.

"Selina gave me some things my mom gave her.''

"Did she?'' He looked more deeply into her eyes, and Clair didn't try to hide her somewhat melancholy happiness.

"I'll show you sometime," she said. "It's odd. She had a pen and a hair clip—I don't remember them, but they must have been special to my mom. Selina was her best friend.''

"Do you have anything Sylvie left you?''

"A couple of books—I've always wondered if some of her things got packed in with mine and somehow got lost when I moved from one foster home to another.''

"I didn't know you planned to visit Selina today.''

"The house was too quiet, and Mr. Hunter reminded me I should stay out of the kitchen when Bonnie's there.''

He pushed his hands into his pockets. "Leota hired

her to cook just after my grandparents moved to Maine.''

Leave it to the Dylans to retire north when most people moved south. "I'm going to call Paul when I get back and ask him to put me to work.''

"You don't want more time to yourself?''

She shook her head. "The inactivity makes me crazy.''

"Clair?'' he said in a sharper tone than usual.

She lifted her chin, in case he was preparing to deliver a verbal blow.

"Thanks for bringing Selina—and for making her feel you trust me.''

"She believes in us,'' Clair said, dropping her voice.

"I didn't know how to thank you for that.''

"Just doing my job.''

With an impatient glance, he tapped the door again. "Ready, Selina?''

"Come on in.''

He brushed past Clair, his warmth for her gone, and she almost wished she'd found a better answer. She'd felt self-conscious. In fact, she was glad her friendship with Selina might help him.

Selina's fever was high. Nick gave her ibuprofen. Her X-ray came back negative, but he prescribed an antibiotic.

"I wish I had samples to give you. Actually, Clair, if you want to get Selina's prescription filled, I'll be glad to drive her home. I was about to close up for the day, anyway.''

"What do you think, Selina?''

"I put my health in Nick's hands. I guess I can take a car ride with him."

"I'll do the prescription if you'd rather." Nick took a blow on the chin with grace.

"You're as touchy as your wife, young man. Just start the car heater ahead of time, and we're in business. I'm freezing."

"That's the fever. It should drop soon."

Clair stopped at Bigelow's first, but their pharmacist had taken his son's Boy Scout troop on a hike. At a new chain store out by the ramp to the interstate, the pharmacist was on duty and grateful for the work.

By the time she returned to Franklin House, Nick and the judge had put Selina to bed and come back downstairs to mind the store. Nick held out his hand as Clair came in. He only did it for show, but Clair tucked her fingers into his, relishing his strength. Funny—the closer she grew to friends like Selina, the easier she found giving in to her growing feelings for Nick.

The judge patted her shoulder. "Dinner's on me tonight, Clair. As a thank-you for what you two did for Selina."

Clair glanced at Nick. His smile, a masterpiece of heart-stopping intimacy, pulled her closer to him. She leaned into the pool of his body heat.

Just doing her job.

EARLY THE NEXT MORNING, Clair drove to the brick-lined entrance of the Saddlebrook subdivision and parked her car in the first cul-de-sac. She strode back to the monstrous flower bed that divided entrance from exit to wait for Paul. Minutes later he nosed his truck to the short curb. His shrewd glance through the truck's tinted windows made her uneasy.

She'd enjoyed last night's dinner with the judge, but Nick's hand, drifting to the nape of her neck, the way he'd leaned into her to laugh at some joke of the judge's, the way his gaze lingered on her as if he couldn't look anywhere else—the whole performance had left her restless, dissatisfied.

"Trouble in Dylan paradise?" Paul asked.

"Time for an Atherton reality check."

"A Fairlove Lovelies reality check." He opened the door and climbed out. "Help me unload the bulbs, so I can move the truck out of the way. Where'd you park?"

"Back there." She pointed at the brick wall that hid her car. "Thanks for letting me help. I need the work."

"For the money?" he prompted with a smirk as he opened his truck's tailgate.

"For the sheer release of physical exertion." She couldn't complain to Nick, but Paul would understand. "Do you know Bonnie Rutherford?"

"I know the family."

His response stopped her. One thing she hadn't expected from coming back. She no longer knew families. She knew names, and sometimes she recognized faces, but Fairlove had changed in twelve years. She felt like an outsider sometimes.

"Here, take the other end of this." They hoisted a large bag of bulbs off the truck and settled it beside the flower bed, both grunting with exertion. Paul reached for another bag. "What did Bonnie do?"

"She throws me out of the kitchen every time I carry a dish through the doorway."

"Bodily?"

"With her attitude. You wouldn't believe the class discrimination that goes on in that house, and I'm on the wrong side of the battlefield."

"What do you mean?"

She sighed. "Never mind. I don't like myself when I whine."

"You're not whining. How is she rude?"

"She's territorial. I'd understand if I were trying to take her job or make more work for her, but I try not to intrude."

"You're trying to change the natural order up there. Forget it. Stay in your place, and they won't feel as if you're muscling in on theirs."

"I don't like my place."

"What'd you think was going to happen, Clair?" He turned the next bag toward her. "Is this too heavy for you?"

She obviously hadn't considered all the implications of being a temporary Dylan. She took her end of the bag and yanked, but Paul took the brunt of the load off her.

"I assumed I'd move in there on my own terms. I didn't know I'd have to adapt to everyone else's idea of who I should be."

"You're Cinderella. Enjoy the palace. Make your own place."

"What do you mean?"

"It's your house, too. Plant something in the garden. Redecorate a room only you use. Tell them who you are."

They dropped the bag at the same time, and Clair stretched her back. Planting or redecorating implied longevity. Nick wouldn't like that. "You don't understand."

"Does Dr. Dylan know how you feel?"

"Why do you always call him Dr. Dylan?" Her frustration bubbled over. "Aren't you the same age?"

"I'm not from here, Clair. I don't know the man. So he's 'Dr. Dylan' to me."

She knew how to fix that problem. "Maybe you should meet him on social terms. He knows a lot of home owners."

Paul looked puzzled.

"People who need landscaping," she said. "People who might need your services."

"Cool. You know I'm always available to network." He pulled a shovel out of the truck. "Don't think you'll get a bonus out of this, though."

"I'll settle for a building contractor. Can you recommend a couple of good ones?"

"I can tell you the one I plan to use when I build my own house. He'll know an architect, too."

"What's his name?" She took a small notebook from her back pocket.

"You won't remember?"

"Stop harassing me and give me the guy's name."

"Tim Hanover. Don't put your little pencil away. I'll give you his number, too."

She practiced Nick Dylan's "back off" look on

him, but she must not have the skill. Paul only laughed.

BEN WELLS HAD INVITED backup to their meeting. As his secretary escorted Nick inside his office, Wilford Thomas rose from a vinyl chair on the other side of Ben's desk. Holding out his hand, Wilford eyed Nick warily. Nick enjoyed his first glimmer of the power his father had found so irresistible.

"Afternoon," the attorney said.

He shook the man's hand. "Wilford, I'm glad you joined us. Apparently, I have business to clear up with both of you."

"I thought Wilford could help me explain why we covered the Atherton house the way we did," Wells said.

"Ben, it's my house, not the Athertons', not my father's. Wilford, that was the last decision you'll make about my property without talking to me first."

"Clear enough," Wilford said, his voice tight. He sank into his chair again, touching his perfect white hair.

"Let's make sure. Why don't you have your secretary schedule a meeting so you and I can talk?"

"About what?"

His voice shook and Nick relented. He'd never respected his father's bullying. "About where we go from here. Maybe we have a conflict of interests, since you're also one of the estate's attorneys."

"Your father never had a problem with my handling his personal matters, as well as his property."

Nick unbuttoned his overcoat and sat in the chair

Ben hadn't offered him. He glanced at Wilford. "I'm not my father. Why don't you set up the appointment and we'll talk. Right now, I have a more pressing problem."

"The insurance," Ben said, coughing. "I can't change the policy now."

Nick stared at the other man, whose naturally florid face darkened. How high did his blood pressure run normally? Would Jeff have asked him to change the policy after a fire? The thought ached between Nick's eyes.

"What I want you to do, Ben, is give me a check for the coverage you two agreed on, and then both of you need to keep your mouths shut if Clair ever mentions a higher figure."

"Is that all?" Ben's relief reassured Nick.

But Wilford, gasping like a fish, found his voice. "What are you talking about?" he exploded. "You don't plan to make up the difference, do you?"

"My family owes her that money, and I want no trouble from you when I make the transfer."

"I can't allow you to give Clair Atherton that much money, Nick." Wilford glanced Ben's way, constrained from saying more about the true state of Nick's marriage.

"My wife's name is Clair Dylan, and I have the money in my personal accounts. I'm not asking your permission. I just don't want you to tell anyone else what I've decided to do."

"I won't allow you to hand over your capital. For Clair's house?" Wilford sputtered. "You're throwing your money away."

"My money," Nick said, rapid-fire, "and I have to use it because you didn't do your job. My decision stands, Wilford, so don't try to interfere with my wife or me." He turned to the insurance adjuster. "When will you have Clair's check?"

Wilford interrupted. "I'll resign my position as your attorney, Nick."

Nick suspected the older man's quitting might save him the eventual, uncomfortable task of firing him. "Do what you have to. Ben, I'd like to get the money into an account for Clair within the week. Is that possible?"

"I'll see what I can do." Ben stood so fast his chair slid into the fake paneling behind him. He thrust out his hand. "I'm sorry we caused you this trouble, Dr. Dylan." He adopted a formal, intimidated tone.

Nick gripped the other man's hand and tried to ignore his own hollow feeling. He'd never used Dylan methods before. He didn't feel powerful. Ashamed, maybe. Not powerful.

"I'm still Nick." His own skin didn't seem to fit just now. "Don't quit, Wilford. We'll work something out. Just recognize I have to make this right for Clair. I can't help myself."

"I'm supposed to advise you. If you won't take my advice, I serve no purpose for you."

Nick nodded, too tired to argue. "I'll try to listen when we aren't discussing my wife's—" He stopped. He'd almost said "future." Just in time, he remembered Ben didn't know the truth. "Past," he substituted.

He didn't care if Ben thought he was helping Clair

build a shrine to her family. Wilford already understood as well as he ever would. Nick picked up his coat and exited the seedy office.

"Wait, Nick." Wilford hurried to catch up. "I'll talk to you later, Ben. Thanks for seeing us on such short notice." Wilford struggled into his coat as he reached Nick's side. He pushed through the door, a significant look backward telling Nick his news was private.

Nick put on his own coat on the sidewalk. "What next, Wilford?"

"I've been approached about putting together a memorial for your father. I tried to explain that you and Leota were still in mourning and might want to wait, but then I realized, if you can persuade Clair to help, this is a perfect opportunity to convince Jim Dale and Greg Andrews that your marriage is based on love, rather than a business agreement."

Jim, the bank president, and Greg, the party chief who'd swung Jeff's every election, were the other two executors. They'd have to believe in the marriage if Nick could persuade Clair to work with him.

"I'll talk to her." He turned up his collar and walked away from Wilford. How did a man induce his wife to build a memorial to the man who'd destroyed her life?

On Tuesday the following week, Clair waited outside Mrs. Peabody's Coffee and Cake and watched men wrapping the town's Christmas garland around signs and Fairlove's three traffic-light cables. On the porch behind Clair, Mrs. Peabody had already set up her faux fir, complete with carefully wrapped empty boxes. The coffee shop was new—only seven years old.

When Clair had lived in town twelve years ago, Mrs. Peabody had been her English teacher. Selina had told her Mrs. Peabody's rich brew and moist, miraculous chocolate cake were luxuries she mustn't forgo. She ought to avoid them on her meager budget, but Tim Hanover had asked her to meet him at Mrs. Peabody's to talk about her plans for rebuilding her house.

A couple of snowflakes and some nonseasonal swearing wafted through the air. Apparently, town-owned Christmas lights were no more reliable than privately owned ones.

"Try it again—plug it in," one of the men called to the guy who controlled the current.

A buzz preceded popping lights and more swearing, and Clair decided to wait inside, out of the cold. A college-age young woman, dressed in dramatic black that contrasted with her pale blond hair, seated her at one of Mrs. Peabody's tables. "I'm Gwen. I'll be serving you this afternoon. What will you have?" She eyed Clair curiously.

More of the Dylan mystique. For once, Clair disregarded her misgivings about the name she'd borrowed. "I'll start with a latte. I might like a piece of cake later, but I'm waiting for Tim Hanover. Do you know him?"

"I can't believe you persuaded him to meet you in this place." She leaned forward. "I love working here, but I can't see Tim wrapping his paws around one of Mrs. Peabody's china cups. Are you looking to hire him to work on your house?''

Clair smiled. This small-town gossip, she liked. ''Possibly. What do you know about his work?''

''He built a barn for my best friend's father. Watertight, airtight and snug as a sauna. That's what my friend's dad says.'' She reeled off her testimonial, then ended with a self-conscious curve of her mouth. ''I'll get your coffee.''

''Is Mrs. Peabody around?''

''She's visiting her sister in Maryland. Were you one of her students?''

Clair nodded. ''A long time ago.''

''She stopped teaching the year before I would have had her.'' Gwen picked up the menu and returned to the kitchen.

The bell over the shop door tinkled. A man of medium height and broad build stepped inside. In a denim jacket and rumpled, dark-brown hair, he looked too large for the chintz chairs and dimity-covered tables. He headed for the front desk, which was out of her sight. Within seconds, Gwen led him to her table.

''Mrs. Dylan?'' The man shifted a large binder to his left hand. ''I'm Tim Hanover. I hope I'm not too late.''

Half rising, Clair shook his hand and gestured toward the chair opposite hers. ''I'm pleased to meet you,'' she said. ''Paul Sayers recommended your work.''

''I brought pictures of my most recent projects.'' He slid the binder around a delicate bowl of water and freesia blooms and turned to Gwen. "I'd like black coffee and some of Mrs. Peabody's cake. And wrap up another piece, will you? My wife won't let me in the door tonight if I don't bring her a slice."

"Glad to." Gwen snapped her notepad shut. "I'll be just a few minutes." She moved away.

"I guessed you'd want an estimate on clearing your land first, so I stopped by your old house." Tim pulled several sheets of paper out of the binder as Clair opened it. He laid one page in front of her. "I'll salvage what I can, but I have to warn you, this won't be an archaeological dig."

He came on like a whirlwind. Clair scanned his estimate. She wanted to start the renovations, but she wasn't ready to turn her back on what she'd had. "Have you cleared many sites like mine?"

His wide mouth turned down. "A school and a barn," he said. "I hate the destruction. I definitely prefer building, but when you work in my job in a place as far from a big city as we are, you have to be flexible."

She pushed his estimate to the side and leafed through the binder pages. Houses of all styles and sizes passed in front of her, some in subdivisions, some standing alone. "How long have you been in business?"

"For my first five years I worked closer to D.C. Then my wife and I had our first son, and we wanted to move out to the country. We liked Saint Joan's University so close—my wife's a little on the artsy side—so we settled here twelve years ago."

"May I have references?"

"Why don't you look at those pictures, pick the houses you like, and I'll ask the owners if you can call them. Dr. Dylan will probably want to talk to them, as well."

She nodded to keep from saying her house didn't belong to Nick. "Sounds good."

"I thought you might try to rebuild the old place. Everyone said you were mighty attached to it. And I do glasswork as a hobby. Might be useful if you want to rebuild."

Clair's lips felt stiff. "I'm not sure I can rebuild it the way it was. I don't have blueprints, and I doubt anyone stored them."

"I can recommend a couple of architects for you. They might be able to work from drawings, or maybe you can just tell them what you want. I'm sure they've seen the house."

"Thank you," she said. "I'd like their names."

They finished their business quickly. Clair chose a few houses that resembled her old one. Tim passed her business cards for three different architects and, over ambrosial chocolate cake, described their work. Finally he left for another appointment.

Clair lingered over the last crumbs of her cake. She glanced up when the bell tinkled again, and she met Nick's intent gaze. She looked away. Sometimes they felt too married.

She lifted her head, pasting on an artificial smile of welcome for the other diners. "Nick."

"I wasn't sure I should come in. Did you finish with Tim?" He took Tim's vacated chair, his long legs bumping against hers.

She jerked away, hypersensitive to his presence, to his ever so potent, familiar scent. "You were watching me?"

"I picked this up today." Sliding his hand inside his lapel, he pulled out a business-size envelope and passed it to her across the freesia. "I wanted to be alone with you when I gave it to you, and I saw you standing outside here."

He folded his broad hands in his lap, over the navy material of his suit. His aloof posture offered Clair space. She slid her fingernail beneath the envelope's flap.

Gwen returned. "Dr. Dylan, can I bring you anything? Mrs. Dylan?"

"I'll have another coffee, please," Clair said, startled as always at the name that bound her to a man who could make her want him with an accidental brush of his leg.

Nick smiled at the young woman, and she beamed back, barely avoiding, Clair thought, melting into a puddle at his feet. "Coffee, too, please," he said. "Black and strong."

With another brilliant smile, Gwen flounced away, her slender hips swaying naturally in her short skirt.

Clair gripped the envelope, wrinkling the edges around a hard, plastic rectangular shape. She should be grateful for the lesson Gwen had just taught her. She wasn't the only woman in town with a weakness for her husband. She hoped the infection wasn't terminal.

"Clair, are you going to open that?"

She finished opening the flap and turned the envelope upside down. A plastic case containing a checkbook fell out. She stared from it to Nick, a slow burn starting. "You aren't suggesting I get a salary from you? I won't use this."

"I opened that account with the insurance money. It's yours to use as you like."

Idly, she flipped open the checkbook and looked at the starting balance. "Good Lord!"

Heads turned all over the room. Nick glanced at the other customers. "It's your money, not mine. It's for the house."

Her tension heightened as she searched his watchful expression. "I didn't expect so much."

"Don't you want your house back?"

"What's going on, Nick? What aren't you telling me?"

He lifted one black eyebrow. "What do you mean?"

Giving in would have been easier, but something smelled funny. "You're defensive. I think you're hiding something from me."

He scooted his chair closer as Gwen came back with their coffees.

"Cream, Mrs. Dylan?"

"No, thank you." She couldn't look away from Nick.

"I'm not hiding anything from you." He took her hand. She jumped, but he tightened his fingers. "Relax. I don't want anyone to know we're arguing." He looked around, and several people had the grace to turn away. "I'm afraid you won't take the money because you're always so determined to do everything by yourself. I know my part in returning your house galls you, but I don't want you to throw your home away. I want to do right by you.''

Clair lost herself in the husky sound of his voice. After a moment she snapped out of her trance.

''You could be lying,'' she said.

He laughed. ''If I admitted it, I'd be a pretty bad liar.''

His response drew a smile from her. Nick stared at her lips, and she struggled against the longing he made her feel. ''Where did you get this money?''

''Ben Wells brought it to my office.''

''I only asked him for an appointment yesterday,'' she said, mystified at such quick work. ''He didn't even call me back.''

''I spoke to him before you.''

Ah. She was Nick Dylan's wife, an appendage with a name she didn't want. ''He works pretty fast for a Dylan, doesn't he?''

''Meaning?'' Nick asked, his tone becoming dangerous.

''Why didn't he bring the check to me? It's my house. Everyone knows it belongs to me.''

''No one knows the house belongs to you. In Ben's eyes, you're my wife, and the house belongs to both of us.''

In Tim's eyes, too, and Ernest Fosdyke's. They all saw her as Nick's wife. She must be doing a fine job.

She tucked her hands in front of her. ''I'm sorry I'm not behaving well, but you were right. I don't like having to accept help. No matter what I do, I can't bring back my family or my house, and I can't change anything by myself.''

"I have more bad news," he said, a mix of dread and frustration in his tone.

"I didn't say this was bad news—I just don't want you to take over my life." His patient expression annoyed her more. "Never mind. We can't see eye to eye. What's your bad news?"

"Wilford told me he's been approached about a memorial for Jeff."

"Who wants to do that?"

"The mayor, I assume, and the town council. Anyway, they want us to help."

Clair pushed her fingers against the table. "You can't ask me to do that. I'd be betraying my family."

"As Wilford said," he went on doggedly, "working with the executors gives us a chance to look convincing as a married couple."

"They'll see us look convincing as a couple who want a divorce if you force me to glorify your father."

"Think before you answer, Clair. You and I can make this memorial what we want it to be. We can create something useful. It doesn't have to be a statue or a fountain. I thought about a community center with a clinic. How about child care with facilities for sick children? We could fill the gaps in this town." Excitement lit his eyes. "This is the best revenge for both of us."

"I see your point." She paused. "But what would my mom and dad say? What will people in town say? That I forgot my family because I married you?"

"We'll announce the project with the idea that a community center lets us honor all our parents—all the parents in this town."

"With your father's name on it."

"I can't help that, Clair. If we don't take part, the council will build the memorial without us, and they will put up a monument to Jeff. I don't want that any more than you do."

His voice cracked as he finished, and unthinkingly Clair placed a comforting hand on his arm. The pain in their pasts seemed to connect them, though what they'd lived with was vastly different. She still mourned the loss of the unconditional love she'd been given—something Nick had never known.

She must be out of her mind, but she knew how deeply Jeff had hurt him, and she realized Nick needed to create something positive out of a damaging past, which gave her the strength to compromise. "I'll do it," she said, shaking inside.

"Thank you." Tucking her hand in his, Nick pulled her up and dropped cash for the bill on the table. "Come on. I'll walk you to your car." His body's warmth surrounded her. His closeness reawakened her disturbing hunger. She wanted to lean into him and just breathe.

Outside, he stopped beside her car. Over his shoulder, she saw curtains flutter as a couple of patrons kept an eye on the Dylans.

"What's between us gives us both a chance to build our own futures," Nick said. "Forget about the past."

"Can you?"

He pressed his lips into a thin hard line, yet they still retained their sensual curve. This close, she could almost feel the texture of his mouth, almost taste him.

Soaked in the heat of each breath he took slowly in and even more slowly released, she recognized desire.

A few flakes of snow gleamed off his dark hair. "Can I what?" he asked, his voice thick. "What were we saying?"

His confusion unnerved her, because she shared it. "Can you forget the past?" she asked.

"I'm trying." He dipped his head toward her. Her pulse thudded in her ears, but she couldn't back away. He grazed her cheek with his as he touched his firm lips to the corner of her mouth. "I'll see you tonight."

Without looking back, he strolled toward his office. She pressed the back of her hand to her face and inhaled, trying to find her poise. Suddenly, as if she'd come to the end of a long empty tunnel, she saw herself as she must look to anyone who'd watched them. The picture of a happy young bride whose husband had talked to her in passionate, quiet tones, kissed her with the deliberation of a man who needed to touch his wife, and then promised to see her again when darkness came.

Closing her eyes, she leaned against the car—long enough to realize she was making a bigger spectacle of herself. Had she really believed she could take back her home and forget the reality behind her marriage? Clair got in her car and avoided the truth that reflected from her gaze in the rearview mirror.

Dr. Dylan's wife looked as empty as she felt. She might never learn how to make or hold the kind of love she'd acted so convincingly with Nick.

CHAPTER EIGHT

A FEW DAYS AFTER he met Clair at Mrs. Peabody's, Nick was dressing for dinner when Hunter came to his door. The older man held up two freshly pressed suits as Nick let him in.

"You're here. I'm glad I knocked. I heard voices in Mrs. Dylan's room, and I thought you were with her."

Feeling caught putting on clothes in his own room, Nick gave up on a tie that refused to knot. "We stay out of each other's way when we're getting dressed. The result of living so long alone, I guess." He dropped the ends of his tie. "Hunter, I've been meaning to thank you for everything you've done to make Clair feel comfortable."

"I enjoy Mrs. Dylan's company." Hunter hung the suits in the closet. "We just have to persuade Bonnie and your mother that she's made positive changes in this house."

Nick looked around the room, which still bore no trace of Clair. He'd put off asking her to bring her things in after that day at the coffee shop. As she was fond of saying, their marriage had become too real.

"She tries, doesn't she."

"You're happy, despite your mother's opposition?"

Nick imagined Clair's reaction to the truth behind that checkbook he'd given her. "I try." He swept a hand toward his dressing room. "I think I'll ask Clair to help me with my tie."

"Have an enjoyable evening tonight." Hunter turned from the closet. "I laid in some caviar for Mrs. Dylan's cat."

Nick laughed. Hunter had secrets of his own, one of them a soft spot for that rogue feline. Turning, Nick knocked on his wife's door. A real husband wouldn't have to knock, and he tried to ignore Hunter, whose indulgent smile betrayed his thought that Nick must still be learning to live in his new marriage.

Clair was in her bathroom. A mascara wand between her fingers, she looked away from the long mirror. "What's up?"

She'd maintained a cool tone he found increasingly annoying since that day at Mrs. Peabody's. Before he could answer her, Kitty emerged from the dust ruffle and ambled over to weave black hair into the gray of Nick's trouser legs. "No caviar here, buddy." He brushed at the hair on his pant leg. "Hunter bought some for him, though."

Clair eyed the cat, her expression disgruntled. "He likes living here—with you and Hunter. He took a lot longer getting used to me."

"You don't want to share Kitty's affections?" The cat belonged to her, as much as it could belong to anyone, and Clair needed hearts of her own. Not that she'd admit it, but Nick still knew his own share of the empty feelings she tried to hide. "I always wanted a real pet—I had a hamster, but he wasn't too chummy. Jeff suggested a dog once, but I didn't want to leave it when I went away to school."

"Pretty responsible decision for an eight-year-old."

"How did you know I was eight?"

"Hunter told me." She turned back to the mirror, pink coloring her cheeks. "Not that we talked about you."

He laughed. "I'm not surprised Hunter shared family information with you. You are family to him."

"We should return to the businesslike footing we started on."

"Whatever you like." He tried to hide a smile. In some dark corner of his psyche, where baser instincts resided, he enjoyed putting her at a disadvantage. She'd kept him there. "There's something I've been meaning to ask. Will you put a few of your things in my room? And I ought to put some of mine in here."

She capped her mascara and dropped it into a basket on the marble counter. "So no one can be sure we don't share? I'd rather ask Mr. Hunter not to come in at all."

Nick considered. "How could we ask him to stay out? Anything we'd say would seem suspicious after this long."

"We want privacy?"

"I've known this kind of privacy all my life. Besides, unless we lock the doors, Leota could come in any time. I'd rather look realistic."

She thought a moment, her mouth tightening. "Okay, but…"

"But?"

"I don't like knowing anyone can come in here at any time."

"I wish I could help you. I can have the locks changed on your doors, but locking them would look suspicious, too."

"Locking them against you or against everyone else?" She stepped into high, pointed heels that flexed her calves and distracted him.

He met her frustrated gaze. "You definitely can't lock the door between our rooms. If you feel you must lock the others, we can use the privacy excuse—though it's a little thin after nearly a month."

"Which brings us back to where we started."

Kitty thought so, too. Apparently noticing Nick's clean legs, he slinked over to apply more hair. "I know you don't like the lies." Nick nudged Kitty with his toe, but then the cat began rubbing its face against the side of his shoe. "We married for good reasons. Do you want to bail out?"

She squared her shoulders. "How would either of us live in this town if we told the truth?"

Her resolve drew him. Her strength worked on him like a damned aphrodisiac. He tried to maintain his detached tone. "Why do you want to live in Fairlove?"

"I used to close my eyes and remember this place until I could feel I was back here. I needed these streets and this air for sustenance."

She stirred, as if surprised she'd spoken out loud.

As she focused on him, he felt as if he'd peeked through the window at her. His reasons for this marriage—to keep all his father had hoarded—didn't seem nearly as commendable.

"I'll just gather a few things I don't use," he muttered, and returned to his room with Kitty at his heels.

Nick gathered an extra shoe brush, his robe and the case for his glasses. When he returned, Clair waited in the center of her room, hands planted on her hips, her eyes following his every move.

Under her gaze, he grew uncomfortably aware of his own body. No woman had ever made him feel self-conscious. He'd relegated those feelings to novels and mushy movies. Kitty, spiraling between his ankles, didn't help. At last, Nick set his glasses case on Clair's nightstand.

"Do you wear contacts?" she asked. Kitty sprang up to sniff the case and then raised his head to stare at Nick, following his mistress's lead.

What? Was she implying he was vain? "Because of my work. Nobody wants my glasses to slide off my nose onto half-finished sutures."

"I didn't mean anything."

He dropped his robe on the only tidy corner of her bed, but she snatched it back up.

"I don't want this in here. You don't use it?"

He saw through her. Leaving his robe felt too intimate to her. So he lied.

"I have another one." He always dressed before he left his room. Leota had never run an informal household. "What about your stuff?"

"I don't have much to spare," Clair said. "See anything I should put in your room?"

"I picked things I seldom need." He was suggesting, in a roundabout way, that they stay out of each other's space as much as possible.

"I don't have much of that, either." She slid her hand beneath her hair.

Her neck arched, long and graceful. Tempting.

"I have a spare toothbrush," he said, wanting to be anywhere except this close to her. "I'll put it in my bathroom." Two toothbrushes seemed a touch intimate to him. He could imagine Clair climbing out of his bed in the morning to use one.

"I'll find something." Dropping to her knees, she peered beneath the bed. Kitty shot off the nightstand to help her.

Funny. Her gorgeous behind ought to have felled him, but somehow, with her head almost touching Kitty's, he was reminded that she was only human, and vulnerable. She and the war veteran Kitty looked kind of cute inspecting whatever they'd managed to lose beneath the bed during their short stay.

"Find anything?" Nick drawled.

"What's so funny?" She looked up and ran into Kitty's steady gaze. "Oh." She grinned with enviable affection and bumped the cat's nose with hers. "What's he looking for?"

"If you ask him, he might tell us. Come out, Clair. We'll cull what you can spare later. Dinner started—" he looked at his watch "—six minutes ago."

"I think my skirt's too tight." Clutching the mattress, she worked her way to her feet in the narrow, black skirt. "I got tired of your mother critiquing my wardrobe every night, but I warn you, I can't afford too many eating-at-home outfits like this."

"You look perfect." He steered clear of the clingy, emerald blouse that outlined her every curve, concentrating on her relaxation of hostilities, instead.

"Perfect?" She checked the tuck of her blouse and started for the door. "Right."

Trust didn't come easily to her. Living up to his end of their agreement was a gift of faith he might be the first man to give her. He held her door, but as she passed in front of him, a faintly floral, seductively winsome scent rose from her thick hair.

Would she care more about the insurance money or his changing feelings for her if the truth came out, and she realized he'd begun to find their marriage inconvenient?

BRANDON PEMBROKE made his living as a hairstylist, but Ernest Forsdyke would have bet he didn't work his magic on just any head. To afford the rent on his tastefully lighted, brick-and-glass shop in Old Town Alexandria, he couldn't subsist on modest styling fees.

Ernest bought a paper from a newsstand at the corner of Campbell Street and hunkered down at a window table in the Old Town Pizza Parlor across the road from Pembroke's shop. An hour early, he'd wanted to make sure whoever had scheduled the appointment didn't see him first.

The arson investigator had finally said he also believed the fire had started near Clair's kitchen, but he wasn't sure anything other than a spark had started it. A personal friend, he'd grudgingly agreed to take another week to go over his findings again, but Ernest realized he might never have more than suspicions to track down.

Finding out who'd dropped the matchbook might be the only active step he could take to ease his own mind. And if he did, he still couldn't tie the matches to the fire. Anyone could claim to have been curious about what Clair was doing with her family's home and gone there for a look. Everyone in town knew she'd moved back in to stay there until her wedding.

He held his newspaper in front of him, not bothering to look at the print. A woman strolled to the door of Pembroke's shop. She wore round dark glasses and a sable coat with the collar turned up to the brim of her netted hat. For a moment, he wondered if the woman was Leota.

No. Less than ten steps behind the sable-clad mystery woman, Leota Dylan ate up the sidewalk with her long strides. Ernest's heart sank. Every angle of her body expressed anger.

He sighed. Had she burned down a house Clair Dylan had described as everything she loved most in the world?

He waited until Leota followed an attendant around the receptionist's desk before he paid for his soda and breadsticks. Dropping his paper on the table, he pushed open the restaurant's heavy glass door and wove around the pedestrians on the wide sidewalk. Against the light, he hurried across the street. He had to find out when Leota's last visit had been without her seeing him.

Pembroke's waiting area amounted to a ritzy living room where the young woman who greeted him eyed his eight-buck haircut with horror. "I hate to tell you this, sir, but you've turned to us in the nick of time."

"Very funny," Ernest said. "I didn't come for treatment." He pulled out his identification card. "I need information. We have to talk fast, and you can't repeat what I ask."

Reading his ID card, she nodded. "Fireman, huh? I thought you were a cop. Do I have to talk to a fireman?"

"Unless you'd rather speak to a cop."

She tossed her carefully disarranged mane. "I guess we don't keep state secrets here." She folded her hands. "I'll trust you won't tell whichever of our customers I'm about to tattle on that your information came from me. How can I help you?"

"Mrs. Dylan—I just saw her come in."

"I know her."

Ernest reached for the appointment book that lay flat on her blotter, but she scooped it up. "When was her last appointment?"

"Date and time?"

"Both. I need to clear her. I'm sure she has nothing to do with my investigation." With any luck, she'd arrived late at Nick and Clair's wedding because her haircut ran long.

"She hasn't been here in about a month."

He'd prefer three weeks, but the woman's memory might be off. "Will you check the book, please?"

"Sure." She paged through the appointments, but the entry she showed him had a date that was almost two weeks before the wedding. "Here she is. How's that?"

Worst news he'd had in a long time. "You're sure she hasn't walked in without an appointment?"

The woman rose, her smile one of pity for his bumpkin sensibilities. "We don't accept walk-in business. Even a long-standing customer like Mrs. Dylan schedules her arrangements with us."

"Not very exclusive, are you?" He used sarcasm to hide his regret for the loss of a long-shot alibi. "Thanks for your help. I'll keep my mouth shut and you'll do the same? Concerning my visit?"

Smiling, she waved long, burgundy-tipped fingers toward his head. "You wouldn't risk Mrs. Dylan's seeing you now? I know just the man to make something of you. You have a beautiful head of hair, but that cut makes you look like you come from the hills."

"The hills of Virginia, ma'am, the hills of Virginia, and damn proud of it. Besides, I'm definitely a walk-in customer." He marched out of the store, his heart heavy. Now he'd have to ask Leota how her matchbook had arrived at the fire.

LEOTA TOOK THE MAIL off her breakfast tray. Two heavy vellum envelopes interested her most. Her invitations had fallen off after Jeff's death, as if she'd turned back into a housemaid. These envelopes meant her friends hadn't forgotten her. They'd allowed her time to grieve.

One of the invitations was addressed to Nick. Dr. and Mrs. Dylan, actually. The one sip of coffee Leota'd taken churned like acid in her stomach.

She opened the matching envelope addressed to her. "Mrs. Jeffrey Dylan," she said aloud, satisfied to hear her name again.

She ignored the small square of tissue paper that fluttered to her lap and scanned the words quickly. The mayor and his wife had invited her to their annual holiday party.

Black tie, too. Clair Atherton owned nothing suitable. She'd feel completely out of her depth. Leota knew from her first years of married life how much like drowning a black-tie party could be for a naive woman who didn't realize she didn't fit in.

Leota couldn't have asked for a better opportunity to study her son's faux marriage. She had to be right about Nick and his charming bride. And she'd prove her case to the other executors.

Clair wouldn't be able to keep up her facade all night, and neither would Nick. Leota refused to believe he *loved* that woman. She tugged the bell pull at her shoulder, and Hunter appeared.

"Yes, Mrs. Dylan?"

Leota passed him Nick's invitation. "Put this in my son's room, please."

Now, to drop a hint or two in the appropriate ears. With any sort of good fortune, she'd evict that little imposter from her house sometime after— she turned the invitation over again—seven o'clock next Friday evening.

FACING THE FULL-LENGTH MIRROR on the door of her wardrobe, Clair eyed her dark-blue velvet gown. Nick had suggested she wear it tonight. She'd bought it as part of her trousseau. He'd warned her they might have to show themselves if the press who'd followed Jeff's every move tailed them on their supposed honeymoon.

Truth was, she loved the dress. It wrapped her body like a lover's caress. The demure lace insert that rose from the tops of her breasts to the corded neckline made her feel feminine and sexy. But the dress wasn't her. She was not a woman who wore a dress like this. Or the matching velvet pumps.

Nick knocked on her door. She swept her hair into a loose knot on top of her head and secured it with her mother's bumblebee. "Come in," she said.

She'd forgotten how he looked in his tux. The suit and his lean body—both spelled power in screaming capital letters that interested her more than the narrow velvet box in his hands. Power attracted her. She'd gone without it so long.

"I thought you might like to wear these." He held out the box.

"I can't accept jewelry from you."

"You can borrow." He opened the lid. "Maybe the necklace won't work, but the bracelet and earrings are perfect."

Sapphires and diamonds winked at her from a white satin nest. Nick was right. Perfection.

"Are they Leota's?" She couldn't imagine Leota lending them, and she didn't want to decide how to handle an offer of Leota's jewelry without her permission.

"They belonged to my grandmother. She left them to me for my wife."

Clair sensed trouble beneath his calm. "You should save them for your real wife."

"Wear them. They'll look lovely on you, and it'll strengthen our position when people see I've given them to you." He lifted the bracelet and beckoned her to hold out her arm.

"What about their sentimental value?" She searched his careful expression. "Don't waste them on me."

"They carry no sentimental value for me yet. They've been in my family for generations, but my grandmother kept them from Leota all her life. Maybe when I find the woman who should have them, I'll care who wears them. Until then, they're only decoration." Remorse tightened his mouth as he realized what he'd said. "I'm sorry, Clair. That sounded as if I don't value what you're doing for me. I do care that you wear them tonight."

"Not for the right reasons, though." She glanced at his robe, hanging on a peg in her wardrobe. "All this pretend intimacy is starting to give me the willies."

His smile hooked her. "Confiding your willies makes all the lies we've told worthwhile. The night we came here, I envied your...comfort level."

She turned away. That first night, she'd held on to him, almost nude in his arms.

Standing behind her, Nick slid his hand from her

elbow to her wrist. He fastened the bracelet where her fitted sleeve ended, at just the right spot to afford the sapphires their best background. They warmed her skin tones. She sought her own reflection again.

Any other woman, swathed in velvet from toe to neck, would look beloved by the husband who lingered so close, his hand possessive on her wrist.

Nick seemed unaware she could see him in the mirror. She shivered at the purpose in his gaze as he followed the curve of her throat.

"My comfort level?" she said, desperate to break the silence.

"With yourself." He eased closer and leaned down to her, but he lifted his head as he breathed in her scent. She could have moved away from him, but this wasn't pretend, and she needed to know how his mouth would feel if he kissed her and meant it.

In slow motion, he brushed his lips against the back of her neck. His mouth, as warm and firm as her every sleep-induced fantasy about him, stirred a heart-stopping response. Her body answered, from lonely places she didn't want to fill for only one night. Especially not with Nick.

He pressed his mouth to her skin again, drawing in her need, caressing bare, sensitive skin, millimeters from his first kiss. Heat fused with want. In the mirror, she saw herself shiver, at the mercy of his slow progress toward her earlobe. Strands of his hair tangled with hers. She forced her free hand to stay at her side, even as she longed to pull him nearer.

"Nick," she finally murmured. She must be crazy

to deny herself. Nick was her legal husband. Everyone believed they'd been far more intimate.

"Do you want me to stop?" he half whispered against her skin.

"It's wrong."

"We both want more."

"We want each other," she said, "and that's dangerous for two people who fully intend not to make a commitment. We're both too old to make this kind of a mistake, and if I'm not from the wrong side of the tracks, I'm certainly not from your side."

"We live in a classless society." Gently he slid his fingers into the curls at her temples and tilted her head to kiss the other side of her throat.

Clair swallowed the deep moan he drew from her. Her nipples rose against the velvet bodice. She cupped his jaw, relishing the hint of stubble not yet visible. So male, so confusing.

"I don't care about social classes, but you'll never mend fences with Leota as long as I'm around, and you obviously want a relationship with her."

He lifted his head. His dark sleepy gaze melted Clair's will, and she clung to him with the hand he still held.

"Do you really want to talk about my family now?" An unexpected teasing note lightened his gruff voice.

She wanted to curl up around him and persuade him to stay with her here, where they didn't have to act for anyone but themselves. She tugged her hand free, her heart racing. "If we're late we'll look as if we're making an entrance."

"Put on the earrings." He turned toward his own room, but looked back. "Unless you want me to help you?"

She'd already begun to take off the gold hoops she usually wore. She tried for a natural smile, willing him out of her room. She needed to catch her breath before she had to share a dark car with him. He'd seduced her nearly beyond endurance, certainly beyond her knowledge of right and wrong.

LEOTA CALLED HER DRIVER early, determined to arrive among the mayor's first guests. Tonight she'd drop the social niceties. She was a mother on a mission. Her son had embarked on his marriage just to fulfill his father's last wishes, and she didn't intend to let that little Atherton tramp become a permanent fixture. Nothing would hurt her more than letting Sylvie Atherton's daughter win.

Tiffany fixtures muted the light in the reception room where the guests gathered. The Christmas decorations ran to white twinkle lights and a few holly wreathes. Leota wasn't in a holiday frame of mind.

Even as she laid groundwork with the other executors, Leota scanned the later arrivals. She spoke to everyone who mattered before Nick and Clair showed up. After she got rid of Clair, she'd persuade Wilford and the others to give Nick another chance at a "real" marriage with a decent, acceptable woman.

Adding to her rage, Nick and Clair turned heads, walking into the room. Young and undeniably beautiful, the two of them, they looked like newlyweds. They were flushed. And they held themselves apart from everyone else, as if they'd interrupted more private commitments to attend the party. Nick kept his arm draped around Clair's shoulders, splaying his fingers across her velvet sleeve, his hold possessive.

His display of husbandly warmth made Leota realize how truly unaffectionate they were with each other at home. Except for that first morning, she'd never witnessed the slightest hint of affection between them.

What had changed them tonight?

Suspiciously, she made her way toward the crowd gathered around her son and his wife. The mayor, Bob Townsend, called for champagne.

"Join me in a toast to the late Senator Jeffrey Dylan's son and his bride." When a waiter brought a magnum and two glasses on a tray, Bob poured for Nick and Clair. Leota snatched a glass off a passing tray. She sipped before Bob raised his glass.

"To a love as timeless as your parents shared both of you. Clair, you may not remember me, but your father was a good friend to me. He taught me political science in high school when most of my other teachers swore only brain surgery would force information into my head. He wrote letters of recommendation for me when I began applying to colleges. He gave me my start. We've missed your family in this town, and I'm glad you've come back, glad you've married one of our town's finest citizens. And most of all, we're glad we're sharing this holiday season with you and Nick together."

Bob raised his glass to Clair, whose eyes gained depth from tears she fought hard. Leota looked away, uncomfortable with her visibly touched daughter-in-law. To her left, Wilford Thomas, overly urbane, stiff with tension, elbowed his way to Nick.

"One more thing," Bob Townsend said. "As most of you know, the Town Council has asked Nick and Clair and Leota to help us build a monument to Senator Jeffrey Dylan. Clair and Nick countered with a plan they've presented through Wilford Thomas."

Leota shifted her weight from one foot to the other. That community-center idea. Jeff would have considered it a complete waste of money. Not only that, he'd never suggested such a facility. Building one now implied he'd left work undone. Nick should have known better.

"I want you all to know that the council has agreed to meet with Tim Hanover to discuss drawing up a plan for the center."

Leota steeled herself to hide her frustration. She even managed to raise her glass to Bob when he found her in the crowd.

"Leota, Nick, Clair—welcome to the Senator Jeffrey Dylan Memorial planning committee. We on the council look forward to working with you."

Everyone drank, and then the women swept Clair into their midst and bore her away. She glanced enigmatically back at Nick. He lifted his glass again to her, and color flooded Clair's face before she gave up and allowed herself to be urged toward the other end of the room. Nick moved off with Wilford.

Something was going on. Leota had to decide fast. Follow Wilford and Nick? Maneuver Clair into being alone with her and try to— No, Wilford had something on his mind. She'd find out more from them if she could just fit herself into a spot she could listen from. She trailed them toward an enclosed alcove.

The other men drifted away in deference to Wilford's unspoken request for privacy. Leota sauntered to a seat beneath the wings of a potted plant.

She sipped indifferently and leaned toward the alcove at the same time. Too bad Wilford hadn't taken Nick out to the terrace where she could have found a better listening post. Only murmurs reached her at first.

"I can't hear you over the music," Nick said to Wilford in a raised voice.

Leota glanced toward the orchestra. She knew just how he felt.

"I said you did it," Wilford's tone accused. That man had always been too uppity.

"Why are you surprised? I told you exactly what I planned."

"I didn't believe you could be so foolish. She won't know how to manage that much, and how will you cope if you need—"

"Stop, Wilford. Do you want to tell everyone in this building?"

"They'll find out if you make many more decisions like this."

"You act as if it belonged to you when you know that amount hardly made a dent."

"You pay me to treat yours as mine."

"I won't discuss it here. I'd like to find my wife."

Leota sprang from her chair and sank into the darkness of a corner. An "amount" meant money. Nick had done something with his personal money. Something for Clair? Put her on a payroll?

How many husbands did that? How deeply did Wilford disapprove? Would he be willing to tell her?

Leota caught her reflection in the long window opposite her. Standing there in her extremely appropriate black dress, twisting and untwisting her fingers, she looked like the wicked witch in a Disney flick. She froze, but then smoothed her hands over her hot cheeks.

Jeff wasn't here to protect Nick anymore. Was it her fault if she might have to destroy the last Atherton to guard her own? Yes, destroy that phony sweet Clair Atherton as she herself had been destroyed. Leota turned back to the ballroom.

She'd been young when she married Jeff, and she'd been beautiful. She'd believed in Prince Charming and living happily ever after. She'd walked into this very room, certain the important people in this town would accept her. Instead, some of these women had treated her like an interloper.

They'd never welcomed her as they had Clair tonight. Maybe they'd taken Sylvie's side all these years. All the more reason to make Sylvie's daughter pay.

Nick kept trying to persuade her that some sort of useless therapy would help her feel better. She knew exactly the catharsis she needed. She wouldn't feel at peace until this Atherton woman suffered as she had. And she needed peace.

As she stood alone in her dark corner, Nick's talk about not letting the past rule them whispered into her memory. How was she supposed to let the past go when it remained so firmly her present?

NICK COULDN'T STOP looking at Clair. Had she ever coped with a table like this, where she constituted a main course? She'd survived the mayor's announcement without a scratch, and now she chatted easily with the others at her table.

She graciously overlooked the fact that their companions appeared to have mixed up wedding wishes with the holiday celebration. Over centerpieces of holly and berries, she accepted extravagant toasts to both the spirit of the season and their happiness.

He hated to admit it, but the moment he'd seen the long table, set with crystal and old silver that bore his family's crest, he'd worried she'd be in over her head. Instead, he was the one who felt nervous.

Especially since Wilford's lecture. An attorney ought to have better control of his composure.

"Nick, I must congratulate you." Bob nodded toward Clair. "She's lovely."

"She's lovely on her own. Nothing to do with me." No truer words had ever left his mouth. Clair was as much her own creation as anyone he'd ever known. She'd made herself the woman he'd married. A woman who fascinated him.

"I like a bridegroom who grasps his good fortune." Bob rose and waved his glass over the Christmas decorations one last time. "Thank you all for coming tonight. We should use this house more than we do. Our citizens deserve to see it."

Nick's grandfather had built the house for the

mayor of his choice just after prohibition ended. Nick had been invited to many dinners here, but he never forgot that the place had been his family's not-so-innocent contribution.

He picked up his dessert spoon. The crest was a Machiavellian scheme. Every sitting mayor who used it had to remember and sometimes acknowledge who held the real power in Fairlove.

Bob went on. "Let's adjourn to the ballroom. Please stay and enjoy the music. Maybe some of you will even take your creaking joints to the floor. Clair, may I escort you?"

Nick offered his arm to Bob's wife in return. They followed her husband and Clair to the ballroom. Bob signaled the orchestra and they began a stately waltz. Nick watched Clair, ready to rescue her at her first look of discomfort, but she matched the mayor's steps perfectly.

"May I?" Nick asked Mrs. Townsend.

He danced the mayor's wife in a pattern that kept Clair in sight. Midway through the song, Julian Franklin tapped Bob's shoulder. The mayor gave Clair up with a courtly bow only an enthusiastic voter could love.

Clair's face lit up as the judge took her in his arms. A stab of jealousy confused Nick as the two swept past and Clair didn't glance his way. The judge's conversation seemed to absorb her. With the Franklins, she'd begun to build a real relationship.

"My husband is just over there, Nick," Mrs. Townsend said. He led her, leaning down to hear her breathy voice. "Tell your mother I'll call during the coming week. I haven't managed to speak to her once tonight.''

"I'll pass on the message." His mother needed friends.

When he turned from handing Mrs. Townsend to her husband, Clair was in front of him.

"Dance with me," she said, her voice urgent.

He stared at her, speechless. She wanted him to hold her? She took his hand and pulled him onto the honey-colored parquet floor. He had to be careful not to step on the long hem swaying so deliciously before him.

He grabbed at his senses. "I'll lead."

"I've been trying to get you alone since before dinner.''

She peered furtively at the other dancers while he found his stride. She laughed, apparently seeing more than he'd intended.

"I've never seen you look so worried." She sobered. "Although this could be serious. I don't know how to tell you without sounding like a gossip...."

"Tell me what?" He flattened his fingers against her back, enjoying the warmth of her body through the soft, soft velvet. "What's wrong?"

"When Wilford pulled you away from everyone else—when we first arrived—your mother followed you.''

"What do you mean?" He hadn't seen Leota. What might she have heard?

"She kind of loitered outside the alcove." Clair ducked her head. "You were right about her suspicions. You and Wilford didn't talk about our marriage, did you?"

"No." What had they said specifically? "Wilford asked me a business question."

He forced a smile that hurt. The insurance fund was ticking like a time bomb. "Whatever she heard won't matter." He wasn't convinced, and Clair's look of alarm didn't surprise him. "I don't think we said anything she could use. How much longer do you want to stay? Being newlyweds, I think we can escape early and only help our cause."

"I'm ready when you are." She relaxed in his arms, and he was content to hold her through this song and maybe the next. She pulled her hand from his shoulder to cover a yawn. "I've enjoyed tonight. Selina's feeling better, by the way—as she was careful to note in a loud voice in the ladies' room."

"Did she?" Selina's endorsement didn't penetrate the guilt he felt about the insurance money.

Clair laughed, her joy real and catching. "I love talking to someone who remembers my parents kindly."

Nick tightened his arms around her. "I wish I'd known them, Clair. You can talk about them with me."

"No, I can't." She pulled away. "I'm not sure they passed their generosity, their belief in not holding grudges, on to me. I like you more than I expected, but we have a line between us."

His face felt like a mask. "You and Leota are two of the strongest women I know, but you waste your strength. You could use it to do good things for people who aren't as strong."

Clair straightened her arms, forcing distance between them. Her green eyes looked as dark as the shadowed windows in the wall behind her. "I'd rather you stopped comparing me to Leota, but I appreciate your honesty." She looked apologetic. "At least you never lie to me."

Nick slid his gaze from hers, the checking account still hacking away at his conscience. What would she do if Leota told her he'd manipulated her?

That first night, he'd feared she'd leave before their year was up. Now, he wanted to protect her from his breach of faith. An honest man would tell her the truth, but how could he without hurting her more?

CHAPTER NINE

WITH CHRISTMAS a week away, the fire chief wanted to end his investigation. The day the arson expert released Clair's house, Ernest arrived at the Dylans' kitchen door before breakfast. He couldn't accept the investigator's conclusions. It was too big a coincidence—Leota's empty matchbook at a fire that hurt her worst enemy.

Bonnie Rutherford opened the door, her hands wrapped in a dish towel. "Chief Fosdyke, what brings you here?" She stepped outside onto the stoop.

"I need to ask you and Hunter some questions."

Her smile faded. "What questions?"

He had no time to beat around the bush. "Do you know where Leota spent the day of Nick's wedding?"

She raked her hair behind her ear. "Even if I did, Mrs. Dylan's whereabouts are no concern of yours."

Damn. Bonnie would protect Leota with her last breath. "She didn't spend the day at home?"

The door opened behind Bonnie, and Hunter stepped out, the perfect picture of a butler. Or at least Ernest's picture of a butler.

"Chief Fosdyke, how may I help you? Bonnie, you may return to your work."

"Thanks, Hunter."

She flashed a killing look Fosdyke's way. He managed not to duck.

"What do you know about Leota's whereabouts the day of the fire, Hunter?"

A disapproving grimace creased the other man's forehead, but he held up his hand. "I suggest you speak to Mrs. Dylan, sir."

"Cut the pompous stuff. I've seen you swear with the best of us around the pool table. What do you think of Clair?"

"I think she's part of a family I've cared for since before she was born. You're out of luck at this door."

Hunter turned and went inside. Fosdyke closed his fingers around the matchbook. Sure, he could ask Leota, but she'd lie to stay out of jail. Still, he had to confront her. He'd force himself to ask the questions.

THE SITTING ROOM DOOR HANDLE slammed into the hand-painted wallpaper behind it as Hunter entered the room. Leota snatched off her glasses and tucked them beneath the book she'd tried to focus on all morning. She cut Hunter a furious look, but her anger faded as she saw his concern.

"What's wrong?"

"Chief Fosdyke from the fire department is here, asking to speak to you."

Leota's fingers lost their ability to grip. Her book and glasses slid out of her hand and fell to the floor. Hunter snatched them off the floor and handed them to her. "Do you want me to stay with you?" he asked.

A familiar suspicion she'd failed as lady of this

house sharpened Leota's tone. "Of course not. What does he want?"

"He came earlier this morning and asked me if I knew where you were when Mrs. Dylan's house burned."

Leota shivered. Rivulets of fear chased each other across her skin. "Bring him in."

"Let me stay with you."

"No. That isn't necessary." Leota set her glasses on the table at her side. "And don't call my son."

Hunter lingered, trying to pierce her emotional armor with a gaze that only infuriated her. Who did her servant think he was?

Finally he left, and Fosdyke came in by himself. "Afternoon." His elderly suit engulfed his lean body like a shroud. "I actually asked for Mrs. Clair Dylan. Is she at home?"

Leota didn't want to hear her house referred to as Clair Atherton's home. "Why do you want to talk to Clair?"

"I had an arson investigator look at her fire." He stopped, obviously waiting for her.

Fear tightened her throat. "My daughter-in-law works for Paul Sayers's landscaping firm. I suggest you inquire there."

"I've brought her some information."

Leota's heart knotted like a fist, but Ernest's expectations still waited in his gaze. He suspected she'd had something to do with that fire. Well, she'd known him since they'd played tricks on each other in Fairlove Elementary's schoolyard, and she'd beaten him at games before.

She put on the faintly interested expression she'd perfected through endless Washington dinners and campaign speeches. "Perhaps you should tell me."

He seemed to ignore her suggestion. "I'll sit with you and wait a few minutes," he said, "to see if Clair comes home. I'd like to talk to her today."

"I'll order coffee." She pulled the bell at the fireplace. "And Hunter can take your coat."

"Thanks, but I'll keep it. This room feels cold. You can't be warm."

"I've been colder." Turning away from him to hold her hands to the fireplace's glow, she remembered another cloud-edged late evening, night surrounding her in cold, sharp air that still whistled though her memory.

"What's your information?" she asked.

He didn't answer at first. He joined her by the fireplace. She couldn't look away again without feeding his doubts.

"You all right?" he asked. "You look like you tasted something bad. Want me to call Hunter back?"

"I've known you all my life, Ernest. Cut the country-boy crap and tell me what you came to say."

He came right back at her, peeling "country-boy crap" off like the topmost layer of an onion. "Why did you show up late to your son's wedding?"

For a split second, she stood in front of the peeling, ramshackle house again. The match she'd just blown out puffed a spiral of sulfurous smoke into the air in front of her face, and then even the smoke disappeared.

But she'd thrown that match into the long green

grass. It couldn't have blown against the dry wooden clapboards. The match had flown in one direction at the same time as the wind had blown her matchbook end over end into the darkness, but she'd stayed on the path. She'd never been close enough to set that house on fire.

"Mrs. Dylan?"

Hunter, thank God, had answered the bell. Leota swung away from Ernest. "We'd like coffee in here. Has my son's wife called to say when she'd be home?"

"I expect she'll be here any time. Is something wrong, Mrs. Dylan?"

"No, just get the coffee." *And get back here with it fast. Don't leave me to spar with this man who's not my friend anymore.*

CLAIR PARKED HER CAR in the gravel lot beside the kitchen. Covered in wet dirt, cold as an ice sculpture, she reached for the mudroom door, but Mr. Hunter opened it, only to take a step back when he saw the remains of her workday caked on her jeans and sweat-shirt.

"I thought I heard someone out here," he said. "Did you fall in a ditch?"

"Just about. We're putting in a sprinkler system. I had to dig the trenches."

"Don't you have a machine for that?"

"It depends on the yard. Mr. Velasco wants his flower beds to create a maze effect." Clair loved the hard work that made coming back to this house tolerable. "We had to dig by hand. Do you mind if I come in?"

"Do you mind if I put down newspapers?"

"I'd rather you did. I'll wait here. Do you want to close the door?"

"Not if you'll be offended."

She'd learned to save whatever heat they managed to trap in the cavernous Dylan house. With an acquiescent nod, she pulled the door shut and stomped her feet to keep warm while she waited.

When Mr. Hunter opened the door again, he'd spread newspaper on the tiled floor and held Nick's robe out to her. Clair looked at it, uncertain what he expected her to do.

"What's that for?"

"I brought it so you could put it on. Isn't it yours?"

Even worn, the black watch plaid looked masculine to Clair. Willing herself to retain a blasé expression, Clair took the robe between two fingers. "Mr. Hunter, are you asking me to take off my clothes here?"

"I thought you might not mind." He looked sober. "We can, of course, follow your trail through the house with a mop and vacuum."

She studied his serious face. "You're teasing me, right?" Before he could answer, Kitty bolted out of the mouth of the back stairs, making a beeline for the door.

"Oh, no, you don't." Clair leaped inside the mudroom, skidding on newspapers, but she managed to shut the porch door before Kitty escaped. She wouldn't feel safe with him on the prowl until someone cleared the rubble from her house.

"Good catch," Hunter said.

"I'm not trying to cage him inside, but he might be too curious about our old home to resist prowling through the wreckage."

"Naturally, you wouldn't want him to injure himself," Mr. Hunter intoned. "Now I hate to rush you, but Mrs. Dylan wants coffee for two. And she and Chief Fosdyke are waiting for you to join them."

"What?" Dropping the robe out of range of falling mud, Clair hauled her sweatshirt over her head and started on the buttons on her flannel shirt. At Mr. Hunter's look of alarm, she bent down to unlace her boots before peeling off anything else that might embarrass him. However, she pictured the fire chief accusing Nick's mother of setting the house on fire, and her sense of urgency built. "Did Fosdyke say what he wants?"

"No, but I guess he'd like to talk about your house. Shall I tell him and your mother-in-law you'll come after your shower?"

"I won't waste time. They'll just have to settle for talking to me in the robe. You might want to shut that door." Clair undressed at the speed of light and finger-combed dried dirt out of her hair.

She had to prevent a Leota-type explosion. She had to keep Ernest Fosdyke from tearing Nick's family apart. Why, she wasn't sure. Maybe because she didn't know how she'd be able to keep her part of their marriage bargain if Nick's mother had burned down her house. Belting his robe at her waist, she opened the kitchen door.

Despite the good manners that sat Mr. Hunter's shoulders like epaulets, he looked as if he had a mind full of bad news. "Mrs. Dylan, I have to ask you what you plan to say to the fire chief."

Clair hesitated, but Mr. Hunter had taken a chance with her. She met him halfway. "I plan to ask him to stay out of our business." She jutted her thumb over her shoulder. "Just leave my dirty clothes, and I'll take care of them later."

"No. I'll wash them." He set a silver coffee carafe on a tray. "And I'll announce you."

Clair shook her head. "I'd better carry that up. Leota may feel she has to put on a show of power for you." Clair gave him no time to argue.

ERNEST CLOSED THE DOOR Hunter had left open. "Don't make me ask you again. Why are you afraid? I'd like to help you."

Leota threw her head back, the perfect pose for both photographs and denials. Did he think she'd break like china? "What do you know about me anymore? Nothing frightens me."

Where had he tucked his undying friendship when she'd come to him pregnant and helpless, carrying Jeff Dylan's child? She'd wanted choices, options, discussion. But her best friend, Ernest, had said, "I'm busy. I'll call you tomorrow."

That tomorrow had never come. She'd decided on her own, and she'd married Jeff. She'd found her own way.

"Tell me the truth," he said. Something interested him plenty now. It seemed he could find time when he wanted. He eyed her with the concentration of a spotlight.

"The truth about what?" Her version of the truth would always support her cause. He couldn't know for sure about the match, and she sure as hell wouldn't admit to dropping it, not at the cost of the life she'd built. The man was crazy.

"What did you do to Clair's house?"

"What are you babbling about?" She'd done nothing. She'd thought about burning down that wooden tomb, but she'd chickened out.

Just like Jeff always said. Character will out. And hers still wasn't strong enough for a real Dylan. She hadn't dared destroy her enemy. Someone else must have.

"You didn't set that fire?"

"Of course not." She couldn't keep the bitterness out of her voice, even as she watched Ernest note it. He'd never understand, but burning the house down would have proved she possessed Dylan courage. "I'm offended you'd suggest I'd set fire to someone's home. What proof do you have?"

"Someone did, Leota."

She refused to believe she had. "Stop harassing me. Either accuse me or leave me alone. In fact, I want you out of my house. Perhaps you could arrange an appointment the next time you need to see Clair Atherton."

"Dylan," he said.

Once again the door opened. "Fosdyke?" Panic

plain on the face that drove Leota mad, Clair swept into the room and slammed a coffee tray on the desk by the door. "What are you doing here? Leota?" Her anxious tone cut Leota like a knife, and she kept slashing. "Are you all right? What did he say to you?"

Leota choked on her answer. Nick's wife, wearing nothing but a fading robe, had run to her rescue. Somehow, Clair knew Ernest believed she'd set fire to that shack.

Even Clair pitied her? Pity implied Clair thought herself better than Leota. Leota summoned the shield of anger that had become her friend.

"What are you doing here in that robe? Perhaps you greet your gentleman callers naked in your own home, but here we have a much higher standard of conduct."

Ernest held up a hand. "Your mother-in-law and I were passing the time of day while we waited for you. We're old friends." He slid in front of Clair, between her and Leota.

Good thing, because Clair was a fraction of a second from learning, firsthand, everything Leota remembered about schoolyard brawling.

"You're taking advantage, Ernest." Ignoring the insult Leota had thought prime for her target, the younger woman faced Ernest like a mother protecting her young. "This is our home. Unless Leota invited you, you're not welcome."

"Damn you," Leota bawled, unable to stop herself.

Both Clair and Ernest snapped their mouths shut and stared at her. Clair's gaze flashed a warning, while Ernest looked like a warden in front of a prize escapee.

Feeling the weight of their vigilance on her chest, squeezing all the breath out of her, Leota stroked her gold bracelets down her wrists. Her demeanor remained steady as the proverbial stone.

"I agree with Clair," she said. The statement cost her. To express such an unthinkable idea all but killed her. The last thing she wanted was Clair's protection. She bit the inside of her mouth. That hurt less.

At last, Earnest nodded. He knew. Somehow he knew about that match she'd tossed into the wind after she'd lit her cigarette. Could it really have started such a powerful fire?

Leota's mouth curved in a bitter smile. Just her luck. But let him prove anything. Just let him.

"All right," he finally said. "I'll go, but both of you know you're making a mistake."

"I'll show you to the door." Clair cinched the robe at her waist, and her belt ripped. She raked Leota with a worried glance. "Then I'll change before this falls off completely."

As Clair led Ernest through the door, Leota slumped to the couch. Her cheeks felt damp. She lifted a hand to her face. When she pulled her hand back, she stared, unbelieving, at the teardrops tinged black with mascara, on her fingers.

She'd been crying.

"STOP, CLAIR. I need to talk to you." Grabbing her hands, Ernest fought Clair's efforts to shove him through the front door.

But she was desperate. "I'll call the police to drag you out of here if you don't go," Clair said. "You made her cry. Would a woman who'd burned my house down cry because you accused her of it?"

"Maybe she cried because she got caught."

"Leota hates me. If she'd done it, she'd take out a full-page ad in the paper." Clair reached for her belt again, but stopped before she ripped the aged material into shreds. "Wait until the arson investigator gives you his report before you accuse an innocent woman."

"If you thought she was innocent, you wouldn't have blown in there. You were afraid I'd worm the truth out of her."

"You think you can get something out of me, too, but do I look afraid?"

He offered the self-deprecating grin she no longer fell for. "You won't talk, but even I'm smart enough to be suspicious of you two," he said. "Here we have a woman who has set a house on fire. Whose house? Her worst enemy's—her daughter-in-law's house. Strangely, the daughter-in-law wants to give the woman an alibi, but the woman hates the daughter-in-law so much, she'd rather stand accused than accept help. Why does Leota hate you so much?"

Clair ignored his theory. "Why did you come?"

"To talk."

"Which you've done." Clair stepped around him to open the door. "Go now."

"I've heard from the arson investigator."

She froze. Literally. The cold wind blew inside her

robe. Another cold wind whistled into her heart. "He said someone set the fire?"

"He thinks a stray spark set it. Something in the kitchen, but the fire was so hot he can't be absolutely sure. You had cleaning materials and a lot of boxes in there, and they fed the fire."

"My parents' belongings." Sad for a moment, she managed to gather her poise. "Why do you look so miserable, and why are you still accusing Leota?"

"Because I believe the investigator's wrong. You don't work at this job as long as I have without honing your instincts."

"Which you'd better ignore if you don't want a lawsuit on your hands. You must know how powerful this family is." She lowered her voice. "You don't want to make an enemy of that woman."

"Why, Clair?"

She couldn't explain the emotional fallout a thirty-year feud caused. "Because you live in this town, and Leota can affect elections and funding and budgets. Just leave her alone."

"I won't lay off the truth." He nudged her hand away from the doorknob. "Neither should you. Call if you start to worry the new house will burn, too."

He closed the door, and Clair slammed both palms into the wood to hold herself up. Her legs swayed, brushing the soft comforting cloth of Nick's old robe.

What if Ernest was right? What if Leota's tears, tears that had truly urged Clair to defend her, came from being thwarted the first time?

NICK WAS deep in conversation with his part-time receptionist when Clair barged into his office. Not that he minded her visiting, but the belligerent tilt of her chin worried him.

"What's up, Clair?"

"Why don't we speak more privately?" She pointed at the door behind his desk.

At the fed-up note in her voice, he stepped away from paperwork that proved Selina's visit had produced a few more patients for him. "What's happened?"

She shook her head, but she barely let him close his office door before she spilled their problem. "Chief Fosdyke thinks your mother set the fire, even though the arson guy told him no one committed arson."

Nick lowered himself to the edge of the desk and gripped its lip as if it might jump out from under him. "Why?"

"I never got a straight answer. Maybe you should talk to him."

"I will. Where was Leota when he told you he suspected her?"

"He told us both. I refused to say anything about her, and I'm afraid I threw him out."

"You defended her?" Her unexpected generosity touched him. He leaned toward her, but stopped when she backed away. She smelled like the soap scent that floated on steam from her shower. A battle light still glittered in her eyes. "Why would you help Leota?"

"I don't think I helped her. I made her so furious trying, she didn't let me, but who knows? Maybe she put Ernest off the track." Clair rolled her head on her shoulders, obviously exhausted. "Don't get your hopes up. The last thing he said to me was that I should call him if I started to worry about the *new* house burning down."

"No wonder you're upset. Do you believe my mother is capable of burning either of your houses?"

Clair slumped into a chair. Before she looked at him again, she drew a hand down her face. "I don't know what I believe. What do you think? You know her better than I do."

"She's not herself." An understatement, and he needed to make sure Leota hadn't set that fire. "What did she say to you?"

"That I shouldn't greet guests naked."

He blinked. "Beg your pardon?"

"I came in from work, covered with mud, so I changed into your robe."

"I still don't understand."

"Mr. Hunter brought it to me. He asked me to change in the mudroom, and then he said Ernest was talking to your mother. I had to stop Ernest."

Clair's appearance in his robe must have made their marriage look genuine, but Ernest's accusations put them all in danger. Nick concentrated on the medical-office smell, even the whiff of cleaning fluid, rather than his fear that his mother might have set Clair's house on fire. "You're afraid he may be right?" His broken voice shamed him.

Clair noticed. He saw by the flicker in her eyes, but she didn't take advantage of his vulnerability.

"I have to tell you something else, Nick. She started crying when he accused her. It's none of my business, but I felt bad for her. Maybe you should talk to her again about therapy.''

''I'll try.'' He started toward the door, then stopped. ''Why is Ernest so certain? Did he find proof?''

''He didn't show me anything, and he didn't talk about it, but he must have a reason. Why would he want to hurt your family?''

Nick met her puzzled gaze. ''I'd expect you to be happy.''

''Why?'' She rose. ''I'm not out to make you suffer. In fact, I've gone above and beyond to warn you. If you think—''

He grabbed her wrist. ''I'm sorry. What I meant was I'm worried about Leota, and I'm grateful you could forgive my family enough to come tell me about Ernest.''

''Please don't think this changes anything.''

''But it does. Your helping my mother is not part of our bargain.''

''No.'' She pulled away, rejecting him, but he couldn't let her go. She stopped struggling, but then he wondered why she was content to leave her hand in his. He didn't understand Clair's responses.

''I don't think I'll be able to stick out the year if it turns out she set fire to my family's house. I was afraid Ernest would make her confess.''

''That explains worry about yourself, but why did you try to protect Leota?''

''I'm not looking for détente. I just want to move in down the hill from you a year from now.''

''And you don't want my mother in jail?''

"Not because of me." She pulled away, distancing herself. "And for once, I have to ask you a favor. I've drawn some sketches of the way I want the house to look, and I've made an appointment with an architect Tim suggested. It might look odd if you don't come with me."

Nick's guilt expanded. Damn that insurance policy. He hated talking about her new house. Every time she mentioned it, he worried she'd find out about the money he'd given her. The more he cared for her, the more he wished he'd talked to her about the money, instead of forcing it on her. He wished he'd been honest with her.

CHAPTER TEN

LEOTA HARDLY SLEPT that night. Clair Atherton's attempt to protect her from Ernest had both angered her and put her off her stride. She'd teach that woman to act like an avenging angel on her behalf. She'd agreed to meet with their memorial committee in a conference room at the courthouse, but she intended to show up only to look for evidence she could use to force Clair out of her life.

Greg Andrews and Jim Dale, the other executors, would be there, along with Wilford. She had to find something to prove Nick and Clair's marriage was a lie.

After they left the next morning, Leota went to the study where Nick had begun to use Jeff's desk. If she had to, she'd search every personal object Nick had brought home with him. Wilford clearly believed he'd given money to Clair. And if the amount was large enough to worry Wilford, there'd be a record somewhere.

Leota tried to imagine Clair accepting money from Nick. If her show of independence was true, she'd throw the money back in his face and leave him for good.

Leota could put down their excessively polite treatment of each other to self-consciousness around her, but she prayed she'd find evidence Nick had paid that woman to marry him. Even Clair had to want an easier life than digging in other people's yards, but she might draw the line at selling her soul for actual cash.

Leota opened the middle desk drawer. A wave of Jeff's cologne slapped her in the face. She leaned away from the scent, dashing off the tears that sprang to her eyes.

She couldn't afford sentiment. She needed ammunition to remove Clair Atherton from her life once and for all. She found nothing that belonged to Nick in the middle drawer, so she moved on to the right-hand set of drawers.

Bingo. He'd set up several files, tax information, bank statements and office expenses. Leota went for the bank statements first.

Her foolish son wasn't devious enough to hide his crime. She found a cash transfer to a new account. He'd also deposited a check from Ben Wells in the same account. The amount made her blink. She'd bet it would spin Clair Atherton's head like a top.

She folded the statement in neat squares, tucked it in her pocket and closed the drawer, but when she turned from the desk, she found Hunter standing behind her, the mail in his hands.

"How dare you spy on me?" Leota demanded.

"Have you taken something that belongs to Dr. Dylan?"

"I'll fire you, Hunter, as sure as I'm looking at you."

"I won't stand by and watch you hurt your son any more. Whatever you've taken, put it back."

"Call him. Tell him I looked in his desk."

Something in his eyes, a certain vulnerability, caused Leota a moment's self-doubt. A moment when she remembered working in this same house, being afraid of the woman who ran it, a woman who had never, ever accepted her.

Her memory of Jeff's disapproving mother only made her more determined. She'd do what she had to do to preserve her place in her own life. After all, she kept the house and her income no matter what Nick lost because of his lie of a marriage. She'd never again play second fiddle to any woman in her own home. She walked past Hunter, the evidence safe in her pocket.

TIM SENT HIS ESTIMATE by courier, and he offered a price Clair couldn't refuse. On the morning she agreed to meet him at the house, she showed up before the backhoes and dump trucks. It wasn't so bad at first. Tim took down her grandfather's door and wrapped it lovingly in a canvas, rain-resistant tarp.

"That's good oak and fine workmanship. I'll store it until you're ready to put it back up. No charge," he assured her. Then he whistled at the backhoe driver, a guy who'd often shared her first-grade lunch box. "Let's go, Nate. Time is Mrs. Dylan's money."

Clair's courage faltered. Nate twisted the controls on the backhoe and headed straight into the remains of her childhood home's front facade. The last standing supports buckled. Blackened boards tumbled into the burned-out shell. A strong odor of wet, charred remains wafted on the dust that frothed around Nate and his machine.

Clair cleared a lump of tears from her throat.

Tim leaned into her shoulder. "You all right?"

"I remember how it looked before."

"You'll put it back to rights. Don't worry. Have you seen the architect yet?"

Oh, yeah. She'd brazened her way through an uncomfortable meeting at which the architect flat-out asked Nick why he had no opinions. Clair nodded, but she didn't look at Tim. Nate backed out and went at another mostly burned wall. More dust, more smoky smell, more damage.

More tears that threatened to fly in front of Tim and Nate and the rest of Tim's interested work crew.

"I have to go," she said.

"Don't you want to watch?"

Clamping her hand over her mouth, she shook her head until strands of her own hair blinded her. How could she explain? How could a man like Tim Hanover, who made his living knocking down other people's pasts, understand?

"Call me when you're ready to pour the new foundation." Completely exposed, utterly childish, she ran for her car. Her tires skidded through the grass as she spun around. Bumping over the driveway, she concentrated on escape.

She should have prepared herself, but how could she? How did a woman prepare herself to sweep the best parts of her life into a Dumpster?

Worst of all, she had nowhere to go now, except

to the Dylan house. She schooled her emotions until she felt as blank as she'd been the night of the fire. She parked in the cavernous garage and worked her way to the front door.

She didn't want to risk seeing Mr. Hunter and Bonnie in the kitchen. She climbed the stairs, avoiding the treads that squeaked. Her life had turned in a new direction today. She'd lost her old home once and for all, and she was seeking shelter in the house of her family's enemy.

A house that had so much become her home, she knew which stairs creaked when you walked on them.

NICK REACHED for the sign Tim held in his hands. The other man ran his gloved finger over the burn that almost reached the *s* on "The Oaks."

"Take this to her," Tim said. "She might cheer up if you tell her we can put it on the new house. I think she almost cried."

She'd hate even almost crying in front of anyone. Nick took the sign, already halfway home in his mind. "Thanks for calling me. I think the fire was almost as bad as losing her parents again."

"Don't you worry, Dr. Dylan. She'll be better when we're building."

Nodding, Nick headed for his car. At home, he parked in front of the house and ran inside. As he took the stairs two at a time, he realized he might be putting on a protector-to-the-rescue act for the benefit of an empty room. His house was the last place Clair could take comfort. He bumped into Hunter at the top of the stairs.

"We have to talk," Hunter said.

The man's troubled expression distracted Nick. "Is something wrong with Clair?"

Hunter glanced toward her door. "I almost asked if I could talk to her, but she's too upset. I need to tell you something."

"Can you give me a few minutes? I want to see my wife."

"I walked in on your mother searching your desk downstairs."

Nick rubbed his forehead. Leota knew. If she'd opened the desk drawer, she'd have found the bank statement, and she'd tell Clair. How had he fooled himself into thinking his personal papers would be safe in this house?

Who was he kidding? If he'd been straight with Clair, he'd have had nothing to hide.

"Your mother needs help, Dr. Dylan. I expect she'll fire me for this, but she seems to want to hurt you and your wife. She'd do anything to hurt you, and her attitude isn't healthy."

"She can't fire you. You work for me now." Nick broke off. "You don't work for me, Hunter. You're part of this family, and you know it." Clumsily, he hugged the other man, and Hunter broke protocol long enough to hug back. "I'll take care of Leota. Thank you for telling me."

"My duty." Hunter cleared his voice. "I'm glad you understand how serious her condition is." He swung away. His feet gathered speed as he descended the stairs.

In case Clair had given into tears, Nick tapped on

her door before and waited to give her a chance to say he couldn't come in. When she didn't, he entered. She lay, sprawled across her bed, her hair hanging almost to the floor. She didn't seem to notice Kitty batting at the strands.

"Clair?"

She lifted herself on her elbows, and Kitty shot into the hall. For once, Nick closed the door behind him. He'd rather even Kitty missed his confession.

"Dinnertime?" Clair hardly moved her lips. Her red eyes betrayed the reason for her unnatural stillness. Nick knelt beside her.

"Tim told me you ran away from the building site."

She took a harsh breath. "Why did he tell you?"

"He thinks you and I are married, and I care about you." He held out the storm-weathered, fire-singed sign. Its acrid aroma wafted between them. He did care for Clair. Not just as the woman he wanted to compensate for his father's sins. He cared for Clair, the woman, whose spirit spoke to his. "Tim thought you might like to keep this for the new house."

Her smile hurt him. He sensed her struggle to produce it. She eased the sign from his hands.

"I helped my dad make this. At least he pretended I helped him. He told me I'd have to make one someday, but I won't now."

"This one will work for a long time to come." He tucked her unruly hair behind her ear. "You can be honest with me. You don't have to work at being okay."

Her bottom lip trembled. If the agony in her dark

green eyes hadn't tied him up so tightly, her wobbling lip might have warned him off. She was too vulnerable. He didn't know how to care for a woman he could easily hurt.

"When they pulled down my house, it was as if my parents and I never existed."

"Everyone you knew before has welcomed you back." He pressed his knuckles against the back of her neck, kneading the tension. "You probably don't want advice from a Dylan, but I know how you feel. You and I have to adapt ourselves to this town and our neighbors. You, because you left, and I, because I want to make a difference as more than the senator's son."

"You and Leota do matter. No one matters more here."

"My name matters. My name has nothing to do with the man I am."

"How can you pretend not to mind? I get tired of acting as if I don't care that every trace of my past is gone. I don't want to be weak, but I can't talk to anyone."

He studied her pale face, her tired eyes. His answer would change their agreement. He wanted ties. "You can talk to me."

"How do I tell you what I feel about the senator? You must have loved your father."

His own feelings about his father went too deep, and they were too convoluted to share with Clair.

His silence seemed answer enough for her. "I knew we couldn't talk about what really matters to either of us," she said.

Watching him as if he were an experiment, she fell onto her back. Her hair splashed over her comforter. She drew her hand across her breasts, her fingers moving as if she were typing, as if she were thinking with them.

"You did love him, didn't you, Nick?"

"I tried to. He was my father."

"Did he love you?"

Nick looked away from her. If she forced him to answer, he'd have to say he didn't think Jeff had loved him. He'd rather not say that to Clair. Her parents had loved her well. She couldn't possibly understand how he had mostly seemed to embarrass his mother and father.

"That wasn't a trick question, Nick." She dropped her hand against his upper arm. "Just as you loved him, because he was your father, how could he not love his son?"

"I can't answer you." He felt exposed. If she knew the truth, that he'd never managed to earn his father's love, would she turn away from him, too?

Without warning, Clair pressed her hands into the mattress and pushed herself to a sitting position. She curved her hand against his cheek. Instinctively, he flinched.

"What?" She started to pull her hand away, but he caught it close again, relishing her touch. "Don't let him hurt you anymore. Just deal with what he meant to you."

"Is dealing with Jeff so easy? How have you been able to deal with what he did to your family?"

She hesitated. "Maybe you don't want to know

what I did." Leaning toward him, she pressed her lips to the corner of his mouth. Her scent invaded his senses, made his heart race as his body hardened. He'd never responded so rapidly, so mindlessly, to any woman. He turned, catching her face between his hands.

"Don't," she whispered.

But she parted her mouth in moist welcome, and he had to kiss her. She tasted like... It was an addictive taste he would always think of as Clair. She kissed as if she meant it, as if the need she made him feel was mutual.

But she touched him only with her mouth. When he was about to lift his head to ask her to hold him, she deepened the kiss, and he forgot everything except wanting her. Until she dragged her mouth away from his. Her eyes had darkened, and her breathing sounded ragged, but then so did his.

Clair slid her fingers disturbingly over her swollen lips. "We can't have an affair."

He couldn't imagine this much hunger dying at the end of anything so inconsequential as an affair. "I'm your husband."

"No." She glanced at him as she rose from the bed. "Paper husbands and wives don't kiss the way we just did. You should go."

"Why?" He stood beside her, realizing for the first time how much taller he was than her. Her strength, her control, lent her an illusion of height. "We can change our minds about what we want. I've changed."

Her smile shone from knowing eyes. She saw

through him to places he hadn't shared with her yet. The feeling unsettled him.

"How much have you changed?" she asked. "You want to sleep with me, but we're strangers. We both know the outward things, facts any stranger can find out about us. We drop tidbits of information when we have no choice, but neither of us says anything that reveals who we are." She opened her hands wide in frustration. "Look at the words I choose to say this to you. When I try to tell you the truth about how I feel, I sound as if I'm addressing a judge."

Too many years of hiding behind a well-schooled expression held Nick silent, but Clair deserved an effort at an honest answer. "I disagree. I want you, and that should be enough. You matter to me, Clair."

"You and I have been married for nearly a month, but we've never been more honest with each other."

Her hair curled around her face, a life force caught in the dark red and gold strands. His fingertips tingled with the memory of touching the vigorous coils. He wanted her, and he knew she'd stay with him if he asked her and meant it.

He held back. His lie about the insurance money still stood between them. He should tell her about the extra money he'd put into her bank account.

But she deserved the house she wanted. He didn't want to be the Dylan who stood in her way because he hadn't checked the insurance personally. He couldn't come clean.

DURING LUNCHTIME one cloudy day a week after he'd spoken to the Dylan women, Ernest and his crew were washing the town's fire truck when Leota went into Franklin House. To a chorus of the other men's insults, Ernest broke off from his work and cleaned himself up.

He slid the matchbook into his shirt pocket and waited for her at the bottom of the bed-and-breakfast's stone steps. In a few minutes, she came out, her color high, her frown sharpening.

He approached her. "I have to talk to you. We can go inside for coffee or we can talk in your car."

"If you think I'm guilty, talk to the police and my attorney. Otherwise, stay away from me."

"I'd rather we spoke in private, but if you won't give me a choice…" He pulled the matchbook from his pocket and opened it.

"What's that?"

"Proof, I believe." He pointed to the appointment she'd scheduled at the Pembroke salon. "I found this on the side of a path from Clair's old house to yours."

"You're suggesting I had my hair done so I could burn down her house?"

He ignored her sarcasm. "I think you made the appointment and noted the time on the matchbook. Sometime after that, you went outside to sneak a cigarette. Maybe without even planning to, you walked through the woods to the Atherton house. You remembered how the sight of Sylvie stuck in your gut. You found yourself facing a lifetime of Clair every day in your face. You lit the match and let it drop, and at the same time, you dropped this."

Unnaturally wan, she stepped back from him.

"What do you mean? You really believe I deliberately set Clair's house on fire?"

His heart began to thump. Leota mattered to him. She always had. "Was it an accident?"

"No!"

She reached for the matchbook, but he pulled it away. He couldn't cover for her. She'd either grown so spoiled living with Jeff Dylan she'd lost sight of right and wrong, or she needed serious help.

"Tell me the truth, Leota."

"Try and prove your theory with a hair appointment on a matchbook."

"I've tried to help you," he said. "I don't want you to go to jail. I don't want you to suffer. Why would you set fire to Clair's house?"

"You aren't helping me. You're harassing me."

"What happened to the lovable, loving young girl I grew up with?"

A shadow of her remained in the blush that spread across her cheekbones, but Leota Dylan, wife of Senator Jeffrey Dylan, turned her head and tilted her chin toward heights his middle-class Fairlove family had never reached. Heights that mattered to Leota.

"You made your choices, too, Ernest. Maybe I don't approve of what you've done with your life."

He gritted his teeth. The woman refused to meet him halfway. "If you don't tell me what happened, I'll have to show Clair the matchbook. If she asks me, I'll advise her to speak to the police."

Leota's expression collapsed in on itself. It didn't matter. No matter how big he talked, he didn't know how he'd turn his old friend over to the police.

"Why do you care so much about Clair Dylan?" Leota's bitter voice made him feel helpless. "Why does she matter so much to you?"

"Can't you hear what I'm saying? I care about you. I don't want you to hurt yourself with any more bad decisions."

"Confessing to something I didn't do—or, let's even say I did it—confessing to a crime, that wouldn't be hurtful?"

"Did you do it?"

"Of course not."

"You know I have to show the matchbook to Clair."

"She usually comes home around six-thirty. I'll tell her to expect you."

NICK CAME HOME late for dinner. He'd stayed in his office to run an IV for a patient who'd let bronchitis progress to pneumonia. Afterward, he'd had to clear up paperwork and call in a reminder for the patient to come back for another IV the next day. By the time he got home and changed for dinner, he found Leota pacing like a tiger in the dining room.

"Where's Clair?" he asked.

"You know how she is. She never leaves a message when she's late."

"She's lived alone a long time." He sat in his chair, and Leota perched on the edge of hers. Neither spoke as Hunter brought in the first course.

"Excuse me, Mrs. Dylan. I wasn't aware the other Mrs. Dylan hadn't arrived yet. Would you prefer to wait?"

"No, I don't think we need to," Leota said.

When Hunter left the room, Nick opened the subject of the bank statement that was missing from his desk. "I'm also used to living by myself. I'm not accustomed to your helping yourself to my personal papers."

She smiled, her brittleness reminding him of Kitty at his least civilized. "I don't know what you mean, Nick."

Her complete lack of remorse galled him. "My bank statement. What do you plan to do with it?"

"You mean the one that shows you added your money to an account you opened with a check from Ben Wells? The only account you and Clair share?"

In that moment, he wanted her out of his life, but he'd learned so much compromise with Clair he'd begun to think he shouldn't burn his bridges for the sake of winning an argument. He couldn't give up on Leota any more than he could give up on his wife. "I didn't insure the Atherton house for replacement value. Since it was my mistake, I'm rectifying it."

"Clair thinks all the money in that account came straight from Ben?"

"You know what Clair thinks, and you know I don't want her to find out the truth. She won't be able to restore the house."

Leota's smile chilled him.

"All the more reason to show her the statement. Don't you know by now I'll do anything to remind her we're her betters?"

"Why do you need revenge? What did Clair do to you?"

She yanked her napkin out of her lap and threw it on the table, exploding. "My husband loved her mother. He never brought himself to love me, and he didn't hate Clair."

"Your husband was my father. What was wrong between the three of us?"

"He probably wished Clair had been his child."

Her suggestion hardly surprised him after all these years, but listening to her was like making himself a target in a shooting gallery. He took a careful sip of wine. "I'm your son, too. Do you want to hurt Clair badly enough to ruin my marriage?"

She slammed out of her chair, her eyes wild. "I guess I'll find out if your marriage is real. She'll leave you if you've cheated on a business arrangement." She leaned across the table, her mouth a frozen, unnatural smile. "You should have married one of the women your father and I suggested. You could have learned to love one of them."

Nick spun away from her, knocking his own chair to the floor. "You need help, Leota. What if I do love Clair?"

"Bringing her into my home was the cruelest thing you could do to me, Nick. Did you think how I'd suffer?"

Because he had, he gained control of his anger. "If you don't see a counselor soon, I'll bring one here. You can learn to cope."

"I won't see anyone. I need the Athertons out of my life once and for all. You didn't consult me before you brought her here. I don't think I'll wait for you to agree we should both be rid of her."

The door opened, and Clair slipped through it, adjusting her skirt. Damp curls weighted down the drier strands of her hair. "Sorry I'm late." She crossed to her chair and sat. "I know this isn't dinner-table talk, but I spread manure on the Saddlebrook flower beds today, so I had to stop for a shower."

Leota sniffed. "The least you could do is quit that job."

Nick watched his wife uneasily. Clair could have demanded enough from him that she wouldn't have had to work. Unbearable tenderness for her expanded in his chest. He couldn't stop what his mother was about to do, but if Clair ever gave him a second chance, he wouldn't lie again.

"I need to talk to you." He should have told her the other night.

"In the study after dinner?" Clair picked up her water glass as Hunter brought in her salad. "Sorry I'm late, Mr. Hunter."

"Not at all, Mrs. Dylan. Did you have a busy day?"

To Nick's surprise, Hunter waited for her answer. He hadn't asked just to be polite. Nick hoped she wouldn't throw Hunter's friendship away if she decided to leave him.

"Manure at Saddlebrook today," she said. "Don't worry, though. I changed at the office, and I'll wash my own clothes."

Hunter flashed a can-you believe-her grimace Nick's way, oblivious to his surprise at their ease with each other. "Did you bring your clothing home?"

"I tied everything up in a garbage bag," she said. "I'm not stinking up the place."

"I'll get the bag after dinner. Dressing?"

"Thank you, but I'd rather do my own…" Adding to Nick's shock, she backed down. "I mean, thanks for waiting on me hand and foot, even though I'd rather ladle out my own dressing."

"As always, I respect your gracious protest." Hunter spied Leota's still-full plate. "Mrs. Dylan, is something wrong with your salad?"

"It's fine." Leota's acid tone fired a warning shot. She resented Hunter's growing friendship with Clair.

Nodding, Hunter left the room.

"Actually, something's worrying me, so I've lost my appetite." Leota raked Clair with a biting gaze. "I mistakenly opened a bank statement of yours, Nick. This cash transfer to an account you started with Ben Wells's check—why did you have to add money to that account? Did Ben try to cheat you?"

Nick hardly believed she'd go this far, even in the face of her opening volley. "Stop, Leota."

"Or maybe you've opened a new policy? Do you own a policy this expensive?" She twisted the bank statement and tossed it onto the table.

Nick stood, staring at the contorted paper. He looked into his mother's dilated pupils. She was ill. She might not be responsible, but he couldn't go on, a long-suffering son who forced himself to hope they'd salvage a relationship out of their disastrous past. "Do you know what you're doing?"

Doubt finally entered her eyes, but at the same moment, Clair dropped her knife and fork. "What about Ben Wells, Leota?"

For a second the older woman held her tongue. Locked in her gaze, Nick saw her first trace of reluctance. But if her conscience had finally come out of its coma, it came too late.

"I've done something you may find unforgivable," he said. On the last word, he made himself look at Clair. Her dread roused his need to protect her. From himself and his lie.

Clair turned to his mother, a measure of her disappointment in him. "What about Ben?"

Leota eyes grew curiously flat. "Ask Nick about the bank statement." She reached for the paper. "Read it yourself." But she crumpled it in her fist and held on.

Nick started around the table, and Clair stood to meet him.

"You gave Ben Wells money? And Leota thinks you did it for me?"

He curved his hands around her forearms, holding her just enough to keep her from running away, not tightly enough to make her feel trapped.

"Let me explain." But when he tried to tell her, all his excuses seemed like plans. He had no choice. She deserved an effort. "I didn't insure the house for replacement value. If I don't add my money to the amount Ben gave you, you won't be able to rebuild your home."

"You gave me that money?" She tried to back away, but he went with her.

"I've told you before—I owe you that money. I owe you more. My father stole more from you."

Horror filled her eyes. He knew what came next.

Rejection. When she pulled away from him this time, he let her go.

"I don't want my house as a gift from you."

"I'm sorry, Clair."

Ignoring his apology, Clair swung her gaze to the woman at the other end of the table. "You told me because you think I'll say something you can use to hurt Nick. Why do you care so little about him? You're his mother."

Nick moved between them, appalled that she could take his side when he'd broken faith with her. "Don't defend me," he said hoarsely.

"Why? Because you feel guilty? How surprised do you think I am? You're a Dylan. I'm an Atherton. You're supposed to work me like a puppet if you can, but if you ever try to again, I'll leave you."

Her accusations splintered in the air around them. "I'm not the kind of man you think of as a Dylan. I tried to make up for a mistake, and I lied to you because you're so stubborn you'd hurt yourself before you let me help you."

Her derisive laughter could have shattered glass. "You made a fool of me for my own good?"

"I care about you. How many ways do I have to show you?"

She slanted a warning glance at Leota, but Nick spread impatient hands on the table. He didn't care what Leota thought. "You're my wife, and I don't want to lose you." Maybe she interested him because she was so different from the women he'd known before, different, too, from his family, but he meant to find out if they could make more than a contract marriage, and to hell with Jeff's will and its terms.

"I won't lie to you again, even to help you, but give us a chance."

"I understand what you mean," Clair said carefully.

"I don't think you do, because I mean exactly what I said." The stakes had changed for him. Whatever happened in the next few months, he no longer believed he could divorce Clair and forget her.

She lowered her voice. "When we talked the other night, I didn't mean to lead you on—"

Leota sprang back to life. "Are we talking sex? I don't want to know what the two of you did to seal your devotion. Young woman, if you're too blind to see he's a Dylan and he can't help himself, I won't have to lift another finger to get you out of my way." She shoved her chair back. "As for you, Nick, I just wish your father had lived to see you crawl to a woman. I don't mind taking everything from you, if it means I get rid of her. You don't care about our family's name. Why should you have its wealth?"

She slammed out of the room and Clair slumped against the wall. Nick breathed deep, holding his wife's green gaze until he reached her.

Her breath warmed his chin as he took her in his arms. "I've had money and land all my life. Suddenly, they don't mean as much. Will you stay?"

"What are you really asking me?"

"I'm not sure." Holding her tight with one arm, he lifted his other hand to trace the curve of her left eyebrow with his fingertip. He kissed her eyelids shut. She nudged him, finding his lips with hers, and she opened to him.

Her passion broke him. She groaned as he cupped

her face and covered her mouth with kiss after kiss, taking, taking until she pushed him toward the table. Hunger, stripped of niceties, too urgent to deny, brought his hands to her breasts. He traced her nipples, smiling at the soft hungry sounds she uttered against his mouth. He needed to please her.

He needed...he needed to make love to his wife on the dining-room table where at least three other people might show up at the worst possible moment. He buried his face in Clair's throat.

She tangled her fingers in his hair. "We aren't ready."

"I'm ready," he said, laughing against her scented skin. Laughing again when she shivered and made him feel idiotically powerful. "Maybe not here in the salad course."

"Maybe not now," she said. She locked her arms around his shoulders. "I'll let you know what you can do with your money."

He lifted his head, searching her gaze for her feelings. "You aren't still angry? The money belongs to you."

"I can't take it, even if I'm just being stubborn."

She sounded tired. He gave in because his family had put her through enough, and her peace of mind mattered to him. What he felt for her was more than need. Maybe this voracious need was simply the beginning of love, a physical expression of the greatest tenderness he'd ever felt toward another human being.

CHAPTER ELEVEN

WHEN CLAIR FINISHED the work on Mr. Velasco's garden, Paul helped her take photos to put in the office portfolio. Snow had begun to fall, making Christmas Eve day cold and perfect in Clair's eyes. She and Paul split up the garden. She began to shoot pictures at the end of the holly hedge they'd set out in back. Paul met her with his camera at the fenced enclosure Clair had designed to hide the garbage cans.

"You did great," Paul said. "I'm a little concerned that outfit from Charlottesville will persuade you you're too good to work for me."

She wrapped her hands around her camera. "You underestimate yourself. You're probably the only landscaper I've ever met who gave me so much autonomy despite my lack of—"

"Why does that degree bug you so much?"

"Because I don't have it."

"Then go back to school and get one. What's stopping you?"

She lifted her eyebrows. "I've been thinking the same thing. Nothing's stopping me, now that I have a steady job and I can afford classes."

"I might be able to offer you tuition reimbursement. Let me talk to Amanda about it." His wife managed the business aspects of his company. "A Dylan on the payroll is free advertising. I have nightmares about you resigning. We could have sold tickets to people who wanted to watch you spread manure out at Saddlebrook."

Maybe she should congratulate him on the free enterprise of his idea. "Offer me a percentage of the gate, and I'll print the tickets for you."

"What do you mean?"

She took a deep breath. Knowing Leota had wanted her to attack Nick, she'd held her temper. By the time he explained why he'd forced the money on her, she'd understood that he and she thought differently, that he'd truly believed he was doing her a favor.

Nevertheless, her heart felt broken in about ten pieces every time the truth hit her. She'd lost her house again.

"Turns out the insurance payment isn't as generous as I thought. I've had to rethink my plans for the house."

"Rethink how?"

"I can't afford to rebuild as the house used to be. I'm economizing with a two-story A-frame." She tried to look at the situation in a "glass half-full" light. She couldn't take Dylan money, and she still owned her land. She was still building a home of her own. "They're framing it today."

"I thought Ben already gave you the check."

"He did, but someone made a mistake on the amount."

Nick's face flashed before her eyes. Hard with passion, blinded by need. She wanted that man, she craved his passion, but the cold light of day had reminded her he'd lied to her. True, he'd done it to help her, but she couldn't live with a man who believed a lie was okay. Since that night in the dining room, she'd devoted all her time to reworking her house plans and avoiding her husband. She didn't want to commit to Nick in the hope she might change him.

"Maybe this is a good thing," she said, still deeply uncertain—about the house and about Nick. "I can make the house the way I want it. I don't have to live in the past, and the new plan has so many angles. On paper it's like I'm building a dollhouse. I have a hard time picturing it full size."

Paul dropped an arm across her shoulders. "Your new idea is the healthiest suggestion I've heard you make about rebuilding, but you sound as if you're in shock."

"I'll be better today after I see the new house is real." She shut the lens on her camera. "Let's get going."

He followed her. His willingness to let her tell him what she wanted him to know made their friendship easy. Nick had tried to force what he wanted on her. Did she need the challenge of figuring him out? She didn't want to get involved. The past stood between them. And the present. She couldn't pretend he hadn't lied to manipulate her.

Paul shut Mr. Velasco's gate behind them. "I guess we're finished here. Do you feel like starting work on Mrs. Dylan's fountain next week?"

She turned so swiftly she almost fell over. "Leota's fountain?"

"Remember? In the greenhouse? The reason you finally told me you were marrying Dr. Dylan?"

"His name is Nick, and I think I must have willed myself to forget about the fountain." She resigned herself. "I'll do it."

"I'll help you."

"You'll help? Am I back on probation?"

"Honestly? I suspect you may need a buffer." He shrugged. "Mrs. Dylan's rules and all."

"You may be right."

"Why don't you go watch them frame your house?" Paul flattened his palm beneath her shoulder blades. "And then take the weekend off. I'm sending everyone else home when I get back to the office."

"Are you sure?"

"Positive. I'd like to spend time with my wife. I'll meet you at the Dylans' on Monday at eight-thirty sharp."

"Merry Christmas, Paul."

"Same to you, and keep well."

She waved her thanks and went to her car. In town, the Christmas decorations, now safely anchored and twinkling, reminded her they'd done nothing to celebrate the holidays at the Dylan house. On a whim, she stopped at Bigelow's and bought a small pine tree Charlie Brown would have recognized. It fit easily in her trunk.

As soon as she turned into her freshly graveled driveway, she saw the workers lifting boards into place. Their hammers rang out like gunshots. Clair parked out of the way and climbed out to huddle in her coat on the hood of her car.

Tim, managing the work, came over. He leaned his hip against the car beside her. "What do you think?"

"Gorgeous," she said, keeping her upper lip stiff.

"You'll fall in love with it soon. The floor plan we've worked out is terrific." He folded his arms. "Do you think you'll rent it out, or will you and Dr. Dylan move in?"

Contemplating Nick in her home, the amount of compromise two such different people would have to learn, Clair nearly spilled the truth about their marriage. "We're still discussing our plans. How are the drawings for the community center?"

"Going on schedule. I'll be ready to present them at our meeting with the Town Council." He turned as another car crushed the gravel in the driveway. "Selina," he said. "She called me to estimate putting a gazebo in her garden now that you've cleaned it up. I'll owe you a commission before long."

Grinning, he strolled back to work. Clair's spirits rose on the strength of Selina's welcoming smile and the size of her picnic basket.

"Paul dropped by. He said you'd be here."

"What did you bring?" Clair called.

"Your favorites. Cucumber and cream-cheese sandwiches and hot cocoa. Scoot over, girl. I'm coming aboard."

They both braced their feet on the car's bumper and set the basket between them. Selina quickly produced sandwiches and two insulated thermoses.

"Should you be out in this cold?" Clair asked her friend.

"Best thing for me." Selina sucked in a breath.

"I'm all better and this air is bracing. So, what do you think of the house?"

With Selina she could be honest. "I'm still terribly disappointed—more for Mom and Dad than for me. I wanted the other house to kind of pay them back. But the more I see this—" she waved a sandwich at the framing "—the more I like it."

Selina studied her face. "You still seem down, though."

She couldn't explain disappointment that went deeper. She couldn't trust Nick. She'd misjudged the growing strength of their unspoken bond. "I'm taking stock. Not just of the house, of my life. I think I might go back to school."

Selina's smile, as she turned her head away, had a secretive quality. "I've been hoping to hear you say that."

"Have you?" Clair sensed more than met the eye. "Why?"

Selina seemed to consider her answer. "The last time I knew where you were was when you left Wellesley."

Clair blushed. "You knew about that?"

"The judge and I sponsored your scholarship. I knew your parents wanted you to have a good education. By the time I knew you'd lost it, I'd lost you. I thought about forcing the state to prosecute that professor. You were barely of legal age."

Clair squeezed Selina's hand, healing warmth stealing through her body. "You gave me that scholarship? Why didn't you tell me?"

"A couple of reasons. I was embarrassed we hadn't

been able to do more for you, and Jeff Dylan was still alive. When we set up the terms, I didn't think you might lose it. Julian felt we should make you accountable, but then, when…under the circumstances, we'd have given you the money. We just couldn't find you."

"I was so embarrassed I didn't want to be found," Clair admitted. "And then I couldn't afford to go back to school. Imagine your doing that for someone who'd become a stranger to you."

Selina hugged her briefly, maneuvering her sandwich so as not to smear cream cheese on both of them. "Never a stranger. Just a little out of touch."

"It was the perfect gift, Selina, and I wish I'd used it wisely. I wish I could give that kind of—" Clair stopped.

For the first time since Leota had told her about the bank account, she felt as if she was in charge again. She knew what she'd do with the money Nick had tried to force on her. Maybe Jeff Dylan would have a community center named for him, but her parents—she glanced at Selina—and her parents' friends, who'd welcomed her home, would also have an effective memorial.

"Selina, do you have your cell phone with you? I need to talk to my attorney."

"What's wrong?" The older woman fished her phone out of the picnic basket and handed it over.

"Nothing. Everything's right again." A sudden flurry of nail guns seemed to punctuate Clair's excitement. She pointed at the rafters reaching for the sky. "And look—that's turning into a house."

NOT A SINGLE Christmas light shone on the three floors of his family's house. Nick remembered the days when their decorations had welcomed him back home from school. Maybe next year.

He unlocked the front door and headed straight up the stairs. Since Christmas Eve came on a Thursday this year, he'd given Hunter and Bonnie the whole weekend off, and they'd both left the house immediately. Nick unknotted his tie. All these Christmases, and he didn't know where Hunter went to celebrate on his own. He had some family in Maine, but Nick had never met them.

Light shone under his bedroom door. He approached in surprise. Clair?

Though she wasn't waiting for him, the scent of cinnamon and mulled wine wafted through the open door between their rooms. Nick pulled off his tie and jacket and tossed them on a chair as he crossed to Clair's door.

She stood the moment she saw him. In a short, emerald green dress that darkened her eyes, she beamed a welcome. Behind her, a small, somewhat bare Christmas tree struggled under the weight of clear twinkle lights.

"Merry Christmas," Clair said. "I have a gift for you."

He grimaced. The day had sneaked up on him. "I'm afraid I don't have one for you."

"You do." Her serenity glowed like the wine she passed him. "You're going to do as I ask with your money." She tried to take a white envelope from beneath the tree, but a black paw snagged it back.

Clair laughed, snatching her hand to safety. "He seems to think he's outside. He loves that tree."

It suited Kitty. "Did you pick it out, or is Paul giving away leftovers?"

"Bigelow's offered me a deal. You want to try for the envelope?"

"I guess I'd better." To his surprise, when he grabbed it, Kitty strolled out to greet his bare-of-cat-hair pant legs.

"The vet says he's marking you."

Nick frowned, not trusting her change in mood. She'd backed away emotionally and developed a "hands off" attitude after the night they'd almost made love in the dining room.

He turned the envelope over. "You've put a gift for both of us in this envelope?"

"A fresh start. You lied to me. I want to use your money for a better cause than a lie."

He pulled out a thin sheaf of papers and skimmed the words. "A grant for mature learners?"

"Angus Campbell said we should call it that. Did you know Selina and the judge gave me a scholarship? I lost it, but I hope there are other young people who make better choices."

"You want to call it the Atherton-Franklin grant?"

"My parents were both teachers, and I owe Selina and the judge for my being so lackadaisical with the scholarship funds they gave me."

Nick began to understand. He resented being manipulated, but maybe Clair owed him that. She'd found a way to forgive him. "How fresh a start are we talking?"

"We go on as if none of this happened."

"I can't renegotiate terms?"

"You're referring to the other night? In the dining room?" Clair set her wineglass on the table. "Our problems come from our inability to think alike. I'd better define fresh start. I don't want to get involved with someone who can't see why I don't want to be lied to for my own good."

"I see." He tilted the envelope. "This doesn't strike you as manipulation?"

"Obviously you don't have to do as I ask, but I didn't want your money. Someone else can use it. I thought we might announce the grant the day we break ground for your father's memorial. Angus and Wilford can iron out the terms by then."

Selfish or not, he'd rather help her than a faceless student who had no claim on his emotions. "I think it's a great idea. I want to set up the grant, but why don't we do that, anyway? You take this money that I owe you, and go back to school. I know you want to."

She looked surprised. "I'm going back to school, but I can pay my own way now."

Annoyance with her boiled over. "God forbid you should let me help you, my own wife."

"In name only." Clair shrugged, a provoking picture of conviction. "I don't forget our marriage is only real on paper. You do. Another example of seeing life from opposing views. Do we have a deal?"

Her idea of a new start felt more like losing a relationship he wanted to deepen. He offered his hand and a smile that hurt his mouth while he learned to live with her rejection. "Deal. I'll say Merry Christmas to you and leave you to your tree."

Clair's eyes widened and she shook his hand absently. "You don't have to go. Have a glass of wine with me. I'll share my tree."

"Thanks, but you're right. We don't want the same things. A tree won't do it for me." At the door, he turned back. "I'll have Wilford set up a meeting with Angus, and we can put this insurance fiasco behind us."

Making a sudden decision only a cat understood, Kitty turned abruptly from Nick's pant leg and plunged into the tree, yanking twinkle lights and vulnerable branches with him.

Clair gazed at her pet, stunned, but Nick decided to find out if the cat was more pragmatic than his mistress about a guy who offered a helping hand. Kitty'd probably choose assistance over hanging himself. Nick parted the complaining cat from the tree and lights and handed him to Clair.

"Good night," Nick said. He didn't allow himself to take hope from the wistful smile that wavered on her lush mouth.

LEOTA HARDLY CAME OUT of her room that weekend. Nick also seemed to disappear after he'd dashed Clair's holiday spirit. By Monday morning, Clair was sick of her own company and eager to work.

With Kitty on her shoulder, she tracked Mr. Hunter to the dining room. An astounding array of silver lay on the table before him. He was polishing a soup ladle. Clair lifted a knife. Its broad base shone like a mirror above the wheat sheaves sculpted on its handle.

"I can see myself. How old is this stuff?"

"Late 1800s. Do you like it?"

Kitty sniffed in the knife's direction as if Mr. Hunter had asked his opinion. "It's beautiful," Clair said, "but if you drop a piece, you'll break your toe."

"I'm careful. May I help you, Mrs. Dylan?"

"I have to set up Leota's fountain in the greenhouse today, and Kitty likes to come with me." After Nick's visit, she hated to ask for anything, but Mr. Hunter waited for her to go on. "Kitty gets underfoot. He might hurt himself." She gave up trying to induce him to volunteer. "Do you mind if I leave him in the kitchen?"

He nodded, his gaze on the spoon he was wiping. "He should be fine in the kitchen. Bonnie's taking an extra day off."

Clair took Kitty to the kitchen, then went to the greenhouse. Leota wanted the fountain beside a bed of tropical plants. Clair was sweeping the stone floor beside the plants when Mr. Hunter brought Paul out.

She stared at her employer's empty hands. "Where's the fountain?"

"On the truck. You have to help me carry it."

"You're a he-man." She put the broom aside.

"Bad weekend?" he asked in an amused tone that worsened her mood.

"It didn't start out that way." Truthfully, she'd missed Nick. She'd actually wanted to share her Christmas Eve with him. Her nice, safe decision to distance herself left her unhappy now.

Paul had brought a dolly, which they unloaded from the truck first. Together, they managed to slide the boxed fountain on the dolly, and they rolled both carefully across the manicured grass to the greenhouse door.

"We'll have to unpack it," Paul said. "It won't fit through in the box." He took a knife from his belt and sliced the box open. "Something happen with Dr. Dylan?"

"A difference of opinion."

"It happens. All part of marriage, but the great times make the bad times hard to take." Paul gave her a comforting smile. "You run the water line. I'll wrestle this inside."

She appreciated his advice, but he couldn't know her marriage didn't work like his. She'd made the right decision. She didn't want to be hurt. Nick had already lost so much in his life she didn't want to add to his pain. Why start a relationship that could only fail?

Clair took the tubing from the floor and eased it along the rock ledge that acted as a retaining wall for the tropical plants.

Paul spoke from the door. "Let me know when you're ready to break. You could give Nick a call— ask him to lunch."

Before she could answer, Mr. Hunter came to the door. "Mrs. Dylan, Chief Fosdyke has arrived, and he's asked for you."

Dread prickled in the pit of her belly. "I'll come. Excuse me, Paul." She followed Mr. Hunter to the study, where the fire chief rose from a Louis Quinze chair.

"Clair."

"What can I do for you?"

Ernest seemed to take note of her defensive tone, but he waited until Mr. Hunter left the room. "I guess Leota hasn't spoken to you?" As she shook her head, he sighed. "We'll do this the hard way, then."

"I'm tired of talking to you about Leota and the fire."

"I waited during the holiday, because I hoped she'd tell you herself." He took a matchbook from his pocket. "I found this on your property."

She refused to touch it. "So?"

"Open it, and read what Leota wrote on the cover."

She did, imagining a sensation of heat on her fingertips. She began to fear his accusations might be true. "Brandon Pembroke. Is he a friend of Leota's?"

"Her hairdresser. She admits the matchbook belongs to her."

Clair cupped the matchbook in her palm. "Where did you find it?"

"At the edge of the path from this house to yours."

The resentment she'd controlled so she could live in this house began to flame inside her. "Leota admitted she burned my house?"

"No, and I can't prove she did, but I believe she's guilty."

Clair prowled to the fireplace. The force of her anger fairly pulled her across the room. "You believe she set the fire?"

Ernest took his time considering. Finally he shook his head. "No, but I'm biased. I think she had the match, and I think something happened that we don't know about. Help me force her to get help."

"I don't care if she gets help. She burned my house. She should rot in jail. I'm tired of her family taking from mine. I don't have to stand for it. I'm not fourteen anymore."

As her voice rose and her control slipped, Ernest backed up. "You'd prosecute your mother-in-law?"

Yes. She wanted to scream, but Nick stood between her and retribution. He'd turned his life upside down to take care of Leota and keep their family together. If she prosecuted Leota, she'd hurt Nick.

"You don't think you can prove she did it?"

"Not even the arson investigator believed me."

"If I try to press charges, the police will investigate."

"Maybe. The papers sure will." He came closer. "You're part of the Dylan family now. Can you handle the gossip?"

She'd borne worse, but she'd promised Nick to stand by their agreement, and Nick had never knowingly tried to hurt her.

"I only wanted you to make Leota get help," the chief said.

"Everyone in this town has a plan for somebody. How do you want me to help Leota? Why should I help her?"

"You love her son, and he wants to help her." The last part of her question answered, he moved on. "Tell Leota you'll turn the matchbook over to the police and ask them to investigate if she doesn't start therapy. She has to learn how to stop hating your family.''

''For her own good?'' She didn't try to keep the irony out of her voice. ''Why shouldn't I make her pay?''

''You should help her,'' Ernest reiterated, ''because of Nick, because one day you'll have his children, and they'll be part of Leota. You have to live on in this town and in this family.''

He might not be the country boy he pretended to be at first glance, but he couldn't see through walls, either. ''You don't understand how I felt about my home.''

''You said it was everything you loved most in the world.''

''Leota Dylan belongs in jail if she burned it down.''

''I believe you love your husband more than that house. I've seen you together.''

Clair cursed her agreement with Nick. And she cursed his family. Would she never be free? No, a silent voice answered in her head. Not after these past two months with Nick, learning to care about him, to see him apart from Jeff and Leota.

She didn't want to give up her ties to Nick. As simple and terrifying as the truth could be, she'd stumbled on her own answer.

She dropped onto an ottoman. ''You said yourself, she might set fire to the new house.''

''Make her see someone who can teach her how to deal with her anger.''

Clair hadn't survived foster care and poverty without exploiting a good brain. If she had to protect Leota because she couldn't hurt Nick, she could also make sure no one burned down her new home.

"Do you want to come with me when I talk to her, or should I confront her alone?"

Ernest assessed her in silence while her fuse burned ever shorter. "I'd better come with you."

LEOTA HAD TURNED UP Andrea Bocelli in her bedroom to drown out the sounds of Clair and that Paul Sayers working in the greenhouse. When the knock came at her door, she expected Hunter with the coffee tray she'd requested. She called out, "Come in."

Clair opened the door, and Ernest came in on her heels. In that moment, Leota understood. Unlike Jeff, she was accountable for her actions. This Dylan name had never done anything for her. Her husband had hidden behind it. He'd even used it against her, to remind her she didn't belong. Now, the pain she'd endured because he'd never freely given her his name or his love was about to bring her down.

"I guess you know what we have to discuss," Clair said, as her face became Sylvie's.

Leota shook her head to clear that face and that time from her mind. She needed all her wits about her. "I'm completely in the dark."

Clair held out the matchbook, flipping the cover open.

Leota stared at her own handwriting. "Are you reminding me I have a hair appointment? Very thoughtful, but I already kept that appointment."

Clair shut the matchbook and dropped it into the pocket of her flannel shirt. "You're going to see a counselor, Leota."

Rage made her ears buzz. "Get out of my home."

"I believe you burned mine down, and I'm telling you now, you'll start therapy, or I'm taking Ernest and the matchbook to the police."

"I happen to know an arson investigator already determined your fire was an accident."

"Don't you mean your fire?" Clair stepped farther into the room, her face tight.

Her resemblance to Sylvie finally began to fade, and she became her own person. Sylvie had never been so forceful. If Leota hadn't been sitting, she might have backed away from Clair.

"This is still my home." But she couldn't find her familiar sense of purpose. "I allowed Nick to move in here, because he wanted to be with me while we both grieved for his father. I didn't ask you to stay, and I don't want you here any longer."

"Imagine what people will say when they hear you're being investigated for the fire that destroyed my house."

Leota froze. "What will Nick say?" she mustered, on the off chance this woman actually cared for her son.

"He'll have to choose." Clair lifted her head. "Do you want him to choose between you and me? I'd rather not force him to do that."

"I'd rather I'd never met any one of you Athertons. Your father was a failure. Your mother tried to steal my husband from me. She never accepted the fact that my husband married me, and that's why your father chose to die. He couldn't face one more defeat, and he couldn't face you or your mother, who never got over my husband." Moisture gathering in Clair's eyes unexpectedly slowed Leota down. "You think you can come in here and carry on where Sylvie left off. Well, I give away no one and nothing that belongs to me. Make Nick choose. I'll be rid of you."

Clair didn't seem to notice the tears that overflowed from her eyes. "Say what you need to, Leota, but I won't take the chance you'll destroy my new house. Bring me proof of your sessions with the therapist."

Turning, she ran into Ernest. He stumbled out of her way, and she didn't lift a finger to hide the fact she was crying.

Leota met Ernest's unnerved gaze. Deep inside her a voice whispered she'd never known the kind of love that could leave her defenseless.

"I'm going after her," Ernest said. "She still loves her parents, you know." He grabbed the door and yanked it open. His eyes accused her. Leota didn't like what she saw of herself in his gaze. "All Clair has left of her family is the way she remembers them."

He strode out and slammed the door behind him. Leota stood there, stunned. He'd left her high and dry once before when she'd needed his help, but she'd never felt so abandoned.

"SELINA, I NEED a room, but this time I don't know how long I'm staying."

"For one, Clair? Can I do anything for you?"

"I'll be alone, but you can't do anything." She must look like hell.

Selina simply handed over the key. "The Concord again."

"Thank you."

Clair locked the door, dropped her coat and her bag and crumpled on the large feather bed. She curled into a ball, trying to find some place in herself where she still felt strong.

Leota had lied. She recited those words over and over, and she tried to believe them. Leota had wanted to hurt back when Clair had backed her into a corner.

She remembered her parents. Of course she remembered them, but they'd lived so long in her memory and in her imagination she'd hoped someone would recall the same vivid life she'd believed in. Selina had seconded her memories, but Selina had tried to protect her in a lot of ways.

Suddenly someone pummeled her door so fiercely the frame shook. Clair rolled over and waited for whoever it was to leave. After a final solid rap, she heard footsteps walk away from her door.

Clair focused on the bed hangings, dark-blue-patterned damask, shot with gold vines. She wouldn't be here if she hadn't married Nick. She'd have rented an affordable apartment. This wasn't her kind of bed or her kind of room. Since she'd married Nick, she'd stopped living her kind of life.

A key, turning in the door's lock, pulled her to a defensive, standing position. Nick came around the door. Concern etched lines into the corners of his eyes. She sank back onto the bed.

"Why didn't you answer when I knocked?"

"Why didn't you say anything?"

"I thought you'd assume it was me. If you didn't want to let me in, making sure you knew I was the one knocking wouldn't change your mind."

"I didn't want to see anyone." She felt tears on her face and wiped them away. She didn't want to look weak in front of him. "Did you go home? Have you seen Leota?"

"Ernest called me from his car. He told me everything." Nick dropped his keys on the lacquered table beside the door. He left his coat on as he came to the bed. "I'm sorry about the fire. I'd like to believe she didn't do it, but she's been so angry. I'm not sure what she's capable of."

"Turns out the fire wasn't the worst thing that could happen."

She covered her face, but Nick pulled her hands away, his touch gentle.

"Leota doesn't know anything about your parents, except they were happier together than she was with my father."

"They loved each other. I won't believe Mom had an affair with your father after she and my dad married. She loved Dad."

"Be sure, Clair. I saw them together, and I'm sure."

She felt his concern for her in the way he stroked his fingers through hers. For once, her instinct to stand on her own fell out from underneath her. She turned her hands, so that their palms pressed together.

"I missed them so much after they died, and then

I had to leave here. I needed the memory of a loving home. Eventually I needed Fairlove to be real so badly I began to wonder if I made it up.''

He was silent, but she felt him beside her. He shrugged out of his coat and dropped it on the floor. Then he sat back against the pillows and pulled her against him. The solid strength of his chest at her back comforted her. She wrapped her arms around his.

''Do you really think you could fool yourself?'' He sounded blessedly skeptical.

''Your mother sounds sure of what she says.''

''Leota's troubled. She's had to fool herself all her life. We're a family that survived by painting a false picture for outsiders.''

''She made me break down completely. I cried all over myself.''

His chuckle reverberated against her back. ''So you're not made of steel, after all?''

She twisted her mouth in an unwilling smile. ''I told Leota she'd either go into counseling, or I'd turn everything over to the police.''

''I owe you one. She won't risk letting 'the public' know what's really happening to her. She especially won't risk going to jail for burning down your house. What could be worse than losing to an Atherton?''

''Lucky for me.'' She rested her head against his shoulder. Tension let go of her as she allowed herself to relax against Nick. ''I didn't do it to hurt Leota. I just don't want her to set fire to the new house.''

''I didn't do you any favors dragging you into my life, did I?''

''I thought you did at the time.'' Twisting her head,

she studied his mouth, the firm full curve of his lower lip, the shaving nick just below his nose. "While we're being honest, you're probably going to be angry with me later for blackmailing your mother, and I understand, but let's deal with it before it makes problems we can't solve between us."

"I thought I'd find you with Angus, drawing up divorce papers."

She allowed herself a nod and looked away from him again. "We're in a mess, but I'm glad you came."

"I'm glad Selina let me in. She never seems sure I'm not my father reincarnated."

"Most people here seem to wonder. Why do you stay in Fairlove?" she asked.

"I live here. My family has been here almost as long as yours." He shook his head, moving his chin back and forth against her hair. "Fairlove feels like home. Nowhere else ever did."

His answer resonated. She'd assured herself they were different, came from different worlds, made different assumptions about life. He'd grown up in a wealthy family that had always won. Her family had lost everything, even each other.

But deep down Nick wanted a home just as much as she did. An emotional home. A house on a plot of land, however well-established, wouldn't do.

She twisted so that they were face-to-face. Throwing consequences out of their small room, she curled against him, wrapping one leg over his, pressing her breasts to the hard muscles of his chest.

Nick's eyes darkened as he lifted his hand to touch

the backs of his fingers to her cheek. Clair studied his gaze, slowly easing closer until kissing him seemed like the most natural thing to do.

He opened his mouth, allowing her to lead him, and she understood her husband for the first time. He knew himself, and he was self-assured enough to accept a woman's need.

His body heat emanated through the cloth of his shirt. Clair slid her hand over his chest, seeking the beat of his heart, the strength of sinews that flexed beneath her fingertips.

He'd come to her when she'd needed him.

Nick sat up, pulling her with him. She reached for his shirt buttons, and he helped her, the friction of his fingers against hers a sensual pleasure.

When his shirt lay open, he flattened her palms against his chest. Clair groaned as she allowed herself to learn the shape of his body. When she pulled the tails of his shirt out of his waistband, he reached for her sweater.

He grimaced at the thermal T-shirt underneath. "How many layers can I expect?" he asked. But he kissed her as she opened her mouth to answer. "Don't tell me. I'll just start peeling."

Clair laughed, pushing her hands around his back. Large and lean, he was not just a virile man. He was Nick, and he was her husband, and she was ready to be his wife.

CHAPTER TWELVE

NICK CAUGHT HER FACE in his hands and stared into her passionate green gaze. Her trust honored him He wanted to be the man who deserved Clair's trust.

She pushed his shirt off his shoulders, her hands stoking a passion he'd never known. He craved her hands on him. He kissed her parted mouth, taking the warmth of her breath into his own body.

She held herself unnaturally still, as if waiting for a beat she heard in her head, felt in her body. Watching her fueled his desire. He ached to push her, but he waited for her. He didn't want his own passion. He was starved for hers. He tilted his head to kiss the vulnerable corner of her mouth, the curve of her cheek.

With a shallow breath that shuddered across his chest, she opened her hands and bumped them over the ridges of his rib cage. He stroked her hair behind her ears, watching her trail a path of heated kisses to his nipple.

His heart seemed to stop, while the rest of his body raced to a finish he held back from. Clair lifted her head to let him pull off her shirt. He pressed his palms to the undersides of her breasts, discovering the firm curves she arched for him.

He opened her mouth, kissing her with need he'd never admitted to anyone. He urged her onto her back, and she helped him with the button and zipper on her jeans. Slowly, enjoying each curve he revealed, he peeled the denim off her body, stroking the beautiful thighs that had so mesmerized him on his wedding night. Clair pushed her panties after her jeans with provocative impatience.

"Now yours," she said, and she watched as he took off his trousers.

Her eyes, the deepest green he'd ever seen, drove him crazy. Her frank hunger battered at his will to last for her. He caught her in his arms, bracing her fall with his body as he slid back onto the bed.

Splaying his hands around her hips, he lifted her above him. She smiled, a siren with secrets she kept close. He hoped she'd soon share some of those secrets.

Her body, lean from working so hard outdoors, struck him dumb. He slid his hands over her thighs, her stomach and then cupped her breasts as she groaned with frank pleasure.

Offering herself, she leaned over him. To his disappointment, she closed her eyes as he rolled her nipple against his tongue. He wanted her completely with him, but she sighed, and he repeated the movement that pleased her, until she whispered his name in a wanting, private tone.

He sat up, bending her over his arm, and she linked her legs behind his back. Behind her, he could see the long length of her back in the dressing-table mirror. He traced his fingertips down her spine.

"Are you mine, Clair?" he whispered.

She didn't answer, but she followed the line of his gaze, and he ducked his head to suckle her breast again. Her throaty groan made him move to her other breast. He loved the texture of her in his mouth. She tasted like life and hope.

She filled him with life and hope.

Behind her back, she slid possessive hands along his legs, smiling at his gasp when she reached his upper thighs. She teased him, shifting finally to touch him where he needed the pressure of her hands. He gave himself up until he could no longer stand her hands on him, but when he turned her onto her back, she laughed, making him a present of her joy.

He nudged her knees apart and leaned between them, kissing her as he pressed against her welcoming body.

"You know where we're going, Clair?"

"Shh. If you talk, you'll frighten me."

He knew what she meant. Making love to her mattered. Tonight was no one-time affair. He needed Clair in his life. Maybe she needed him.

She twined her arms around his neck and arched to take him inside. He'd never felt such heat. He felt drenched in her. He made her his wife.

She moved with him, her desire more honest than any truth he'd ever known. He groaned, trying to hold back, but she muttered her frustration. His need and hers became the same.

He recognized her as if he'd been waiting for her. Suddenly, with a small cry, she caught her breath, stopped breathing altogether. Her body clenched. He gave himself up, stroking into her, only to collapse in the most intimate pleasure he'd ever known.

She curled around him, shaking in his arms. Turning into the welcoming heat of her body, he kissed her forehead.

She pressed her mouth to his breastbone, touching her tongue to the moisture on his chest. "Salty." Her chuckle raised goose bumps on his skin. "But I'm cold and tired. Will you stay?"

He tightened his arms around her. Eventually, he'd have to let her go. But for now, she filled his arms. "It's early to sleep."

"I'm guessing we'll wake up again later."

He stretched to turn off the lamp. Moving together, they pulled the bedding over themselves. Clair curled her arm around his neck. Breathing the seductive scent of her skin, he fell asleep.

He awoke in darkness. Clair lay on top of him. Her hair covered his face as she traced his collarbones with her lips. Already hard, he moved inside her. She loved him sweetly, rocking against his body until he arched into her in a release that shook him even as she shuddered against his body.

"Don't move," he said, when her heart against his slowed to a normal pace. He was glad she couldn't see his face, the need he couldn't have hidden from her, need that made him feel exposed in ways he hadn't confessed. "I want to lie with you like this."

"Yes."

NICK'S CELL PHONE RANG beside the bed. Clair reached blindly, but Nick managed to scoop it off the floor. Nick flipped the phone open and put the receiver to his ear.

"Yeah?" he growled. After a moment, he sat up, pulling the sheet with him. "This is Dr. Dylan. No, don't worry about disturbing me, Mrs. Bateson. How far apart are your pains?"

Clair curled her knees up to her chest as he waited for a response. He dropped his hand on her shoulder, but then twisted his fingers gently into her hair. She turned his palm up for a kiss.

"I think you'd better go to the hospital. I'll meet you there. What?" He waited again. "No, I won't be offended if you keep trying Dr. Morgan. I'll call the hospital and see if they can't find her for you." With that gently spoken promise, he shut the phone and turned his head toward Clair in the darkness. "I'm sorry to leave like this."

"I'll look forward to meeting the baby."

"I'd better take a quick shower." He kissed her swiftly, and she sank back into her pillows with a sigh.

She refused to think of last night as a mistake. Neither of them had sworn undying love, but she believed he'd taken their lovemaking as seriously as she had. The future felt different. Undecided, but different.

She'd almost fallen asleep again when Nick opened her door, and a triangle of light crept across the floor. She burrowed into her pillow. "Are you leaving?"

"I need to tell you something." His tone, impersonal, considering the circumstances, put her on guard.

"What's wrong?"

"It was what you said, about meeting the Bateson's baby. I couldn't stop thinking…I want you to know, if you're pregnant, I won't abandon you. We'll stay married."

Her mind reeled. Here she lay, dreaming of love, and he could suggest a marriage to protect his family honor? Nick, more than anyone, should recognize the waste. Maybe she'd only mistaken him for a man who could put his father's twisted teachings behind him.

She pulled the sheets to her chin. "Let's forget you said that."

"We weren't exactly careful." He came into the room, tucking in his shirt. "Physician, heal thyself."

"You weren't thinking. I didn't think, either." She pushed her hand through her tangled hair. "We should have covered the health basics, but I'm not…you don't have to worry about illness."

"Neither do you," he said. "Nevertheless, if you're pregnant, I want to be a father to my child."

"You sound like you're making the kinds of promises Jeff made to Leota. I don't need your sense of duty, and I don't want that kind of father for my children." Impatiently, she shook her head. "Why discuss this? I'm not pregnant."

"You could be, and we need to talk."

"You're supposed to go deliver someone else's baby." She was seconds away from throwing him out of her rented room.

"I'll see you tonight at home."

"Not if you want to talk about this."

He sat on the edge of the bed, but when he reached for her hand, she held back. He grimaced his frustration. "I've said this all wrong, but can't you try to see what I mean?"

"I don't like your instincts. You think like a Dylan."

"I have to go." He measured each word with regret.

"I don't want you to stay married to me because we might have made a mistake. I don't want you to be an angry man who feels he was trapped in a marriage. Would you want your child to grow up feeling unwanted?"

"I don't want anyone else to pay for my mistakes."

Mistake? The word plunged into the soft, exposed parts of her heart, the parts she'd given to Nick. "I don't want to be your mistake. I can take care of myself."

"You didn't last night."

"You'd better go."

"If you'd listen to me calmly and hear what I'm trying to say to you, we could come back from this."

"I don't think so. You and I are business partners again. Nothing more."

ON THE DAY the memorial committee had scheduled to meet, a snowstorm blew into town, twisting leftover Christmas decorations and loose newspapers around Fairlove's noted federal architecture.

Leota had left home early. Nick and Clair had reached an impasse. The anger she felt simmering between them had to be real. Neither stayed longer than necessary in a room with her, but she looked forward to seeing them together in full view of the executors today.

When she arrived at the courthouse, Mayor Townsend greeted her in the rotunda. "I believe Dr. Dylan is waiting." Deep in an apparently impromptu conference with the school superintendent, Bob waved for an assistant who showed Leota to the correct conference room on the second floor.

Leota stood back as the woman opened the door. Dr. Fortnam had asked her if rage-filled thoughts plagued her. She'd lied and said no. Vehemently. He hadn't believed her. He'd asked her to try to turn her anger into acceptance.

"Can I bring you coffee, Mrs. Dylan?"

Leota took one of the deep, cleansing breaths Dr. Fortnam had practiced with her until she'd nearly passed out. Then she stepped inside and met her son's bland gaze. "Morning, Nick. No, thank you, young woman. I see ice water on a tray over there in the corner. I'll serve myself."

"The others should start to trickle in."

Nick closed the file in front of him. "You left the house early."

Was he putting her off or pretending not to know she'd gone to her Clair-imposed doctor's appointment? She plastered on a false smile. Anger management. So far, her anger still managed her.

Dr. Fortnam often reminded her she could go to jail for dropping that match. She shouldn't have told him the truth about the fire, but he might be the only human being she'd ever know who was willing to believe she'd dropped the match accidentally.

"Leota?" Nick set the folder away from him. "Are you all right?"

Fortnam had persuaded her she needed to show her son she could learn to cope better. Giving in to Nick's and Clair's demands didn't have to mean failure.

"I saw your doctor friend, Fortnam."

A pleased smile lightened his expression. "You saw him today?"

Oddly, she wanted him to be pleased. She wanted to believe her son cared more about her. She couldn't let him see how his concern mattered to her though. She met his softness with aggression. Maybe he'd finally come to his senses about that woman. "I brought the bill, if you need to see it."

"I believe you." He lifted his hands, placating her. "I'm glad you went. You'll try to keep an open mind?"

"What choice do I have?"

"Open, not resigned, Leota."

"I'm tired of you calling me by my first name. How do you think other people look at us when they hear that?"

"I don't care how other people look at us." Nick rolled his chair back and poured two glasses of ice water, one of which he handed to her. "You should try not caring."

"If you don't care, why did you marry Clair?"

He paused, water glass in hand. "I won't talk about my wife with you."

"You would have contested your father's will if you didn't care what people thought about our family."

Taking his seat again, Nick set his glass on a coaster at his elbow. "I'll tell you this much. I first saw Clair planting flowers at her old house. You know, those purple and pink things that were growing beside the door before the house burned down?"

"I saw them." His remark about the fire annoyed her, but he didn't seem to want her to confess her supposed sins.

"I watched her for half an hour before she realized I was behind her. She was singing and digging, and she looked more content than I've ever felt. I wanted to look at my life the way she looks at hers."

"You didn't know how bitter she was then?"

"I didn't realize everything our family had taken from her. How much did you know?"

Leota sipped her water. "I knew nothing about the mortgage until the people in the moving vans began to load up the Athertons' belongings." She turned to the window. "That was the day I knew I'd lost Jeff to Sylvie Atherton forever. He couldn't have kept hating her all those years if he hadn't truly loved her."

"Jeff's blindness didn't make you unlovable."

Leota faced her grown child, enraged that he should try to make her feel better about his father's indifference.

"What?" he asked clearly confused at her expression.

The mayor opened the door and brought Wilford, the city councilmen and the other two executors, Jim Dale and Greg Andrews, at his heels. They all took their seats. Bob looked to Nick.

"Clair's on her way?"

"I expect her any time." His casual tone drew Leota's interest. A different note than the one he and Clair struck at home. "She was scheduled to replace a broken water pipe this morning."

He didn't even seem embarrassed that his wife stuck like glue to her menial job. Leota tilted her chair, picking up the pen beside the yellow pad in front of her. What kind of son had she raised?

Dr. Fortnam had asked her that same question, but she didn't feel despair when she asked herself. Strange how the absence of a familiar sensation could feel almost like pain.

"Here's Clair." Bob looked through the window into the hall.

Leota forced a smile. Clair appeared at the door, her long curls damp, her navy corduroy skirt too short. Nick smiled at her the way he always did—as if he'd like to be alone with her.

"I'm sorry I'm late. I had to go home for a shower. Tim, I'm so glad to see you. I noticed the roofers working on the house, but I don't think they're putting up the shingles I asked for."

"What?"

"They seem lighter, more gray than black."

"Excuse me." Tim stood, pulling out his cell phone. "I'll stop them, and we'll go by after this meeting if you have some time."

At least she and Paul had finished the fountain. From now on, Leota would hire another landscaper if she had to find one in New England.

"If we can all get ourselves on the same page," Bob Townsend called, "let's discuss the suggestions

Nick and Clair and Tim have brought us. What we have here,'' Bob said, ''is a haven for the children of Fairlove. I don't know if we can afford a day-care center, a playground and a clinic, but I say we ask for a plan that includes our wish list and trim from there. Tim, what's your availability?''

''I've done windows, floors and walls at Clair and Nick's, so I'll soon be grateful for another project to work on while I wait for the subs to do their finishing touches.''

Nick cut in. ''Before we start to trim our ideas, I'd like to take the plans to our estate attorneys. Even though you all suggested the memorial for my father, Clair and I brought up the center. I think the senator would have wanted to help our children, but I don't believe he'd want the town to absorb the cost. We own some land at the north end of town that would make a perfect site, and this idea is important enough to us that we'd like to find funds to salt the pot with.''

Leota bit her tongue to keep from swallowing it.

FOR TWO WEEKS, Ernest tried to call Leota, but she refused to speak to him. Finally he stationed himself outside Mrs. Peabody's on Leota's bridge day. She spied him the moment she came out, and she turned in the other direction.

''Leota, wait. I just want to ask how you are.''

''I'm fine. I'm seeing a doctor I don't need. I'm living in a house with a woman you helped blackmail me, and my son doesn't seem to live there anymore.''

''What do you mean?''

''His office is so busy he's had to hire his receptionist back full-time. Seems that busybody Selina Franklin went around telling people they should go to him for treatment or they'd lose his services altogether." She tapped her finger against her cheek. "Or maybe he and Clair have argued. He's hardly ever home. I wonder if he's sleeping back at his house again."

"Without Clair?"

"Makes you think, doesn't it? No one believed me when I said their marriage wasn't real. Do you want to be my witness against them?"

"I don't think the counseling has begun to help you yet."

"I told you I don't need it."

"Don't you love your son?"

"Because I love Nick, I want him to have a good marriage. I don't want him pretending with Clair Atherton, just to keep a pile of bricks and some land."

Ernest's eyes narrowed. "You'd sell your soul for that pile of bricks. As far as I'm concerned you did sell your soul when you married Dr. Dylan's father." His accusation startled him. He'd never realized how little respect he had for the senator. "Don't throw your son away. You'll lose that boy if you don't stop trying to ruin his marriage."

"That boy is thirty-two years old and none of your business." Leota twisted away from him. "Stay out of my life, Ernest. If you couldn't show up when I needed you, I don't want you now."

Shocked, he watched her flounce away. "Leota," he shouted, turning every head on the street except hers. "When did you ever need me?" Had she tried to reach him? Had he let her down? When?

"I asked you to meet me the day I knew I was pregnant," she said.

"I was a kid, just a teenager."

She shrugged. "We all have excuses for the mistakes we make that hurt the people we love." She walked away, and he stared after her. If she knew he'd cared about her, why wouldn't she stay to argue their differences out?

In the four weeks that had passed since she'd made love with her husband, Clair had recognized changes. The weather had already begun to warm in these longer February days. Nick had retired to his dignified but detached corner in their silent battle, and she missed him deeply.

Most of all, she feared she had morning sickness.

At first, she blamed her nausea on her unrequited need for a man who could turn his back on her. A test would tell her the truth, but she was afraid to take it. Despite her brave talk that night at Selina's, she'd backed herself into a decision she didn't want to make.

To take her mind off Nick and herself out of his house, she'd begun to devote her nonworking hours to her new home. Tim had been right. She'd fallen for the new house. She found herself humming as she cleaned her windows. Maybe half the size of its predecessor, her new home was cozy, where as the other house had been a record of her family's history.

A grinding sound on the gravel announced the arrival of one of Tim's trucks. Clair strolled out to the porch as Tim himself stepped out of the driver's seat. He waved and went around to the back of the truck, where he began to unwrap a large square object.

"What'd you bring?" she called, shielding her eyes from the cold sun.

"A surprise. I kind of hoped you wouldn't be here. You couldn't go away and pretend you haven't seen me, could you?"

"Not if you have a gift." Her curiosity piqued, she jumped off the porch and hurried across the hard ground.

"Be a good sport. I need to set it up so it will look perfect when you see it."

"You really want me to go away?" The heavy packing cloths hid a mysterious lump. "Can you even carry this by yourself?"

"I brought a dolly, and I think I can manage. What were you doing inside?"

"Cleaning windows."

"Go upstairs and do the ones in the master bedroom. When I yell, you can come down here and sand the porch.'"

"Sand it?" She turned back doubtfully.

"The painters dripped paint on it when they did the porch ceiling. Hurry up, Clair, before it gets dark."

She went, feeling a bit more optimistic. Surprises could be cool.

A couple of crashes and some pretty impressive swearing floated up the narrow stairs and down the hall to her bedroom. Smiling to herself, Clair finished cleaning the windows and then sat cross-legged in the middle of the floor.

Three more bedrooms, one hardly bigger than a closet lay down the hall, but this room she'd already claimed for herself. She tried to picture the bed she'd ordered, a sleigh bed that would fit a family of four.

She tried to picture her family-to-be. Two children, a boy and a girl? Two boys? Two girls who'd never know the loneliness, the fear she'd fought along with the other pangs of adolescence. Those girls looked familiar. Long, shiny, straight black hair. Blue eyes that never darkened with more knowledge than little girls should possess.

Clair stood up and tossed her cleaning cloth at the window. Her imaginary daughters looked too much like Nick. How could she think of sharing a child with him?

When she'd most needed him, he'd taken up familiar Dylan ways. He'd lied to her about the insurance money, and the moment he'd awakened in the bed they'd made love in, he'd offered to save the day for her just as his father had for Leota. What if Nick couldn't help being like his father? She didn't want a child they'd made to trap him into a lifelong commitment.

She rubbed her hand across her belly. Stress could cause this sensation of constant nausea. Only, stress had never affected her this way before.

"Okay, Clair. Come on down. Don't come in here, though."

Tim had thoughtfully set up the sander for her next to a mask. Clair slipped the mask over her nose and mouth and flipped the switch on the machine. With the work she did for Paul and Tim, she'd soon be ready to star in one of those do-it-yourself shows.

She concentrated on the roar of the sander, the bits of sawdust spraying out from under it. She managed to put Nick out of her mind, becoming one with her work. After she'd been sanding in one direction for about ten minutes, she turned. Tim, standing in the doorway, startled the living daylights out of her.

He laughed at her ridiculous shriek and pulled the sander plug. "Come with me, tough woman."

Making a rude face, she followed him inside to the library. The window he'd installed where her plain, square, picture window had been took her breath away. Squares of stained glass transformed the orange sunset into jewel tones in the shapes of buildings that had graced Fairlove's Main Street for a hundred years. In the center of the window, Tim had rebuilt her old house in glass.

Tears grabbed at Clair's throat. She turned to him, her hands open wide.

"Thank you." She couldn't think of another word. "Thank you."

He nodded toward the window on the left side of the room. "He asked me to make it."

Clair looked. Outside, despite his nonchalant stance and attitude, Nick couldn't quite hide his uncertainty about his welcome. "My husband?"

"Yep. Why don't you go thank him? I kind of rushed, and I'd like to make sure everything's set in case we have a storm."

The walk to Nick was one of the longest trips she'd

ever made. She didn't know what to say. She was still angry that he'd already made their decision, as if she were just a body he'd slept with. Suffering from a painful contradiction, she still craved the sight of his face, the husky tone of his voice. Though she dreaded being near him she was angry he found staying away so easy.

He started toward her when she was still ten feet or so away. "Do you like it?"

"I love it. It's beautiful."

"It's Fairlove. You didn't think it was cheesy?"

"I was away for twelve years. I think it's a perfect homecoming gift." Would asking if he'd ordered it before they'd argued be ungracious? "I'm not sure I can—"

Weariness cloaked his face. "You will accept it."

"I'm going to try to say this without offending you, but when you tell me what I will do, you annoy me."

"What am I going to do with—"

"Thank you for the window," she interrupted, sliding her hand down her shirt to flatten her palm against her belly. They might have a larger problem to solve.

"Truce?"

"Huh?"

"Can we agree on a truce, Clair?"

"I guess we'd better. We have to present a united front at the groundbreaking next weekend. Did Wilford show you the papers on opening the grant for applicants?"

"You could have given me the papers."

"I haven't seen much of you. Where have you been the past few weeks?"

"Working. Word must have gone around that I don't kill my patients. I've delivered three babies."

"A population explosion." She dug the toe of her shoe into the ground. "Thank you again for the window. Would you like to come in and see it?"

To her surprise, as she turned away from him, he took her hand. She started to tug away, but stopped herself. Nick glanced past her to the house. "For Tim's benefit."

Tim beamed at them both from the doorway. Clan felt the weight of her false status as Nick's bride as she led him past the builder.

She preceded Nick into the library, then watched him look down at the floor at the gemstone patterns of light. Nick's smile, when he finally turned his gaze to the window, weakened her resolve to keep herself safe from him.

He glanced at Tim. "I can't believe you were able to do this in such a short time."

"I surprised myself. My bill will surprise you."

"Whatever you charge, I'll gladly pay."

Nick's honest enjoyment made her forget the obstacles between them. If only they could both forget the years of disappointment he'd suffered at his father's hands, the pain Jeff's bitterness still caused him. She wouldn't court that kind of parenting for her child, and what else could Nick know?

Tim pounded Nick's shoulder. "I'm kidding. Apart from a few extra supplies, the bill will be what I quoted you."

"At your prices, my father would have asked you

to put a Fairlove building in each window of his house.''

Tim chuckled. ''Real vote getter, huh?''

Laughing, Nick slid his arm around Clair's shoulders, the way any loving husband might. She wanted to pull away. His touch had become oppressively familiar, but she'd made a bargain, and she'd stand by her promise.

''JEFF AND LEOTA sent him away when he was just a little kid. They didn't value him. How can I trust a man with that kind of upbringing to be a good parent?''

Two days before the groundbreaking ceremony, Clair had turned to Selina in an attack of panic and guilt. Selina looked dumbfounded. ''Are you sure you're pregnant?''

''I took three tests. They all turned out positive.''

''You have to tell Nick. I can't believe you'd consider keeping his baby a secret.''

Selina's disapproval spooked Clair. ''Please don't say anything to the judge. I don't want anyone to tell Nick. I'll tell him when I'm ready.''

''So you said. Have you seen your doctor?''

''No. Who would I see? Nick must know every doctor in this part of Virginia. They all volunteer at Staunton.''

''He has a right to know about his baby. Didn't you consider what kind of father he'd be?''

She might have if she'd ever intended being foolish enough to risk pregnancy. ''I didn't think.''

''Nick's been a good husband to you.''

"Wait until he's faced with early-morning feedings and dirty diapers. Wait until he has to answer a question for the sixtieth time."

"You need him to answer one question now. Give him a chance to tell you he wants to be a father to his child."

"I can't explain, Selina. It was something he said." That he wouldn't abandon her if she was pregnant. She didn't want him to see her as someone he owed. "I could imagine him being as miserable about the baby as his father was about him. I refuse to allow any son or daughter of mine to feel abandoned."

"Don't wait too long, Clair. You need prenatal care. You should establish a relationship with the doctor who'll deliver your baby."

First, she had to figure out her relationship with her baby's father. Nick had a right to know, but did she have the courage to tell him? The moment she did, she'd find out whether he was a Dylan or Nick, the man she'd almost trusted.

CLAIR'S FINGERS SHOOK as she fastened her earring, preparing for the ground-breaking ceremony. Nick opened the bedroom door behind her and came into the room. She ate him up with her eyes. Her hunger for him had nothing to do with how handsome he invariably looked in the dark suits he favored. After that day at her house, she had to keep maintaining her distance from him, because she had to hide her morning sickness—which didn't seem to keep regular hours.

"Hi," she said in a softer tone than she'd intended.

"Are you ready?" His glance matched hers for appetite.

She didn't doubt he cared for her in some way, but she was no bright, shining deb in her first season, the kind of wife Leota and Jeff would have chosen for him.

Clair had to assume, for her child's sake, that Nick might revert to type and think she wasn't good enough to mother his baby. Looking away from him, she stepped into her shoes.

"I'm ready. Mr. Hunter's riding with us?"

He nodded, his expression slightly defensive. "He's part of the family."

"Did Jeff think so?"

"I've tried to explain Jeff to myself. He thought the way his parents taught him. I'd like to believe he started life in a different time, and he couldn't help the way he judged people."

Clair's heart ballooned and fell. "You're excusing him?"

"I'm trying to understand him."

"But do you feel empathy?"

"Are you testing me? What do I win if I pass?"

He probably thought she was still holding a grudge for his "morning after" promise. Heaven knew she firmly believed he'd threatened her with a life like his.

But her conscience prodded her. Until she told him about their baby, he didn't stand a chance of changing her mind. If she told him and he couldn't be a good father, she would risk her child's emotional future.

"We should go." She ignored his biting question

about winning. "We don't want to be late climbing the stairs to the podium."

"This is your last chance, Clair. Let me give you the first grant for school."

Their talk about college for her seemed far in the past, and even though her baby made her education more important than ever, she said, "I wish I could say yes, but I can't accept payment for our marriage."

"How many times do you have to base your decisions on your need to be independent?"

"I don't know, but I'll meet you in the car." She was so tired and nauseous she prayed they'd reach the community-center site before her nausea turned into a crisis.

NICK LOOKED OUT over the crowd. Despite the cold, most of Fairlove's citizens huddled in chairs the council had set up on the Dylan-estate land he was about to donate. He and Clair had insisted everyone in Fairlove be invited to today's presentation. The faces in front of him belonged to his past and his future. He'd delivered two of the babies fussing on their moms' shoulders.

And he'd fallen in love with the slight woman in the red dress and blue coat whose physical presence he felt behind him.

Clair had lost weight. His concern for her nagged at him, but he pulled the microphone forward.

"Good morning, and welcome. Today, we celebrate two events. I'd like to tell you first about the Atherton-Franklin Grant for Living. This is a special grant designed for mature learners who can come up with college tuition, but need help with living expenses.

"My wife suggested this grant, because she herself could have used this kind of assistance. She's a courageous woman who has learned from the mistakes she made in her young-adult years. She'd like to prevent other young people from going without education, and I admit to you all, I admire her more for bringing this need to public attention than I would for all the degrees she'd like to have earned."

The applause that met his words surprised him. As he waited for it to die, he turned to look at Clair. Her warm smile bridged the gaps of distance and mistrust between them. Though he was reluctant to tarnish the unexpected moment of understanding, he turned back to the crowd.

"The town council has given us an opportunity to help the town in another way. They proposed a memorial to my father."

He stopped. Now came the part he dreaded, the part where he had to paint his father as a man capable of thinking of a center to benefit the children in the town Nick had grown to love. He closed his eyes. He had to describe the kind of father he hoped he might be one day.

THE CATCH in Nick's voice drew Clair's gaze to the back of his neck and shoulders. The tension she saw there made her wish she could protect him. He didn't like people to know he felt vulnerable.

She glanced to her left at Mayor Townsend, whose bland expression indicated he was not paying atten-

tion. To her right, Leota perched as if she might eject
from her chair at any moment. Leota's usually sharp
expression had softened, a change Clair had first noticed in the town council meeting. Had Nick finally
begun to get through to her?

Nick turned his head away to clear his throat, but
the microphone caught the faint sound. Clair edged
to the front of her seat, fighting an urge to go to him.

"Most people I meet call my father 'the senator,'
and he always was. I never knew him when I didn't
have to share him with the people he worked for.
You, and the other citizens of Virginia. But home,
where his heart returned most, was a place he unin-
tentionally neglected. When our town council came
to my wife and me and asked us to help, we wanted
to do what he would have done if he'd had the time."

He took a long sip of water. Again, he turned away
from the microphone, but he couldn't conceal his
shaking hand. His courage suggested Clair might be
wrong when she assumed he was like his father. Had
Jeff Dylan hidden his true nature from everyone? Was
she the only person listening to Nick who knew the
truth?

"We asked the council if we could build a center
for our children, yours and mine. We want to build a
playground and a clinic where we can provide affordable and thorough care. Most important of all, and
this is personal to me, I want to make sure no child
ever has to leave this town because she has no one
to care for her. Here, in our home, we can provide
what public services can't. We can treat each child as
an individual, make the time and the effort to keep

our extended family together. From now on, when my father's name comes up, I'd like us all to think of the good we can do each other in this place named for him—the Senator Jeffrey Dylan Community Center.''

Silence met these last low-spoken words. Clair gripped the arms of her chair and pushed herself to her feet. She felt Leota's movement behind her, but she didn't care what Leota or anyone else thought. She walked to her husband, more aware than ever of the astounding strength that enabled him to bare his soul in front of all these people.

She pressed her hand to the center of Nick's back. He jumped, but then he faced her and reached for her hand. He covered the microphone with his other palm.

''I should have told you what I was going to say,'' he said.

''No.'' She thought of the child she carried, the child he didn't know about. She wanted to believe in Nick. ''I wish someone like you had stood up for me all those years ago.''

Nick leaned down and pressed his lips to her temple. He held her at his side as he addressed the crowd again.

''Please, all of you, come back to this site to help us build the center. Selina Franklin found a book on building playground equipment, so we already have plenty of work to go around. Come when you can. All hands are welcome.''

Now the applause returned. Enthusiastic applause. Clair let Nick lead her away from the center of the podium. Lost in new faith for the man who'd given that speech, a man who could not have been more unlike Jeff Dylan, Clair indulged in the unexpected serenity of her relief.

She could tell Nick about the baby. He'd protect their child. If he believed in the extended family he'd described, his child would be precious to him. She could believe in him. He'd consistently put his mother first. He'd even tried to help Clair when she'd needed him.

Leota's stony face seemed to rise out of the crowd that had climbed onto the podium to congratulate Nick. Ice-cold hatred shone diamond hard from her eyes, and Clair finally understood.

Leota believed Clair and Nick's marriage was real—that they'd both learned to love. And she could not allow her son, a Dylan, to be happy with an Atherton.

Clair wrapped her hand in the cloth of Nick's overcoat as she realized Leota would use any ammunition to destroy an Atherton, and she didn't care if her son's body became a spoil of her war.

Clair's bubble of relief burst. A real wife would stand with her husband, to protect him, even against his mother.

"How could you?" the older woman hissed at her son. She used her elbows to maintain her position in front of him in the crowd. "Do you know what you just did to your father's memory? How long will it take the national reporters to note he never did anything for this hick town? How long until they point out the differences between his record and what you just said he'd want? You've glorified your priorities at your father's expense, and I won't let you get away with it. I'll tell everyone the truth about your marriage. You *paid* Clair Atherton, and you know I can prove it.''

''Stop it, Mother.''

Clair saw Leota's hesitation, saw her look at him, closely, as if she finally recognized the depth of Nick's pain. ''Why did you call me that?''

''You're trying to hurt Clair, but if you do that you'll drive a wedge between you and me, Leota. Talk to me privately. You know my feelings about providing services for this town can't hurt Jeff's image. Come home with us now. Don't say anything more.''

Leota pointed at Wilford. ''After he tells you what to say? No thanks.'' She took a silent poll of the white-haired men and women, the town council and the executors, who'd closed ranks around them. ''Explain your marriage to them, not to me.''

''Nick,'' Bob Townsend began, ''we want to end this kind of talk here. You and Clair are newlyweds. Are you having problems?''

Nick hesitated with a searching, hungry look at Clair. She lifted her hand to her stomach. She carried proof that would stop the executors from taking anything from him, but she didn't want him to find out about the baby this way. Clair slid a glance toward Leota. What would that woman do to her grandchild? With all the force of her will, Clair silently begged Nick's mother to back down.

Meeting Clair's eyes, Leota's fury erased all signs of her softening toward Nick. ''I want to talk to the executors about the two of you and your separate rooms. They'll be interested in the nights Nick doesn't come home and the fact you're barely speaking to each other.''

Clair turned to Nick. Would he forgive her for not telling him about their child before now? Before Leota left her no choice.

She took his face in her hands and willed him to believe in her love for him, which all but robbed her of the ability to speak. "I'm sorry to tell you like this," she said. He caught her arms, his concern for her cutting bone deep, making her feel she'd betrayed him. She glanced swiftly at the people around them, not stopping at Leota, before she turned back to Nick. "I'm pregnant."

His face blanched. Unspeakable happiness flamed in his eyes. Clair felt its power, and for a second, she thought they were going to be all right.

"A baby?" His voice was a deep river that would support her all their lives together. Abruptly, a frown drained the happiness from his face. "But...how long have you known?"

Clair broke free of his hold. She turned toward the tent behind the podium. "Not long. A few weeks. Could we speak in private? I'd like to explain."

"A few weeks?" He shook his head. His trust in her drained from his dark blue eyes. "You have nothing to explain. Just tell me why you waited until now. Make me believe you planned to tell me sometime."

CHAPTER THIRTEEN

NICK LED his wife to the tent. Awareness of her pregnancy kept his touch gentle, though he was furious and hurt. "Answer me." The tent flap had hardly closed. Nick watched every movement Clair made. She danced around a chair, putting it between them.

"I thought I couldn't trust you. I knew how your parents treated you, and I didn't want to risk having my baby grow up in that kind of family."

His heart ached at her lack of faith, at her opinion of him. He put his hand to his chest. She should have known him better. After all this time, she should have known he wasn't like his father.

"Jeff made you think you weren't good enough," Clair continued. "Leota resented you. They sent you away to school when you were only eight years old. When you told me you'd stay married to me if I was pregnant, I heard you say you'd be there for me and my child the way Jeff was for Leota and you."

He gripped the back of the chair. "I haven't treated you the way Jeff treated anyone. Why hasn't my care of you told you what kind of man I am?"

"I did realize, when you were talking out there, that you weren't the man I feared. I was going to tell you when we left here. I know how lame that sounds, but I would have told you."

Nick pushed the chair aside. "I'm tired of trying to prove I'm a good man—to Jeff and Leota, to you, most of all. I've kept my promises to you, except for that damned insurance money, and I've made that up and then some."

"We've become friends. Until now we've stood by each other. That didn't make us a good parenting team in my mind."

"A team? What are you talking about? I'm talking family. Haven't you felt the times I've gone out of my way to be fair to you because of what my family's done?"

"I need to trust your instincts, but when push came to shove, your choices frightened me."

Fear felt like a good excuse to take his child from him? He stared at the woman he'd loved and saw a stranger. "You can't look past what you think you know about me to see who I am. I want to be your husband, but you're hiding, because you'd rather be alone than commit. I'd protect you from anything that could hurt you, Clair, but I won't let you pretend I'm not the man who should be my child's father."

"Give me a chance, Nick. I made a mistake."

"What kind of chance did you give me? How did you plan to hide my child from me? How do I know you aren't still lying about what you want? Remember, we don't think alike. Your words." He shook his head as if he'd come to a decision. "I suggest we make an arrangement, like the prenuptial contract. After our year is up, we'll stick to visitation terms for taking care of the child.''

He made blindly for the tent flap. Outside, the cold and his neighbors' interest made him want to knock something down.

CLAIR RAN THE GAUNTLET of community curiosity. She didn't care what anyone thought. She had to reach Nick before he drove away. She grabbed the handle on his car door and pounded on the closed window as he turned the key in the ignition.

He looked as if he'd let her break the window before he'd put it down to talk to her. At last he gave in. ''What more can you say?''

''Don't go.'' She shook the handle in her frustration. She refused to believe nothing could make this better. ''Can't we talk until we find an answer?''

''Your answer was to hide my child.''

She risked everything. ''Don't leave me, Nick.''

''I was never with you. Not so much that you noticed who I was.''

He backed the car out and swung it toward the road. Clair's legs wobbled. She almost sank to the ground, but her miserable pride saved her from collapse. She didn't want to show anyone her heart was breaking.

She started walking. Nick had reached out to her from the moment she'd met him. She'd pushed him too far, and she'd inflicted hurt on him beyond anything Jeff had done. She'd asked him for guarantees, but she hadn't been willing to look at possibilities.

Selina's car pulled up beside her and the window

on the passenger side descended. "Let me give you a ride, Clair."

"I need to go back to his house."

"You'll ask him to start over?"

"I have no choice."

"Come on, then. Hurry before those reporters catch up."

In silence, they drove as far as her new house. "Could you slow down?" Hoping against all logic that Nick might have gone there, she looked for his car, but the house stood silent and still. Not yet a home. "Okay, better go on."

At Nick's house, Selina pulled to one side of the drive. No sign of Nick's car here, either, but maybe he'd parked in the garage. "Do you want me to come in?" Selina asked.

"No. I have to handle this on my own." She heard Nick's accusation that she couldn't commit. He always thought she'd cut off her nose to spite her face. "But I may come back to your place later. If he doesn't want me to stay."

The Dylan house stood as empty as hers. Not even Leota or Hunter had returned. Clair wandered from room to room. Every sound sent her to the window. In the study, Kitty dropped off a bookshelf to wind treacherously between her feet. Clair fed him, grateful for his company in the silent house.

She no longer understood what had so frightened her. She no longer felt her old compulsion to keep herself safe with independence.

She only knew she loved Nick Dylan. She would fight for him if he gave her one more chance.

FOR HOURS, NICK DROVE through the hills around Fairlove. Clair's inability to see him hurt more than all his parents' petty betrayals combined. They'd simply been bad parents, too self-absorbed to care for a child who'd craved their love.

But Clair wasn't a self-absorbed person. He'd seen her step outside her own best interests more than once. But not for him. She'd accused him of returning to type, but she'd run from him because of the way he'd phrased a promise. She'd heard it as a threat.

Her reasons for not telling him about the baby hurt more than the fact that she hadn't. When he'd lied about the insurance payment, she'd blamed their inability to view the world the same way. Was this any different?

He needed her to believe in him. He needed her belief before he could trust her love.

Nick peered through his windshield at the night sky. He'd promised to stay married to her, but he'd wanted to ask her to make their marriage real. Was he willing to throw away a bond that had made him believe in his own ability to love?

No. But he was angry, even though he understood the patterns that had made her decide not to trust him. He also understood that she, of all people he knew, would protect her child with everything she had.

Still, he had to make sure she loved him. She'd come to him for a house his father had stolen from her family, a symbol that meant more than boards and plaster to her. She'd stayed with him because of strings he'd wrapped around her.

Now he had to know she wanted him because he

was the man who loved her, the man she was supposed to spend the rest of her life with. If she believed in him, he'd fight to gain and keep her trust from now until doomsday.

Nick turned toward Fairlove. He opened the glove box and pulled out his cell phone. Wilford answered on the first ring.

"Nick, don't ever do this again. I've been worried about you."

Nick shook his head in the darkness of his car. Slowly but steadily, he was working toward caring relationships. "I have a task for you."

"Glad to help."

"You won't be, but I don't want an argument, and I don't care how many judges you have to drag out of bed. I want you to sign Clair's house over to her now. As in today." He tilted the face of his watch, but the dial looked blank. "Whatever time it is."

"I'm on it, Nick."

Wilford's meek agreement startled him, but he took it in stride. "Can you do it tonight, Wilford?"

"What do you think you pay me for? Can you give Leota a call? I finally persuaded her to go home, but she's worried you'll wrap your car around a tree or something. She's blaming this afternoon on Clair, but I think she finally sees her own part in the chaos."

"I'll call her."

Nick dialed, and gratefully listened to the answering machine in the kitchen. He told Hunter he was all right and asked him to pass the news along to his mother or Clair if they showed up.

By the time he arrived at Wilford's office, the attorney had his deed in an envelope. Nick thanked him and drove to Clair's house. Their home soon, if she was truly willing to try again.

No one answered when he knocked. She must have gone to his house. He hoped so. After this afternoon, she wouldn't go back there if she wasn't serious about him.

In his own driveway, Fosdyke's car sat behind Clair's. Nick parked his car, his relief at knowing Clair was home tempered by unease for Leota. If Fosdyke had found better proof, he'd have brought the police.

Leota's voice reached him the moment he opened the door. "Nick will never give me a chance to apologize."

Upstairs, a door opened. Nick smiled as he recognized Clair's quick steps, but Fosdyke's response to Leota distracted him.

"He'll forgive you. If he didn't love you, he wouldn't have moved back into this house."

Nick looked up as Clair rounded the landing. Her wide, welcoming smile sent a bolt of unexpected desire through him, which he restrained. They had to sort themselves out before they made love again. He lifted his index finger to his lips to ask her not to speak.

She nodded, looking wary as Leota went on.

"I don't know if I married Jeff because I loved him or because he was a way out of a poverty-ridden life as a nobody in this town. He only married me because I was pregnant. Instead of resenting Jeff, I blamed my son."

Her admission tore at him as if he were still a child. But he preferred her honesty to the pretty family pictures they'd made in the past. Leaving Clair in the hall, Nick stalked into the study and asked Leota the question he'd never dared voice.

"When will you stop resenting me? When will we salvage what's left of our family?"

Leota spun around, tears starting to her eyes. "I'd like to stop now, Nick. I can learn to control what I feel."

A grown man, he ached because his mother couldn't love him freely. "Why do you have to control yourself? What did I do to you?"

"Nothing. You don't know what life was like for me, what I gave up for you. You weren't to blame, but Jeff told me in small ways every day that he could have won Sylvie back if I hadn't gotten pregnant. Then, you weren't the kind of son he wanted. You were always at odds with him, and he blamed me." She choked off a sob. "None of your father's and my selfishness and resentment is your fault, but I'm trying to explain the way it seemed to me."

Her old viewpoint only hurt him, but tonight, he was determined to salvage his life. "If you can accept me, can you accept Clair?"

"I owe you both a thank-you for not sending me to jail. I'm not a new woman here, but I am tired. I don't want to hurt you any more, Nick."

He tried to feel gratitude. Instead, he still wished she could love him. "Did you burn down Clair's house?"

"I'm not sure I want to know that."

He turned to see Clair behind him. He moved to stand by her shoulder and said, "I don't think she did it on purpose."

Leota slid her index fingers beneath her eyes, to blot her mascara. "Thank you for that, too, son."

Nick's eyes stung with sudden tears as she called him "son." He needed his mother, as she needed him. She looked squarely at Clair.

"I was smoking a cigarette down by your house— I'd just gone there for a look—and I dropped a match in the grass. I thought it was out, but it must not have been. It must have blown against your house. No one will ever trust I didn't do it on purpose. I won't blame you or Nick if you can't."

Nick believed her. For what it was worth, he believed her.

Clair didn't answer Leota at first. Finally she said, "You understand my child makes a connection between us we can never break?" Her calm swelled Nick's pride.

"You'll let me see the baby?"

"Until the first time you say a hurtful word. Also, Leota, you can't malign my parents. I plan to make sure their memory stays alive."

"I'll stay in therapy, and I'll try my best to be a better grandparent than I've been a mother."

Nick left Clair's side to go to Leota. He'd moved back into this house he couldn't love, hoping for the change Leota had just promised to make. He wouldn't let her go. "You can still be a mother if you want. I haven't stopped being your son."

"You forgive me?"

Her quavering voice made him want to protect her. "I forgive you, but I'll have to learn to trust you. Just as Clair will." He curved his hand around her shoulder. For the first time he could remember, his mother didn't flinch away from his affection. "I'm glad I moved back here."

"Nick." She covered her face to hide her tears. He held her, watching Clair's eyes tear up behind his mother's back. "I care about you, too, Nick. I didn't know how much until I hurt you this afternoon. I forgot you in my anger at the past, at Clair and her family." She wiped her eyes dry. "I know now that I have to deal with Jeff and my life here, instead of blaming my unhappiness on you and Clair."

His heart warmed by her effort, Nick hugged her, but let her go before she could feel pressured. "Clair and I still have some conversation to finish, so I'm taking her upstairs now. We'll see you at breakfast in the morning."

"Good night," Leota said through trembling lips.

When Nick turned back to Clair, he found she'd gone. Ernest stood, frozen at the door, as though they'd caught him sneaking out. He offered a sheepish smile.

"She must have wanted to let you talk to each other alone. I'm on my way, too."

"No, don't go." He glanced at his mother. "Unless you want to be alone?"

"No, I'd like Ernest to stay." She took a deep breath. "If you can spare the time, Ernest."

Nick said another good-night to them both and made his way to the stairs.

Ernest's voice floated up. "You haven't eaten anything this evening, Leota. I'd like to take you out." He sounded as if he feared being rejected, too. "I left my fire truck at the station."

"Too bad. A ride in your truck would have proved I'm sincere."

Nick laughed. Apparently his mother heard him. She called another half-tentative good-night.

CLAIR LET OUT HER BREATH as her doorknob turned. He'd come home to her, as well.

"Clair?"

He stepped inside, and she felt safe. For now. How different her world seemed because she could admit she loved Nick.

"Can I tell you again how sorry I am?" she said. "I don't know where we stand."

He pulled an envelope from his lapel pocket. "Read this, and I guess we'll both see."

Warily, she slid her finger under the flap and pulled out a folded packet of papers that Nick took from her and unfolded. He handed her the deed to her house and land. He'd signed it over to her. Disillusionment fell on her, heavy as a lead blanket.

"Why did you do this?" She refolded it. "I don't want it. You should have talked to me."

His gaze narrowed, but she couldn't tell if he was hopeful or angry. "I thought you'd want it. I didn't attach strings."

"No strings?" She waved the papers, fear making her sharp. She didn't want to lose him. She didn't want to believe he'd try another game with her. "You tried to force money on me when the insurance settlement didn't match what I needed. How is this different? I don't want a gift. We aren't going to trade access to a baby for my house.''

Nick pulled her around to face him, locking his hands on her shoulders. ''You don't understand. I'm giving you the house because I don't want an unfair advantage over you. I'm trying to ask you to stay married to me, but I don't want you to do it because I own your house.''

She searched his eyes and found tenderness. ''It isn't necessary. The house is yours, too. You can keep it. I'd like to live with you in it.''

''And the commitment?'' he asked.

''I can't be more committed to you.'' She took his hand and laid it against her belly. ''This is a life we created, and I want you with me. Maybe I was wrong about our not thinking alike. If you'd just burn that deed and trust me, we could learn to be two halves of a whole.''

''I gave you the deed because I love you.'' He knelt at her feet and pressed his mouth to her belly. ''I love our child, and I want all of us to move into The Oaks for that fresh start I tried to interest you in before.''

Hope rose again in her, like a balloon full of the sweetest, lightest air. She dropped to her knees beside him. ''As long as we're equal partners from now on.'' She wrapped her arms around him. ''I love you dearly, but I'm afraid we're going to drive each other crazy for the rest of our lives.''

He laughed into her hair. ''We don't have to think

alike. We'll learn to ask questions before we leap to conclusions.''

She kissed him, drawing passion from him, offering her own. She tasted her tears, but she let them flow. She wasn't ashamed of loving her husband enough to cry. This man, her strong husband whose bravery had put hers to shame when she'd needed it most, wanted to belong to her.

''How did you decide to come back?'' she asked.

''I love you. I've always wanted a life different from my parents. I married you knowing I was hurting my mother and destroying my father's last plan for me. I never expected I'd love you for yourself. All my life, I wondered—like other kids wonder about the bogeyman—whether my father was right about me, but he was wrong about everything. He never loved my mother. He never loved me. He never gave enough of himself to understand love. I may have to learn to be a good husband to you as we go.''

''I'm sorry I misjudged you.'' She wished she could erase those days and weeks. ''I thought I could make this marriage on my terms, but you kept changing what I wanted. You were kind to your mother, no matter how she behaved. You didn't hold grudges against the people who didn't trust you. You kept trying to make me see I didn't have to be a loner anymore. I've never known a man who gives the way you do, but I thought the real you was in your mistakes.''

''Let's put all our mistakes behind us. We'll probably come up with new ones, but for tonight, let's forget the past and celebrate our future.''

He stood and pulled her onto the bed with him. She savored the rush of his desire. His kiss, both gentle and demanding, worked its magic. She felt freedom she'd only read about in stories she hadn't believed.

She leaned back, licking her bottom lip. Nick's brooding gaze excited her as he watched the tip of her tongue. "Hmm," she said. "You taste different without all those secrets and doubts between us."

"An arousing turn of events."

"How aroused are you?"

Answering with deed, rather than words, he shrugged off his jacket and pushed it off the bed. Then, he opened the buttons on her blouse and bared her swollen breasts to his hungry mouth. With a replete, masculine sigh, he traced his tongue along a blue vein that radiated from her nipple. Clair pushed his hair away from his forehead.

"These veins," he said, tracing another, "they'd tell me you were pregnant if I didn't know. But how much weight have you lost?"

Laughter bubbled out of her. "I just drive you mad with lust, don't I, Doctor?"

He grinned, his mouth moist against her skin. "Believe me, you do."

"Convince me."

He did.

EPILOGUE

LATE-AUTUMN WINDS pushed leaves across the lawn Clair had lovingly tended all summer. They collected against the golden oak door, now firmly back in its place of honor. From his basket a safe distance from his father's step ladder, three-day-old Sam Dylan made baby exclamations at the clouds that passed overhead.

From his post in front of the basket, Kitty pricked his ears at the unfamiliar sounds issuing from his charge's mouth.

"Let me just check on him, Nick," Clair said. "Don't climb the ladder yet. We have to put up the sign together. That's the tradition."

"I don't care about tradition. Should you be climbing a ladder at all yet?"

Clair grinned at her overprotective husband as she leaned over their son. "Hey. At least I'm not trying to do it by myself."

She ran her index finger down her son's nose. Perfect. Like his father's must have started out. "I hope he's not cold out here."

"Dress a baby as you would dress yourself, and then take off a layer."

"Maybe I'll take off a layer next time we bring him out."

Clair pressed a kiss to Sam's perfect nose and joined her husband beside the ladder he'd opened at her restored front door. She took the sign he held up.

"I would have talked about changing the name if you'd wanted to," she said, running her finger over a curlicue on the *S* in Oaks.

"Why would we change?" Nick looked at the trees around them. "They're all still here."

"Thank you." She kissed his nose too. "Let's do this before the others arrive. This is just for our family."

"Take your end."

They each started up one side of the ladder. As they reached the rungs that put them even with the sign, Nick brushed tears from Clair's face. He replaced the tears with a warm kiss. Smiling at him, she lifted the chain on her side of the sign Nick had burned in Tim's shop. Nick took the other chain and they slipped both ends onto the iron arm at the same time.

Her mouth still trembling, Clair stroked her husband's jaw as the sign swung free. "Thank you."

He cupped her head and kissed her, and she forgot the ladder and the cold air and the fact she'd given birth only three days ago.

"Thank you," he said. He pushed the sign with his finger. "For this home and our son. For love I count on each second of every day."

She let her tears fall. "Our life together is so much more than I hoped for," she said, and Nick helped her from the ladder to take her in his arms.

"I love you." He tightened his embrace. "I never knew how much I could mean those words." He kissed her deeply. After a few moments, they both turned to Sam. "Are you ready to meet your grandma?" Nick lifted the baby to look into his blue, wondering eyes.

Sam squeaked a little. Clair reached for him anxiously, and Kitty scrambled to his feet, as well. "Careful, Nick," Clair said. "He's awfully new."

Nick tucked him close and turned him toward Clair. "Tell your mom you're tough as nails."

"He doesn't have to be tough. We'll be tough for him." Clair leaned against her husband, looking up at their house. "I remember when I thought a few boards and some glass would build a home. I didn't know I needed you, too."

He placed his hand on her shoulder. His gold wedding band reminded her how much she liked marriage.

"I'm just glad we both figured out in time," he said. A car at the edge of the drive made him grow serious. "Leota's here with Ernest. You sure you're up to this?"

"Sam needs to know his grandma, and she needs to know Sam." She looked up. "As long as we don't talk baby-sitting."

His face blanching in mock horror, Nick handed the baby to her and watched as Leota crossed the yard, holding a blue box. Beside her, Ernest cupped her elbow with a proprietary air.

"Presents, Sammy," Nick gloated, leaning over Clair's shoulder. "What do you think of our boy, Ernest?"

"He's fine." The other man held out his hand.
"May I touch him, Clair?"

She glanced self-consciously at Sam before she answered. "I know I'm an angsty new mom, but would
you mind washing your hands first?"

"Not a bit."

"I'll come with you." Leota paused to look at
Clair. "If you don't mind if I hold him?"

"Better hurry, He's due to fall unconscious at any
moment, and Selina and the judge are on their way
over. Selina's pretty bossy."

A smile softened Leota's lovely features from the
inside out. "Thanks, and, Clair?"

"Uh-huh?"

"Don't stop being an angsty mom. I wish I could
go back and be one myself."

Nick put his arm around Leota, and Clair sensed
the effort he put into speaking. A muscle twitched in
his jaw. "You're doing all right, Mother," he said.

Beaming, Leota went with Ernest. Nick picked up
Sam's basket and Clair carried the baby into the library where the Fairlove window overlaid the air with
warm color.

"Leota's changed," Clair said, lowering her voice.

"You're still not sure whether to trust her?"

"I don't let myself think like that. She's tried so
hard."

Nick nodded, his gaze reflective. "Why don't you
two sit down—get this weight off you."

Clair cuddled Sam in her favorite chair. The door
squeaked open, and Kitty muscled into the room. He
lifted his nose, sniffing for the baby. Instead of seeing

Sam as a rival, he'd put the infant nearly on a par with his favorite caviar. He prowled to Clair's chair and lifted his front paws to peer at the baby.

"Still here, 'kay, old buddy."

Kitty glared at Nick for not taking his watchful efforts seriously. Then he turned and marched back to the door, where he resumed his position of protector, sitting regally, ears perked.

Clair leaned into Nick's solid shoulder, trying not to laugh. Ernest and Leota skirted the cat warily as they came back into the room. Leota, especially, seemed not to welcome him.

"You don't leave him alone with Sam, do you?"

"Not so far. Kitty hasn't learned how to use the phone yet." Nick tossed Clair a heart-stopping grin.

Leota tried to quell him, but they'd both moved beyond quelling days. "Let me sit down." Leota took the chair across from Clair's, and Clair stood again to place Sam in his grandmother's arms.

The infant closed his eyes to settle in for a nap. From the floor, Kitty grumbled his dissatisfaction with his charge's new location. Clair stayed close to Leota's shoulder to ease Kitty's anxiety.

"It's not that I don't trust you, Leota. I'm trying to show Kitty I do."

"He's like a dog." Ernest eased behind Leota's chair. "I think I'll just hide my ankles back here."

"Sam," Leota said softly, "you sure look like your father."

"Does he?" Interested, Nick moved behind her other shoulder.

"Remarkably. I'll get out your baby photos. Clair,

I thought you might want to name him for your father."

"I wouldn't do that to you, Leota." She smoothed the blanket back from Sam's dear bald head. "Besides, we don't want him to be a Dylan or an Atherton. He needs to be…Sam. Just our Sam."

Nick took her hand. Lifting her gaze to his, she didn't have to speak again. Nick understood. Of all the men in the world, the one she shouldn't have loved, loved her, and together, they'd made a family.

He pulled her toward the fireplace, away from Leota and Ernest and curved his arm around her neck. "I have some new terms for you."

She nodded, loving him with her eyes.

"What do you say we get married again?"

Clair slid possessive hands around his hard waist, shivering at the friction of his cotton shirt against her bare forearms. "That's a nice idea, but why do we need to? We have a baby we both adore. We're sharing a house we built almost with our own hands. We share a life in a town where we both contribute. I trust you with my son. I trust you with my life. How could our vows be more real?"

He studied her face and then lowered his mouth to hers. He tasted of Nick, spicy, hot-blooded, patience and abiding love. He buried his face in her hair.

"I take you, too, Clair Atherton Dylan. I take you and Sam and this sweet, sweet future we've given each other."

Presenting...

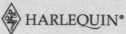

HARLEQUIN®

RX PRESCRIPTION ROMANCE

Get swept away by
these warmhearted romances
featuring dedicated doctors
and nurses.

LOVE IS JUST A HEARTBEAT AWAY!

Available in December
at your favorite retail outlet:

SEVENTH DAUGHTER
by Gill Sanderson
A MILLENNIUM MIRACLE
by Josie Metcalfe
BACHELOR CURE
by Marion Lennox
HER PASSION FOR DR. JONES
by Lillian Darcy

Look for more
Prescription Romances
coming in April 2001.

If you enjoyed what you just read,
then we've got an offer you can't resist!

Take 2 bestselling love stories FREE!
Plus get a FREE surprise gift!

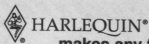

HARLEQUIN®
makes any time special—online...

eHARLEQUIN.com

shop eHarlequin

- ♥ Find all the new Harlequin releases at everyday great discounts.
- ♥ Try before you buy! Read an excerpt from the latest Harlequin novels.
- ♥ Write an online review and share your thoughts with others.

reading room

- ♥ Read our Internet exclusive daily and weekly online serials, or vote in our interactive novel.
- ♥ Talk to other readers about your favorite novels in our Reading Groups.
- ♥ Take our Choose-a-Book quiz to find the series that matches you!

authors' alcove

- ♥ Find out interesting tidbits and details about your favorite authors' lives, interests and writing habits.
- ♥ Ever dreamed of being an author? Enter our Writing Round Robin. The Winning Chapter will be published online! Or review our guidelines for submitting your novel.

Tyler Brides

It happened one weekend...

Quinn and Molly Spencer are delighted to accept three bookings for their newly opened B&B, Breakfast Inn Bed, located in America's favorite hometown, Tyler, Wisconsin.

But Gina Santori is anything but thrilled to discover her best friend has tricked her into sharing a room with the man who broke her heart eight years ago....

And Delia Mayhew can hardly believe that she's gotten herself locked in the Breakfast Inn Bed basement with the sexiest man in America.

Then there's Rebecca Salter. She's turned up at the Inn in her wedding gown. Minus her groom.

Come home to Tyler for three delightful novellas by three of your favorite authors: Kristine Rolofson, Heather MacAllister and Jacqueline Diamond.

HARLEQUIN®
Makes any time special ™

#1 *New York Times* bestselling author

NORA ROBERTS

brings you more of the loyal and loving,
tempestuous and tantalizing Stanislaski family.

Coming in February 2001

The Stanislaski Sisters

Natasha and Rachel

Though raised in the Old World traditions of their
family, fiery Natasha Stanislaski and cool, classy
Rachel Stanislaski are ready for a *new* world of love....

*And also available in February 2001 from
Silhouette Special Edition, the newest book in the
heartwarming Stanislaski saga*

CONSIDERING KATE

Natasha and Spencer Kimball's daughter Kate turns her
back on old dreams and returns to her hometown, where
she finds the *man* of her dreams.

Available at your favorite retail outlet.

Silhouette®

Where love comes alive™

HARLEQUIN®

AMERICAN ◆ ROMANCE®

and **Muriel Jensen**

present

WHO'S THE
DADDY?

*A*t a festive costume ball, three identical
sisters meet three masked bachelors.

*E*ach couple has a taste of true love behind
the anonymity of their costumes—but
only one will become parents
in nine months!

Find out who it will be!

November 2000
FATHER FEVER #858

January 2001
FATHER FORMULA #855

March 2001
FATHER FOUND #866

HARLEQUIN®
*M*akes any time special ™